THE BOSTON GIRL

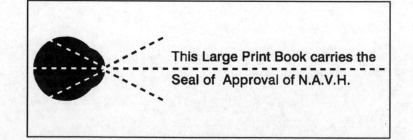

THE BOSTON GIRL

ANITA DIAMANT

THORNDIKE PRESS

A part of Gale, Cengage Learning

GALE
CENGAGE Learning·

Farmington Hills, Mich · San Francisco · New York · Waterville, Maine
Meriden, Conn · Mason, Ohio · Chicago

GALE
CENGAGE Learning®

LIBRARY OF CONGRESS CATALOGING-IN-PUBLICATION DATA

Diamant, Anita.
  The Boston girl / Anita Diamant. — Large print edition.
    pages ; cm. — (Thorndike Press large print basic)
    ISBN 978-1-4104-7597-8 (hardcover) — ISBN 1-4104-7597-2 (hardcover)
    1. Jewish women—Massachusetts—Boston—Fiction. 2. Feminism—Fiction.
  3. Boston (Mass.)—History—20th century—Fiction. I. Title.
  PS3554.I227B68 2014
  813'.54—dc23   2014039551

Published in 2014 by arrangement with Scribner, a division of Simon & Schuster, Inc.

For Robert B. Wyatt and S.J.P.

■ ■ ■ ■

1985

■ ■ ■ ■

NOBODY TOLD YOU?

Ava, sweetheart, if you ask me to talk about how I got to be the woman I am today, what do you think I'm going to say? I'm flattered you want to interview me. And when did I ever say no to my favorite grandchild?

I know I say that to all of my grand-children and I mean it every single time. That sounds ridiculous or like I'm losing my marbles, but it's true. When you're a grandmother you'll understand.

And why not? Look at the five of you: a doctor, a social worker, two teachers, and now you.

Of course they're going to accept you into that program. Don't be silly. My father is probably rolling over in his grave, but I think it's wonderful.

Don't tell the rest of them, but you really are my favorite and not only because you're the youngest. Did you know you were named after me?

It's a good story.

Everyone else is named in memory of someone who died, like your sister Jessica, who was named for my nephew Jake. But I was very sick when you were born and when they thought I wasn't going to make it, they went ahead and just hoped the angel of death wouldn't make a mistake and take you, Ava, instead of me, Addie. Your parents weren't that superstitious, but they had to tell everyone you were named after your father's cousin Arlene, so people wouldn't give them a hard time.

It's a lot of names to remember, I know.

Grandpa and I named your aunt Sylvia for your grandfather's mother, who died in the flu epidemic. Your mother is Clara after my sister Celia.

What do you mean, you didn't know I had a sister named Celia? That's impossible! Betty was the oldest, then Celia, and then me. Maybe you forgot.

Nobody told you? You're sure?

Well, maybe it's not such a surprise. People don't talk so much about sad memories. And it was a long time ago.

But you should know this. So go ahead. Turn on the tape recorder.

My father came to Boston from what must

10

be Russia now. He took my sisters, Betty and Celia, with him. It was 1896 or maybe 1897; I'm not sure. My mother came three or four years later and I was born here in 1900. I've lived in Boston my whole life, which anyone can tell the minute I open my mouth.

■ ■ ■ ■

1915–16

■ ■ ■ ■

THAT'S WHERE I STARTED TO BE MY OWN PERSON.

Where I lived in the North End when I was a little girl wasn't so quaint. The neighborhood smelled of garbage and worse. In my building to go to the bathroom, we had to walk down three flights from our apartment to the outhouses in back. Those were disgusting, believe me, but the stairways were what really scared me. At night, you couldn't see your hand in front of your face and it was slippery from all the dirt and grease. One lady broke a leg on those steps and she never walked right again afterward.

In 1915, there were four of us living in one room. We had a stove, a table, a few chairs, and a saggy couch that Mameh and Papa slept on at night. Celia and I shared a bed in a kind of narrow hallway that didn't go anywhere; the landlords chopped up those apartments to squeeze in more people so they could get more rent. The only good thing about our place was that we had a window that looked out on the street so there was a little light; a lot of the apartments faced the air shaft, where it was always the middle of the night.

Mameh didn't like it when I looked out the window. "What if someone saw you there?" she'd say. "It makes you look like you have nothing better to do."

I didn't understand why it bothered her but I kept my mouth shut so I wouldn't get a smack.

We were poor but not starving. Papa worked in a belt factory as a cutter and Celia was a finisher at a little shirtwaist factory upstairs over an Italian butcher shop. I don't think we called it a sweatshop back then, but that's what it was. And in the summer, it was steaming hot. When my mother wasn't cooking or cleaning, she was mending sheets for the laundry across the street. I think she got a penny apiece.

Together, they made enough money for rent and food. Mostly I remember eating potatoes and cabbage, and I still can't stand the smell of cabbage. Sometimes Mameh took in a boarder, usually a man right off the boat who needed a place to flop for a few nights. I didn't mind because she didn't yell so much if one of them was in the house, but they made Celia nervous.

16

Celia was "delicate." That's what Mameh called her. My sister was thin and had high cheekbones like my father, blue eyes, and fine brown hair like him, too. She would have been as pretty as the drawings in the magazines, but she was so shy that she winced when people talked to her, especially the men Mameh pushed at her.

Celia didn't like to go out of the house; she said it was because her English was bad. Actually she understood a lot but she wouldn't talk. My mother was like that, too. Papa managed a little better, but at home we only spoke Yiddish.

When Mameh talked about Celia to the neighbors, she said, "Twenty-nine years old already," like it was a death sentence. But in the next breath she'd brag, "My Celia has such golden hands, she could sew the wings on a bird. And such a good girl: modest, obedient, never gives me any trouble."

I was "the other one."

"The other one is almost fifteen years old and still in school. Selfish and lazy; she pretends like she can't sew." But I wasn't pretending. Every time I picked up a needle I stabbed myself. One time, when Mameh gave me a sheet to help with her sewing, I left so many little bloodstains she couldn't wash them out. She had to pay for the sheet, which cost her I don't know how many days of work. I got a good smack for that, I can tell you.

You wouldn't know Celia and I were sisters from looking at us. We had the same nose — straight and a little flat — and we were both a little more than five feet. But I was built like my mother, solid but not fat, and curvy starting at thirteen. I had Mameh's thin wrists and her reddish-brownish hair, which was so thick it could break the bristles on the brush. I thought I was a real plain Jane except for my eyes, which are like yours, Ava: hazel, with a little gold circle in the middle.

I was only ten years old when my oldest sister, Betty, moved out of the house. I remember I was hiding under the table the day she left. Mameh was screaming how girls were supposed to live with their families until they got married and the only kind of woman who went on her own was a "kurveh." That's "whore" in Yiddish; I had to ask a kid at school what it meant.

After that, Mameh never said Betty's name in public. But at home she talked about her all the time. "A real American," she said, making it sound like a curse.

But it was true. Betty had learned English fast and she dressed like a modern girl: she wore pointy shoes with heels and you could see her ankles. She got herself a job selling dresses downtown at Filene's department store, which was unusual for someone who wasn't born in this country. I didn't see her much after she moved out and I missed her. It was too quiet without Betty in the house. I didn't mind that there was less fighting between her and Mameh, but she was the only one who ever got Celia and my father to laugh.

Home wasn't so good but I liked going to school. I liked the way it felt to be in rooms with tall ceilings and big windows. I liked reading and getting As and being told I was a good student. I used to go to the library every afternoon.

After I finished elementary school, one of my teachers came to the apartment to tell Mameh and Papa I should go to high school. I still remember his name, Mr. Wallace, and how he said it would be a shame for me to quit and that I could get a better job if I kept going. They listened to him, very polite, but when he was finished Papa said, "She reads and she counts. It's enough."

I cried myself to sleep that night and the next day I stayed really late at the library even though I knew I'd get in trouble. I didn't even want to look at my parents, I hated them so much.

But that night when we were in bed, Celia said not to be sad; that I was going to high school for one year at least. She must have talked to Papa. If she said something was making her upset or unhappy, he got worried that she would stop eating — which she did sometimes. He couldn't stand that.

I was so excited to go to high school. The ceilings were even higher, which made me feel like a giant, like I was important. And mostly, I loved it there. My English teacher was an old lady who always wore a lace collar and who gave me As on my papers but kept telling me that she expected more out of me.

I was almost as good in arithmetic, but the history teacher didn't like me. In front of the whole class he asked if I had ants in my pants because I raised my hand so much. The other kids laughed so I stopped asking so many questions, but not completely.

After school, I went to the Salem Street Settlement House with a lot of the other girls in my grade. I took a cooking class there once but mostly I went to the library, where I could finish my schoolwork and read whatever I found on the shelves. And on Thursdays, there was a reading club for girls my age.

This is probably where the answer to your question begins.

"How did I get to be the woman I am today?" It started in that library, in the reading club. That's where I started to be my own person.

THREE CHEERS
FOR ADDIE BAUM.

The settlement house was a four-story building that stood out from everything else in the neighborhood. It was new with yellow bricks instead of red. It had electricity in all the rooms so at night it lit up the street like a lantern.

It was busy all day. There was a baby nursery for mothers who worked, a woodshop to teach boys a trade, and English classes for immigrants. After dark, women would come to ask for food and coal so their children wouldn't starve or freeze. The neighborhood was that poor.

Miss Edith Chevalier was in charge of all that and a lot more. She's the one who started the library groups for girls: one for the Irish, one for Italians, and one for Jews. Sometimes she would look in and ask what we were reading — not to test us but just because she wanted to know.

That's what happened on the day my club

was reading "The Midnight Ride of Paul Revere" out loud. I guess I was better than the others because after the meeting, Miss Chevalier asked if I would recite the whole poem to the Saturday Club. She said a famous professor was going to give a lecture about Henry Wadsworth Longfellow, and she thought a presentation of his most famous poem would be a nice way to start the evening.

She said that I would have to memorize it, "But that shouldn't be a problem for a girl of your ability." I'm telling you, my feet didn't touch the ground all the way home. It was the biggest thing that ever happened to me and I learned the whole poem by heart in two days so I'd be ready for our first "rehearsal."

Miss Chevalier was a small woman, a few inches shorter than me, which meant less than five feet. She had a moon face and chubby fingers and coppery hair that sprang straight up from her head, which is why some of the girls called her The Poodle. But she had one of those smiles that makes you feel like you just did something right, which was a good thing since I was a nervous wreck when I went to her office to practice.

I only got halfway through the poem when Miss Chevalier stopped me and asked if I

23

knew what *impetuous* meant. She was nice about it, but I wanted to sink through the floor because not only did I not know what the word meant, I had mispronounced it.

I'm sure I turned bright red, but Miss Chevalier pretended not to notice and handed me the dictionary and said to read the definition out loud.

I will never forget; *impetuous* means two things. "Rushing with great force or violence," and "acting suddenly, with little thought."

She asked me which one I thought Mr. Longfellow meant. I reread those definitions over and over, trying to figure out the right answer, but Miss Chevalier must have read my mind. "There is no wrong answer," she said. "I want to know your opinion, Addie. What do *you* think?"

I had never been asked for my opinion, but I knew I couldn't keep her waiting so I said the first thing that came into my head, which was, "Maybe he meant both."

She liked that. "The patriots had to be impetuous both ways or they wouldn't have dared challenge the British." Then she asked, "Would you call yourself impetuous, Addie?"

That time, I knew she was asking for an opinion. "My mother thinks I am."

She said mothers were right to be concerned for their daughters' welfare. "But I believe that girls need gumption, too, especially in this day and age. I believe you are a girl with gumption."

After I looked up *gumption,* I never let anyone call Miss Chevalier The Poodle again.

I told Celia and my parents about the big honor of reciting for the Saturday Club, but when the day came and I put on my coat, Mameh said, "You're not going anywhere."

I told her they were waiting for me and that I had practiced and they couldn't start without me but she shrugged like it was nothing. "It's too cold. Let someone else get pneumonia."

I couldn't believe what she was saying. I argued and I begged and finally I was yelling. "No one else can do it. They're counting on me. If I don't go, I won't be able to show my face there again."

Mameh said, "When I was your age I didn't step a foot outside without my mother, so close your mouth before I get mad."

Celia said, "Let her go, Mameh. It's not far. She can wear my scarf."

My mother almost never snapped at Celia,

but she said, "Stay out of this. That one sits in that school while you're killing yourself at work. She's already ruining her eyes from reading. No man wants to marry a girl with a squint."

"Maybe I don't want to get married." The moment I said that, I ran behind where Celia was sitting so Mameh couldn't slap me. But she just laughed. "Are you so stupid? Marriage and children are a woman's crown."

I said, "Like for Mrs. Freistadt?"

Mameh didn't have an answer for Mrs. Freistadt. She lived across the street. One day her husband came home from work and said he couldn't live with a woman he didn't love, so after twenty years and four little girls, he walked out. Just like that.

The wife didn't speak English and she didn't know how to do anything but clean and cook. They got so poor — she and the daughters — everyone in the neighborhood was ashamed for them.

Talking about Mrs. Freistadt was the last straw for Mameh and she came at me with both hands, slapping and cursing and saying things like "Ungrateful worm. Monster. A plague you are."

I was jumping around to keep away from her, which made her even madder. "My father would have taken a strap to you," she yelled, and finally got me on my cheek with a loud slap that made Celia wail as if Mameh had hit her instead of me.

My mother had me against the wall, holding my wrists, and I was hollering, "Leave me alone," when Papa walked in and told her to let me go.

Mameh screamed, "You don't do anything and I'm not having another whore in this family."

"Don't use that word," he yelled. "Betty is a good girl."

Someone started pounding on the door. "Shut up in there."

Celia had been crying the whole time, but now she started banging her forehead on the table. She was saying, "Stop, stop, stop," and hitting her head hard enough that we could hear the sound of her face on the wood.

Papa grabbed her by the shoulders. "Lena, she's hurting herself."

Mameh let go of me to look and I ran.

The cold wind on my face felt like it was washing away everything that happened upstairs. I walked fast and whispered the poem to myself in time with my feet.

Listen my children and you shall hear
Of the midnight ride of Paul Revere,
On the eighteenth of April, in Seventy-five;
Hardly a man is now alive
Who remembers that famous day and year.

I was almost calm when I got to the settlement house, but it was a big shock to see all the chairs and benches in the big meeting room full of girls, talking and laughing with each other.

The Saturday Club was different from all the other clubs. It was bigger — fifty girls instead of ten or twelve — and all the religions were together. They were older, too; some were in high school but a lot of them had jobs. They also held elections and ran their own meetings. I was only three or four years younger than most of them, but to me, they were practically grown-ups.

Miss Chevalier was at the door and sent me to sit in the front row while she waited for the professor. She said he should be there any moment, but five minutes passed and another five and another and I was getting more and more nervous. My hands were shaking when he finally got there. He looked so much like the pictures of Longfellow — with the white beard and long hair — it was as if he'd come back from the dead.

28

Rose Reardon, the club president, banged a gavel and made some announcements. I didn't hear a word and Miss Chevalier had to tap me on the shoulder when it was time for me to go up to the platform. My knees were like rubber.

I had a lot to remember — and not just the words. Miss Chevalier had given me a lot of directions to "add to the drama." This was the North End of Boston, where every schoolchild knew "The Midnight Ride" and we were all pretty sick of it.

Miss Chevalier gave me a big smile and a nod to start me off.

I remembered to begin as if I were a little out of breath, like I had a surprise to tell. Then I tried to make Paul Revere seem like a real person, tapping my foot to make it look like he was impatient to get going. I whispered about the graves being *lonely and spectral and sombre and still,* making it sound spooky. At the end, I went very, very slow.

In the hour of darkness and peril and need,
The people will waken and listen to hear
The hurrying hoof-beats of that steed,
And the midnight message of Paul Revere.

I counted to three and bowed my head

like Miss Chevalier showed me. There was a big round of applause and even a "Three cheers for Addie Baum." Miss Chevalier put her arm around me and introduced me to the professor, who said I'd done the Great Man proud.

Then he gave his talk. And, boy, did he talk. It was not only long but also so boring it was like listening to a clock tick. Girls started yawning and looking at their fingernails and even Miss Chevalier had to pretend she was paying attention. When he stopped to blow his nose, she stood up and clapped as if he were finished. Everyone else clapped, too, but I think it was to thank Miss Chevalier for rescuing us.

After the lecture, I was the belle of the ball. Girls I didn't know came over to say what a good job I'd done and ask where I worked and did I want another cup of punch or a cookie.

Miss Chevalier introduced me to Miss Green, the artist who ran a pottery studio in the settlement house. The two of them lived in an apartment on the top floor. They had the same first name so everyone called them the Ediths.

They were about the same height, but Miss Green looked like a sparrow compared to Miss Chevalier, who was more of a pigeon. Miss Green tilted her head the way a bird would, and looked me over with round, bright bird eyes.

"Miss Chevalier has told me so much about you," she said. "I hope she's talked to you about going to Rockport Lodge this summer. It's just the thing for a girl like you."

Miss Chevalier explained that Rockport Lodge was an inn for young ladies in a seaside town north of Boston. She said it wasn't expensive and some members of the Saturday Club went regularly.

Miss Green said, "You must know that the Frommer girls have been there a few times."

I guess she thought that all the Jewish girls knew each other, but I only met Helen and Gussie Frommer that night. Helen was the older one, a real peaches-and-cream beauty. That could have been hard for Gussie, who had a big nose and a mousy complexion, but you never saw two sisters who looked out for each other like those two.

Helen was sweet, but Gussie had the big personality; she walked me around the room and introduced me to just about everyone. When we got to Rose Reardon, she said, "Madame President, don't you think Addie should join the Saturday Club? Miss Chevalier brought her, so you know she'll be all for it."

Rose said, "Of course you should join!" She was a healthy girl with auburn hair and pretty green eyes and a gap between her two front teeth. People used to call her kind of a face "a map of Ireland."

"You should come to Rockport Lodge, too," she said. "In the evenings we do skits and sing songs and some of the girls read poems — right up your alley. And we don't go hungry." She patted her stomach. "Three meals a day and cake at supper."

I was having such a good time, it was hard to think about going home, and I was one of the last ones to leave. I walked outside with Filomena Gallinelli, who said that she couldn't imagine standing in front of so many people the way I did. "You looked like you were enjoying it."

"I was terrified," I said.

"Then you must be a great actress."

I had seen Filomena around the settlement house and thought she was gorgeous; dark eyes, dark hair, olive skin — a real Italian. She wore her hair in a long braid over her shoulder, which was completely out of fashion, but she could get away with it, not only because it looked good on her but also because she was an artist. Filomena was one of a few girls who had full-time jobs in the Salem Street pottery studio. She was Miss Green's favorite and nobody minded because she was so talented.

She asked if my name was really Adeline because of "Sweet Adeline," the song.

I told her no. "Just Addie. It was my sister Betty's idea and my father liked it because it sounded like his grandmother Altie."

She said she envied me for having an American name. "Filomena is too long and no one can pronounce it."

I said, "But your name fits you; it's beautiful and unusual. Addie is just plain and ordinary."

"What are you talking about?" she said. "You've got a nice shape and beautiful eyes. No one who's ordinary can recite like you did tonight."

After we said good night, I was too keyed up to go home, so I kept walking and walking — up and down Hanover Street, looping around the high school, making a big circle around my block. The cold didn't bother me because my mind was going a million miles an hour. I wondered what Miss Green meant when she said "a girl like you," and if I could be friends with Gussie, Helen, and Rose. I remembered the applause and every compliment and how friendly Filomena had been. "See you next week," she said.

It had been the best night of my life, and if I hadn't walked into a puddle and soaked my shoes, I would have walked all the way to Rockport Lodge — wherever that was.

WHAT ARE FRIENDS FOR?

I'll never forget when I took your mother to see *The Wizard of Oz*. You know the scene when everything changes from black-and-white to color? That's what it felt like the first time I went to Rockport. Everything was in color, everything was new, even things I'd seen my whole life.

The ocean, for example. Boston Harbor was a few blocks from where I grew up, and sure, the water there was filthy and the docks were smelly and dangerous, but how could I not know about low tide and high tide? I had never seen a cloud change the color of the sea in a second, or heard water crashing so loud you couldn't hear the person standing right next to you.

That first week I was at Rockport Lodge, I saw corn growing out of the ground, and goats, and lighthouses. When I closed my eyes at night, I could still see fireflies blinking. I couldn't get over those fireflies.

It was the first time I ever slept in a bed by myself. And the sheets? Ironed! It felt like sleeping on silk. I got my own towel and a pillow that smelled like flowers. So many new smells: beach roses, seaweed, smoke from a bonfire. I ate hot dogs and cherry pie and saltwater taffy that got stuck in my teeth.

It didn't cost a lot to go to Rockport Lodge in 1916. I think it was seven dollars for a week, which was seven dollars more than I ever had. When Miss Chevalier found out that I couldn't afford to go, she gave me a job as her assistant. Actually, she made a job out of thin air.

I took her letters to the mailbox, I helped in the baby nursery when one of the regular attendants was sick, and I put away books in the library. I swept up in the pottery studio, too, where I got to watch Filomena and the other girls paint Miss Green's designs on the plates and vases they sold in a little gift shop they ran on the ground floor.

When Miss Chevalier ran out of things for me to do, she had me sit in her office and read books by Charles Dickens for us to talk about. I got very friendly with her dictionary.

She paid me fifty cents a week, but I was

getting so much more than that. I had a private class in literature, the chance to watch artists work, and time to read. I didn't appreciate it at the time, but what did I know? I was fifteen years old.

I didn't say a word to anyone at home about what I was doing. I would have told Celia, but my sister could never keep a secret or tell a lie. My parents didn't know what a vacation was. And what was I going to say? That I was earning money so I could go away and do nothing? That I had money but wasn't helping to pay the bills, when Celia handed over every penny? I did feel guilty about that. I tried to make up for it by eating less. I'm sure nobody noticed.

The day I went to Rockport was my sixteenth birthday, July 10.

I didn't have to do a lot to get ready. I could wear just about all the clothes I owned and the rest I stuffed into an old pillowcase I bought from a ragman's cart for a few pennies. I left a note in Celia's shoe to say I was going on a vacation with some nice girls I knew. I also left two dollars — all of my spending money — even though I knew it wouldn't make any difference to my mother. I put chicken fat on the door hinges so they wouldn't squeak in the morning; I was very proud of myself for thinking of that.

I didn't close my eyes at all the night before I left. I was out of bed the second it started to get light and I held my breath until I got to the stoop and stopped to put on my shoes.

It was strange to be outside so early. The streets were completely empty and quiet. Not even the milkman was there. No one. It was spooky.

Without the people, I could see how dirty it was. There was garbage piled all over the place and I saw rats running in and out. In the gutters there was all kinds of filth, the worst you can imagine. I ran as fast as I could to get out of there and down to the harbor where Gussie and Helen and Rose were waiting.

Most of the girls were taking the train to Rockport but Miss Chevalier had gotten boat tickets for us. It was a gorgeous day — the sea was calm and the sun was warm — and I stayed at the front railing for the whole trip. I didn't want to miss anything. I wish I'd been keeping a diary, but I still remember how the water was slapping against the hull of the ship and that to me it sounded like clapping. A seagull flew down and hung in the air maybe ten feet from my shoulder and I could see all the little markings on his wings and how his eye looked like a gray marble rolling around in his head. By the time we got to Gloucester, my face hurt from smiling.

When we got close to the dock, Rose started jumping up and down and waving at a heavyset woman in a big hat.

"I can't believe they sent Mrs. Morse to get us," she said. "She is the best cook in the world."

Mrs. Morse didn't seem so excited to see us. She hurried us into a real old-fashioned horse-drawn cart, and we had to sit on the floor between sacks of flour, with our feet hanging off the back.

It's good that we were wedged in so tight because whenever we hit a bump in the road everyone flew up in the air — like in a roller coaster. It was kind of fun but my behind was plenty sore by the time we stopped.

Rockport Lodge was more beautiful than I had imagined; a big white-painted farmhouse with black shutters, two stories, and porches on each side of the front door. Vines with button-size red roses climbed through the railings, almost up to the upstairs windows, where white curtains puffed in and out. Next to the house, there was an orchard with benches in the shade.

Filomena met us at the door and said that she had asked to have me as her roommate. "I hope that's okay with you."

I couldn't believe it. Since we met at Saturday Club, we had only said a few words to each other in the pottery studio. I was a little bit in awe of her, not just for her looks and her talent, but also for her self-confidence.

Filomena was the only girl in the studio that Miss Green trusted to decorate the really big vases — the ones that went to art shows and sold for a lot of money. I know some of the other girls would have liked the chance to do that, but she didn't apologize for being chosen. I don't mean that she bragged. Filomena just knew who she was, which wasn't so easy back then. I guess it's still not easy, is it? It took me until I was almost forty before I knew what I wanted to be when I grew up.

I followed her up the front stairs to a long hallway where all the doors were open and I could see girls unpacking and changing clothes, talking and laughing like it was a party. Our room was at the very end.

"It's small but there's only the two of us; some of the others have four girls crammed in."

The room was just big enough for two

narrow beds, a bureau, and one wooden chair. It was all very plain: white walls and a worn wooden floor, but the light from the window bounced off the walls and made the white bedspreads seem to glow.

Filomena stretched out on one of the cots, but I didn't want to wrinkle anything so I stayed by the door.

"When you bring up your valise, you can put your things in the bottom drawers." When Filomena said "valise," I dropped my lumpy pillowcase and thought, Oh, no. What am I doing here?

But she caught on right away. "Aren't you smart to pack light. I always bring too many clothes and part of the fun is sharing."

That was so nice of her I could have cried with relief, but thankfully, someone rang a bell downstairs.

"That's lunch," Filomena said. "They're always telling you how fresh air works up an appetite, and they must be right because I'm always starving when I'm here."

In the dining room, there were six big oak tables all set with plates, glasses, silverware, and white cloth napkins — which I'd only ever seen in movies. Filomena pointed me to where Rose was sitting with Helen and Gussie Frommer. "See you later," she said, and went to a table full of dark-haired girls who could have been her cousins.

Rose was sitting next to a pale, skinny girl with green eyes, carrot-colored hair, and a million freckles. Rose said, "This is my roommate, Irene Conley. She's from Boston, too." I said hello but Irene shrugged and looked right past me. Rose, who always had a smile on her face, glared at her. "Do you have a toothache or something?"

Irene shrugged again and crossed her arms.

Helen asked if I was settled in my room and did I need anything. She was like a mother hen, as nice as she was pretty, and that day she was wearing a pink shirtwaist that made her look like a flower. But when I started to say how good she looked, she stopped me. "Has my sister introduced you to everybody? Gussie is the mayor of Rockport Lodge."

Gussie was plain as a brick but people liked her because she made them feel important. Whenever she met someone new, she wanted to know everything about them. Helen teased Gussie about her "cross-examinations" but it was flattering to be asked to talk about yourself. At my second Saturday Club meeting, Gussie got me in a corner and asked about school, my favorite movie stars, my family, and what I thought about the temperance movement. When I said I didn't understand it very well, she explained how it was a good idea that couldn't work.

Gussie never forgot a name or anything you told her. She would have made a great politician.

When she noticed me looking over at Filomena's table, she said, "They've been friends forever. The Italians stick together, like everyone. The girls behind us all come from one club in Arlington. The table next to them is one hundred percent Irish. Sometimes there's a Jewish bunch, but our table is like the Saturday Club, all mixed together."

I said, "Like mixed nuts."

Rose laughed. "I love that. We should call ourselves the Mixed Nuts — crazy enough to talk to anyone who talks to us."

Gussie made a toast with her water glass. "To the Mixed Nuts."

Before lunch, we met the women who were in charge of Rockport Lodge that year. Miss Holbrooke and Miss Case reminded me a little of Miss Chevalier and Miss Green. They were much younger and didn't look anything like the Ediths, but they were smart and wore sensible shoes. And no lipstick.

Miss Holbrooke had on a pair of navy-blue bloomers that were so out of date it looked like she was wearing a costume. She had big, gray teeth and a long mane of coarse sandy-colored hair that made her look like a horse, and she wore a whistle around her neck on a string that hung straight down her chest. She was in charge of all the outside activities: lawn tennis, archery, croquet, visits to town and other "attractions" as she called it, and bicycling.

Miss Case was so blond that her eyebrows and eyelashes were practically invisible. She was smaller and quieter than Miss Holbrooke, but she was the boss. I remember she carried around a ledger book and held it out flat in front of her, like it was a desk.

Miss Case said that we would say grace before eating. Rose and Irene bowed their heads and folded their hands, but Gussie, Helen, and I sort of froze. Miss Case closed her eyes and thanked God for the food, for the people who gave money so we could enjoy the blessings of God's green earth, for good health, and the United States, and that we owed it all to Jesus Christ.

I asked Gussie if they always did that.

"They always pray," she said, "But I never

heard anyone say that last part." Jews never said "Jesus" or "Christ" out loud. We weren't supposed to go inside a church, either. Like it was a contagious disease.

I actually didn't think much about being Jewish as a kid. In my neighborhood, there were Jews and Italians and Irish and everyone got along pretty well. Sometimes the boys got into fights and some of it had to do with religion. But it was pretty much live and let live, as I remember it.

I got a little self-conscious when I saw Helen and Gussie take the ham out of their sandwiches and eat just bread with mustard.

But I was hungry and I ate the meat, and it wasn't the first time. I was hungry a lot when I was young and I never turned down food — including things I knew were not kosher. Nothing bad ever happened to me and a lot of it was delicious. So I ate everything they put in front of me at Rockport Lodge. Except for the pickles. Who ever heard of a pickle that was sweet and soft? *Feh.*

After lunch, they sent everyone upstairs to put on shoes and hats to get ready for a hike. I didn't have a dictionary so I asked Rose what a hike was.

She said, "Hiking is the same thing as

walking, only hotter and twice as far as you want to go. But usually, you're glad you went."

I didn't have a hat or another pair of shoes so I just went to wait on the porch. The only chairs out there were made out of wooden twigs woven together. I couldn't believe something like that could be comfortable, which shows you what a greenhorn I was; all excited about a wicker chair.

Rockport Lodge was on the road between Gloucester and Rockport, but I only saw one car pass by. It was so quiet that I could hear the bees buzzing around the roses and a bird singing from far away. Someone upstairs called, "Has anyone seen my hairbrush?" In the kitchen, there was chopping. Every sound was separate — like framed pictures on a wall. I thought, Aha! This is what you call *peace and quiet.*

Rose came outside wearing an old straw hat and canvas shoes. Irene was with her, but it was obvious that she didn't want to be there. Rose told me, "I promised if she came with me this one time, I wouldn't bother her again."

Miss Holbrooke brought a stack of newspapers and started folding them into three-cornered hats. She tried one on and some of the girls giggled. "I know it's not à la mode, but I will not have any of you fainting from heatstroke on your first day."

It turned out that the only girls without hats were Irene and me. She got stuck in one with advertisements for ladies' corsets on all three sides. I was lucky: I only got the baseball scores.

Miss Holbrooke blew her whistle and said, "Away we go." She had a loud, high voice that carried just as far as that whistle.

There were about twenty of us girls. We followed her through the orchard next to the lodge and onto a dirt road with fields planted in long rows on each side. Miss Holbrooke told us which were squash plants and which were corn, but she was even more interested in the stone walls. She called them relics. "An American Stonehenge, if you will."

I looked it up later.

At the end of the road, we found ourselves right on the coast, looking straight out to sea. The sun was so bright on the water it was like staring at a million tiny mirrors.

I heard Irene whisper, "Holy mackerel."

I whispered back, "Amen."

She smiled in spite of herself, and you never saw a cuter pair of dimples.

■ ■ ■ ■

Miss Holbrooke led us past a row of mansions, most of them with two or three balconies that faced the ocean. One of them had a fairy-tale turret. Rose sighed. "You'd never get me off that porch."

We took a path around the back of Rockport and up a hill to Dogtown, which is a big woods right in the middle of Cape Ann, where Miss Holbrooke said she had something very special to show us.

The farther we got from the water, the hotter it was. I was wearing a long-sleeved shirtwaist and my shoes were pinching, so I hoped her special treat involved ice cream or lemonade.

It was cooler when we got to the forest, and Miss Holbrooke said, "We'll be there soon, girls." We started walking faster and everyone tried to guess what wonder we were going to see. A waterfall? Blueberries?

But when she stopped and said, "Here we are!" I didn't see anything special — just trees and shrubs and rocks.

"Where are we?" said Gussie.

Miss Holbrooke walked over to a huge boulder and patted it as if it were a puppy. "We have reached our first erratic and one of my favorite specimens. Isn't it a beauty?"

Nobody said a word until Irene muttered, "We came all this way to look at a stupid rock?"

I was sweaty and thirsty, my legs ached, I had blisters on both feet, and I thought that was the funniest thing I'd ever heard.

Miss Holbrooke spun around and gave me the fish-eye but I couldn't stop laughing. I covered my mouth and turned around but by then Rose was laughing, and she had one of those big belly laughs that got everyone else going.

Miss Holbrooke was furious. Then she was offended. And then hurt.

"I suppose not everyone has a taste for geology," she said.

"Thank goodness she's not the cook," Irene said, and I cracked up all over again.

Irene didn't come to supper that night. Rose said she'd gotten a bad sunburn. "But it's her own fault for throwing away the hat. I'm washing my hands of that girl."

I said, "She's not so bad, but it makes you wonder why she's here at all."

Rose had found out that much. Her brother had sent her and paid her way. "I told Irene that makes him a saint in my book, and she gave me a look that would have boiled an egg."

After supper, Miss Case opened her ledger to tell us about the schedule for the week, and it all sounded wonderful. There was going to be a breakfast cookout, a trip to Good Harbor Beach, blueberry picking, shopping in Rockport and Gloucester. We were going to a town dance, too, which got everyone whispering and giggling.

That's when I noticed Irene peeking in from the hallway. She had a cloth pressed against her forehead and I went out and asked if she was okay.

She said she was fine. "If Mrs. Morse hadn't sent into town for ice, I think my nose would have peeled off."

"It looks like it hurts," I said.

Irene shrugged, but then she hid her face in the towel and started to cry.

I sat down with her on the steps and she told me the story of how she had come to America with her older brother five years ago and the two of them had taken care of each other. But he'd gotten married and his new wife, "the cow, Kathleen," wanted Irene out of their apartment right away. Without a word to Irene, the wife got her a job as a live-in maid in Worcester. "Do you have any idea how far that is from Boston?" Irene said.

The brother wouldn't stand up against his bride, so he sent Irene to Rockport as a kind of peace offering. Irene called it "the old heave-ho."

"I was in service once, and never again. The lady of the house thinks she owns you and calls you a thief if you eat the crusts she leaves on her plate, but it's her who steals your days off. I'd sooner walk the streets."

I said there had to be something we could do to help. She shook her head and said, "You're a good kid," and then she went upstairs alone.

I walked straight over to Rose and told her what was what with Irene. She called the brother a no-good bum and a few other things and said, "I feel terrible about what I said about the poor girl." She went upstairs and told Irene that she would be staying with her until she got on her feet; no arguments and no thanks needed. "What are friends for?" Rose said.

And just like that, the chip on Irene's shoulder disappeared. Her dimples became the envy of everyone and her impersonation of Miss Holbrooke had us rolling on the floor.

"Allow me to serve you a taste of scenery," Irene said, in Miss Holbrooke's voice, which was singsong and fruity, sort of like Julia Child's, come to think of it.

"Now, who wants a piping hot slab of granite?"

It still makes me laugh.

You Have a Good Eye.

The best part of that week was my time with Filomena.

We stayed up late every night talking, talking, talking. She seemed so grown up, I couldn't believe that she was only nineteen — just three years older than me.

We started with our families and I still remember all of her sisters' names: Maria Immaculata, Maria Teresa, Maria Domenica, Maria Sofia, and she was Maria Filomena — the youngest and also the only unmarried one.

Her parents died when she was a baby, so Mimi — Immaculata — raised her. The whole family lived within a few blocks of each other in the North End, and when I met Filomena, she was staying with Sophie — Maria Sofia — and sharing the couch with two of her three boys. Filomena said she looked forward to coming to Rockport Lodge just so she could sleep without a squirming child waking her up.

Filomena left school when she was twelve and went to work sewing in a factory. A few years later, she started going to the Salem Street Settlement House on Saturdays. "I told Mimi that I wanted to improve my English," she said, "but really it was just to have a little time when I wasn't at work or taking care of someone's baby." Miss Chevalier noticed her sketching in the library when she was supposed to be reading, "But instead of yelling at me, she took me to meet Miss Green. And here I am."

Not so different from my story, right?

Miss Green sent her to the Museum School for a drawing class. "I owe her everything," Filomena said. "She taught me pottery and design and gives me art books to look at. She says that being an artist is more than a job or a skill; it's a way of walking through the world."

I didn't understand what that meant until a few days later, when we went to the Headlands, which Miss Holbrooke said was the most beautiful view on Cape Ann.

Irene rolled her eyes. "Stone soup, anyone?"

But Miss Holbrooke was right about the Headlands. It's a special place — up high, maybe a hundred feet above the sea, with water on three sides.

You know where I'm talking about, right, Ava? It's the place I always bring people who've never been to Cape Ann. You can see for miles up and down the coast. It's got a nice view of the boats in Rockport Harbor and most of the town, too. The first time I saw all those white clapboard houses and the church steeple I thought about how much I owed to Paul Revere for getting me there.

Miss Holbrooke called it picturesque and I knew exactly what she meant without having to look it up. It was like one of those tinted picture postcards: a perfect blue sky and fluffy white clouds, sailboats, and even a few ladies with parasols.

The lodge girls scattered around to pick flowers or sit on the rocks and talk. Rose and Irene climbed halfway down the bluff, which almost gave Miss Holbrooke a heart attack. Filomena went off by herself to draw, but I tiptoed over and peeked at her sketchpad.

She was drawing the pile of rocks in front of her, which seemed like a dull subject. But when I looked again, I saw she had made the same shapes into a woman's body, lying on her side, completely naked. I'd probably never seen a nude picture before and I must have gasped. Filomena turned around and held it up so I had a better view. "What do you think?"

Before I could answer, Miss Holbrooke came running toward us, yoo-hooing for Filomena to come with her. Two ladies had set up easels to do watercolors of the harbor. "You should meet them; they are painting the most charming little harbor scenes."

Filomena wrinkled her nose. "Miss Green says 'charming' is a trap that women artists should avoid at all costs."

Miss Holbrooke said, "These ladies are very accomplished, I assure you."

Filomena stared her in the eye and said, "Miss Edith Green is an instructor at the School of the Museum of Fine Arts and she is the one who told me to focus all my attention on drawing this week. I'm sure you agree I should take her assignment seriously."

Miss Holbrooke couldn't say no to that and walked away with her tail between her legs.

"Did Miss Green really say that?" I asked.

Filomena laughed. "She could have. Edith Green thinks everything rests on drawing. You can see it in the designs on the pottery."

"I like the way you do the trees," I said. "It's just a few lines but they seem alive."

"That's exactly right," Filomena said. "You have a good eye."

That was a compliment I never forgot — obviously.

Toward the end of the week, Filomena switched tables and joined the Mixed Nuts. Gussie teased her and asked if she'd gotten kicked out of the Italian club for hanging around so much with the Jews and the Irish.

"I just need to talk about something besides weddings," Filomena said. "They're getting married this year! All of them."

Helen said, "Your time will come."

"Not me," said Filomena. "I'm never getting married."

Rose said she was too pretty to be an old maid.

Gussie didn't like that. "Filomena may want to do other things with her life. For example, I am going to college."

"And after that, she's going to law school," said Helen.

"But don't you want a family?" Rose asked.

Gussie said, "Helen's going to have children; I'll borrow hers."

Helen blushed and Irene said, "Looks like

she already knows who the father's going to be."

"Don't embarrass her," said Rose. "Besides, she'd tell us if there was someone, wouldn't you, Helen?"

"My sister can have her pick," said Gussie. "What about you, Rose? Irene? Any prospects? Addie?"

"Addie's too young to think about that," Filomena said.

I was too young but it was impossible not to think about marriage. Mameh talked about Celia's "prospects" all the time, and at every Saturday Club meeting, there was talk about weddings the girls had been to or weddings they were going to. Even the Ediths, when they heard about an engagement, acted like it was some kind of victory — and they were all for women's rights and education.

I wasn't so sure about marriage. I knew my parents were miserable, and from what I heard in the air shaft, other married people said horrible things to each other all the time. On the other hand, who wouldn't want to be in love and have a man look at me the way Owen Moore looked at Mary Pickford? I used to leave those movies feeling sad that nothing like that would ever happen to me, but I always went back for another happy ending.

In the magazine stories, I could imagine myself as one of the smart, spunky girls chased by men who loved them for their brains and gumption. Those girls were airplane daredevils, or race car drivers, or even doctors, but in the end they gave it up for love and marriage.

When I asked Filomena what she would do if she fell in love, she shrugged. "I know that being a wife would mean giving up art, which is what makes me happy. When I say I don't want to get married, my sisters tell me I'm being selfish, and maybe I am. Or maybe there's something wrong with me."

I said I didn't think there was anything wrong with her.

"I wish my sisters were more like you, Addie," she said. "Betty and Celia are lucky to have such a good listener in the family."

Actually, my sisters and I didn't talk much. They were so much older than me, for one thing; Celia was so quiet, and as for Betty, I saw her once in a blue moon and only when she was sure Mameh would be out of the house and she could sneak in and visit. Even then, she mostly talked to Celia and Papa.

LIKE NOTHING I COULD ACTUALLY TOUCH.

I didn't know my father very well. It wasn't like today, when fathers change diapers and read books to their children. When I was growing up, men worked all day and when they came home we were supposed to be quiet and leave them alone.

Papa was a good-looking man; he had a long, thin face, with light-blue eyes and brown hair like Celia's. He was particular about his clothes, that they should be clean and neat. Whenever he saw a Jewish man in the street dressed sloppy, he said, "They'll think we're all peasants."

What I knew about him mostly came from Betty. He grew up in a little shtetl that was hardly even a town, just a place with an inn, a synagogue, and a market once a week where people bought and sold everything. Papa's family had cows, so they weren't the poorest, but they didn't have enough money to send him or his brothers to school.

Instead they learned with their father, my grandfather, who'd studied at some big yeshiva as a boy. I remember Papa had a very old prayer book; maybe it was from his family.

When Papa was eighteen or nineteen, there was a cholera epidemic that killed his father and brothers, so he was in charge of his mother and two sisters. He sold the cows so the girls could get married, and then his mother matched him up with Mameh, who was from a poor family but managed to get her a horse for a dowry, which meant Papa could make a living moving and hauling things around.

Betty and Celia were born over there, though they were called Bronia and Sima then. My mother was pregnant with a third baby when someone accused my father of stealing a silver cup from the church. In those days, that was the same as a death sentence for a Jew, so he came to America with the two girls. They were maybe ten and twelve years old but they went to work with him so he could keep an eye on them. When Papa got a letter that said Mameh had had a baby boy, he left them alone at nights and took another job to get the money for her ticket faster.

When Mameh came, she got off the ship

alone. Nahum — she had named the baby for Papa's father — had died on the trip over. They had thrown his body into the sea.

All around them, people were smiling and happy to be in America, but she was sobbing and Papa was tearing his clothes.

Betty and Celia were there, too. What an awful memory that must have been.

Mameh had another boy in America, but he died when he was three days old and I never knew his name — if they even gave him one. After I was born, there were no more babies.

My mother thought coming to America was a terrible mistake and she never let Papa forget it. "We should have stayed where we were," she said. "Your son wouldn't have died on that miserable boat. Our daughters would be married and I'd have grandchildren on my lap."

Usually my father didn't answer but sometimes he got fed up. "You would have been better off if they'd killed me?" he said. And then he would leave the house and go to his little shul, a few blocks away, where nobody yelled at him.

He was home in the evening, gone in the morning, like a shadow. Like nothing I could actually touch.

YOU MUST BE
THE SMART ONE.

I threw up on the boat all the way back to Boston from the lodge, but it wasn't from seasickness. All week, I hadn't let myself think about what was going to happen when I got home, but at that point I couldn't think of anything else and that's what made me sick to my stomach.

What if Mameh wouldn't let me back in the house? None of my friends had a place for me, I had no idea where Betty was living, and I was not going to ask Miss Chevalier — not after all she'd already done for me. My only hope was that Celia would stick up for me and get my father on her side, and that would mean a huge screaming fight at the least.

Walking up the stairs to our apartment, I felt like a criminal going to be hanged. But when I got to the door, I heard teaspoons clinking in glasses. That could only mean there was sugar on the table, which meant

63

there was company, which almost never happened.

When I looked through the keyhole, all I could see was a man's back and my father rubbing his chin, which meant he was either uncomfortable or mad. Mameh was pouring tea and smiling her company smile, but she must have noticed the door rattle or something, because before I knew it she was in the hall, pinching me by the ear and talking so fast I could hardly understand her.

"You listen to me. You're going to say you were staying in Cambridge to help out a woman who had a baby. Your sister is getting married, thank God, and he doesn't need to know about you."

"Betty is getting married?" I said.

"Don't you dare say that name to Mr. Levine. Celia is the one getting married."

I couldn't believe it. I never heard Celia say a word about her boss, good or bad. I said, "But Mr. Levine is too old."

"Forty is not so old. His wife is dead a year and he has two little boys without a mother. He sees what a hard worker your sister is: so clean, so nice and quiet. He's got a good business, so she won't want for nothing. Today he brought over coffee and a bottle of whiskey for your father. So you say, 'Mazel tov' and not another word."

When Celia saw me she jumped out of her chair and ran to give me a hug. She was wearing maybe the first new dress I'd ever seen her in — with flowers that brought out her blue eyes. She looked beautiful.

Mr. Levine stood up. "Nice to make your acquaintance, Miss Addie. Celia says such nice things about you." He was a small man — maybe an inch taller than me — with a narrow face and a reddish-brown goatee that made him look like a fox.

He said, "Aren't I lucky to marry into a family of such pretty girls? It will be nice for Myron and Jacob to have a sister, too."

I said I would be their aunt, not their sister.

He laughed and said, "You must be the smart one."

Celia took my hand and said I got all As in school.

So Mameh had to say that she was sure Mr. Levine's sons were even smarter.

"You have to start calling me Herman," he said.

"What is your real name?" Papa asked. "I need it for the ketubah — the marriage contract."

Levine waved away the question like he was brushing away a fly. "Hirsch, I suppose."

Papa made a sour face. This was the kind of man my father called a gantze ganef — a real thief.

Levine reached for the whiskey bottle and said, "Let's make a toast to August twenty-second."

"I still don't know what's the hurry," Papa said.

"What should they wait for?" said Mameh. "They aren't youngsters."

My mother and Levine started talking about the wedding. The ceremony was going to be in Papa's little shul around the corner. Levine said he'd pay for honey cake and wine.

"But I will buy the herring," Papa said. "You can't have a wedding without herring."

Levine smiled in the snobbish way Miss Holbrooke did when one of the Italian girls had said her mother's cooking was better than the food at the lodge.

Levine said he was thinking about joining Temple Israel and Papa gave him the same look back. "You mean the big German synagogue where they throw you out if you wear a yarmulke?"

"The rabbi there is very smart," Levine said. "I can make good connections for business and my sons will meet a better class of people." He winked at me. "And Addie will like it because the women sit with the men, like human beings."

"If you want a church, go to a church," Papa said, and the words hung in the air like a bad smell. My mother got nervous and said that maybe the bride and groom would like to go for a walk together.

Celia said, "And Addie can come with us." See how she looked out for me?

I walked a few steps behind them and watched. Celia looked comfortable holding his arm, and he patted her hand a lot but they didn't say much to each other and I couldn't tell if there was any feeling between them.

We were on Hanover Street, which felt like a carnival after Rockport. There were a lot of people walking and talking at the top of their lungs — in three or four languages, mind you. We walked past a shop window where a group of girls were watching a man take the clothes off a dress dummy. One of girls said, "That's what I call fresh," which made me wonder if Celia knew anything about the birds and the bees. She was so shy about everything.

My mother never told me about sex. When I got my period, she slapped my face and showed me how to wash the towels we had to use. You don't know how lucky you are in that department. I found out about what happened between men and women from a couple of girls in the schoolyard — and they had different versions.

On our cot that night Celia said, "At least you'll have more room when I go."

"But I'll miss you," I said.

She said we would see each other all the time. "Mr. Levine's apartment is only a few blocks from here."

"You don't call him Herman?"

She said she wasn't used to it yet. For three years she had known him as Mr. Levine.

I didn't understand how it all happened so fast. I was only gone a week.

Turns out, it had started in May, when Mrs. Kampinsky, who lived downstairs, told my mother that Levine was looking for a wife and Mameh said why didn't he look right in front of him?

"He asked if he could walk me home after work," Celia said. "I met his sons a few times and Jacob, the little one, seems so sad. Levine asked if I would mind taking care of them and promised that I would have a good life with him."

I asked if she was in love with him.

"Not yet. Mameh says you learn to love someone when you make a life together. She says a man who loves his children is a good man. Myron is six and Jacob is almost four, and they need a mother. And like Mameh says, I'm almost thirty years old and who knows if I'll ever get another chance like this? He'll take care of me and Mameh and Papa when they get old."

I could hear my mother's words coming out of her mouth, so I said, "Did she push you into this? You can still change your mind."

She said no, that she had decided for herself. "He asked me a month ago and I told him I wanted to think. I didn't even tell Mameh until you went away. When she found out where you were, she started screaming that the settlement ladies had sold you to be a white slave and wanted Papa to go to the police. But when I told her about me and Mr. Levine, she had more important things to think about."

I had the horrible feeling that she'd said yes just to protect me. I even asked, "That's not why you're marrying him, is it?"

She said no. "Actually, I feel bad because once I'm gone, you'll have to leave school and I know how much you want to keep going."

She was right. My parents didn't make enough money to pay the rent and everything else. Without Celia's pay I was going to have to get a full-time job.

I felt like a rock had fallen on my chest.

Celia whispered, "I'm sorry, Addie."

I said it wasn't her fault, which was true. I also said it was okay, but that was not true.

MAZEL TOV.

When Levine found out about my sister Betty, he invited her to the wedding. Mameh started arguing, but he made that wave with his hand and said, "Don't be so old-fashioned. I want to meet one of these New Women. Anyway, Celia wants her there."

When Betty walked into the apartment a few nights later, my mother wouldn't even look in her direction. Betty grinned at me. "Who knew little Addie would turn into such a spitfire? Going off on an adventure like that without telling anyone? Atta girl."

I didn't really know Betty. What I remembered most about her was the fights she and Mameh had about her not coming home right after work or about going out at night with friends. The funny thing is, except for the fact that she was younger and curvier, Betty was an exact copy of our mother: same brown eyes, same wavy brown hair, and the same broad nose. They talked the same, too, as if they knew the answer to everything, shaking their heads up and down a lot, which made you nod back, as if you agreed with them — even if you didn't.

Betty was a big talker. She told us all about her job at Filene's and how she had moved up from wrapping packages to sales-girl quicker than anyone could remember.

"You see this skirt?" Betty said. "I got it practically free. A lady brought it back to the store and said it was ripped when she bought it. I think she tore it herself but the store has to pretend like the customer is always right, especially the ones who spend a lot of money. So that means us girls get some nice bargains."

She asked Celia a lot of questions about "this Levine" and came right out and asked if she really wanted to take care of his two children and his house. Mameh got mad. "Of course it's what she wants. It's what every woman wants."

Celia said that we shouldn't worry and that he was a fine man.

Betty started coming over a lot and she usually brought presents: tobacco for Papa, a scarf for Celia, stockings for me, chocolate drops for Mameh. But no matter what she brought or how Celia tried to make nice, it always ended with a fight. Mameh would

72

complain about America; how the apples had no taste and children didn't listen to their parents — even the air was worse here. "People get sick from everyone breathing the same air. In our village we had room at least. The air was clean."

Sooner or later, Betty would smack the table and say, "Enough, already! I remember what it was like over there and the air smelled like cow shit. And the floor in the house was made of dirt. Can you imagine such a thing, Addie? Filthy and disgusting! In America, at least it's the twentieth century."

When they started fighting, Celia shriveled up like a plant without enough water. Sometimes I wondered if she was marrying Levine just to get away from the noise and the tension.

Celia said she wanted to make her own wedding dress, so Levine bought her a beautiful piece of white satin. But a few days before the wedding, when it still wasn't done, Betty said she would help with the finishing and made Celia try it on.

The dress was a plain shift that fell from her shoulders to her ankles, with long sleeves and a flat collar. Betty threw a fit. "You can't wear that. It looks like a nightgown."

Celia said it would be better when she attached the sash. "Then maybe you'll look like a shiny nurse," Betty said. "I'm going to buy the fanciest veil I can find and some lace for the collar and around the hem. You are going to be a pretty bride or I'm not coming to this wedding." Celia giggled, and for a moment I saw them as children: the bossy big sister and the little sister who would follow her anywhere.

Celia's wedding day was sunny and beautiful, so Mameh had to spit three times to ward off the evil eye. "Rain is what brings luck," she said. Betty rolled her eyes and fussed with the veil, which had little pearls sewn all over and covered most of the dress and made Celia look like a princess.

Before we left the house, Betty took me aside and asked if Mameh had explained to Celia what happens on the wedding night.

I said, "Probably not."

Betty groaned. "That isn't good. I'm telling you, Addie, our Celia is not a strong person. We have to keep an eye on her, you and me."

But now that Celia was leaving, I realized how much she had watched over me and had put herself between my mother and me. It was going to be awful without her.

■ ■ ■ ■

Celia took Papa's arm as we walked around the corner to the little storefront synagogue, where Levine and his sons were waiting by the door. The boys looked miserable in new shoes and starched shirts and the groom was blinking as if he had something in his eye.

"Where's your family?" Mameh said.

Levine only had a few second cousins in America, but their children had gotten mumps, so the whole wedding party was just the eight of us, including his boys.

The shul was in a store where they used to sell fish, and since we were there in August and it was hot, the smell came back. I had only been there for High Holiday services, when it was crowded — especially in the back, where the women sat. But that day you could hear an echo, and it was so dark it took a minute for my eyes to see the old men standing next to the table with the food.

Papa said hello to each of them and asked about their wives and children. He prayed with these men before work every morning, so it was like his club. Mameh didn't want them at the wedding — she called them schnorrers — moochers. But I was glad they were there. I thought they made things a little more cheerful.

The rabbi came running in and apologized for being late. He had a long white beard with yellow tobacco stains around his mouth, but he had young eyes and clapped Papa and Levine on the back and said "Mazel tov" like he meant it. He picked four men to hold the chuppah poles and called for Levine and Celia to stand with him under my father's prayer shawl, which was the canopy.

The rabbi sang the blessings, Levine put a ring on Celia's finger, and they sipped from a cup of wine. After Levine stepped on a glass, the old men clapped and sang "Mazel tov."

The whole thing was over in a few minutes.

The rabbi shook hands with everyone, even Celia and the little boys, and left as fast as he came. "He has a funeral," Papa explained.

We ate bread, herring, and honey cake and the old men toasted the wedding couple three times with big glasses of Levine's whiskey. Celia stood beside her new husband and ate a few bites of cake, but when Jacob started whining and rubbing his eyes

76

she said maybe it was time to go.

We walked with them to the end of the block and watched as they turned the corner.

Betty was crying.

Mameh said, "What's the matter with her?"

Papa patted Betty on the cheek. "My grandmother used to say it isn't a wedding if nobody cries."

The apartment was one hundred percent sadder after Celia left. No one smiled at me when I walked in the door, and even though I had the bed to myself, I didn't sleep any better.

My parents fought constantly. Mameh went back to blaming Papa for the baby who died on the boat. "If you had waited with me until he was born, maybe he would still be alive."

Then my father would say, "If we stayed and I was killed, then you and all your children would have died with the rest of your family from typhoid or from Cossacks. And if you'd let me take the other boy to the hospital here, he would still be alive."

That was the first I'd heard about the baby who was born in America before me. He was small and weak from the beginning, but my mother wouldn't let him out of the house. "No one comes back alive from the hospital."

He called her stupid.

She called him a failure.

Night after night, they blamed each other and cursed and wore each other out. Papa started going to shul right after supper. Mameh muttered over her sewing until she had a headache. I stayed on my cot as much as I could, and when the days got shorter and it was too dark to read back there, I fell asleep early and got up before the sun. I didn't mind. That way, I got out of the house before the bickering started again.

THIS DAUGHTER OF YOURS IS A FIRECRACKER.

Betty said she could get me a job at Filene's. "The floorwalker has a little crush on me."

I liked the idea of getting out of the neighborhood and working in a department store. I wouldn't get dirty or ruin my hands and strain my eyes like I would in a factory — if I could even get a job in one.

But it turned out that Filene's wasn't hiring, and since I didn't know how to type or operate a switchboard, I went to all the tearooms and sandwich shops I could walk to, but nobody was looking for waitresses. I didn't have any luck in the stores or movie houses, either.

One Sunday when Betty, Levine, and Celia were visiting, Mameh complained about how lazy I was. "She thinks she's too good to get her hands dirty. Ethel Heilbron's daughter has the brains of a donkey and she's making good money in a shoe factory."

"It's not Addie's fault, Mameh," Celia said.

Levine said, "She'll find something. I read in the newspaper about how a Jewish girl is running the whole library in East Boston." Jewish success stories were one of Levine's favorite topics.

"Look at me. I'm not even born here and I own a shop with twenty workers. Just yesterday, I went to buy buttons from Glieberman and he had a girl writing down the orders so he could sit on his tuches like a big shot. And let me tell you, compared to me, Glieberman is a small-time operator."

Betty said, "But if Glieberman has a secretary, how does it look that you don't have a girl, too?"

Levine shrugged. "He's spending a lot of money just to show off."

"It's not showing off," she said. "It's professional. Besides, I read in a magazine you've got to spend money to make money."

"I heard that, too," he said.

Betty winked at me. "And it just so happens that you have the perfect girl right in front of you. Addie has good penmanship and an A in arithmetic. Tell him how you worked in that settlement house lady's office. You were kind of a secretary there, weren't you?"

Suddenly everyone was looking at me like I was a cow for sale.

Levine slapped the table so hard that the cups rattled. "Mr. Baum," he declared. "This daughter of yours is a firecracker."

"She could start this week," Betty said.

Now everyone looked at Levine, who rubbed his beard and glanced at Celia. "What do you say, Mrs. Levine?"

She was bent over some mending and didn't answer. So he said it again, louder. "Celia, would it make you happy if I hire Addie?"

When she realized he was talking to her she looked up and said, "Yes?"

"Of course yes," Betty said, who was very proud of herself for coming up with the idea. She kept talking, and before Levine or I knew what had happened, she arranged for me to start the next day. When I showed up at H. L. Shirtwaists at seven o'clock the next morning, it took him a minute to remember what I was doing there.

His "factory" was one big room on the second floor over a butcher's. There were maybe twelve sewing machines, a couple of pressing machines, some tables for cutting and finishing, all crowded together. And in those days, people didn't take that many baths, so you can imagine what it smelled like.

Levine didn't have a real office, just a corner near one of the back windows where he had stacked some packing crates to make a separation. His desk was a door on top of more crates, and on that was a big mess of papers and envelopes and scraps of material.

I picked up a receipt and remembered how the secretaries I met at Rockport Lodge talked about their bosses like they were little children who couldn't wipe their noses without help. I said, "Maybe I can straighten this up for you."

Levine was blinking like he always did when he got nervous and said, "Just what I was thinking."

By the end of the day I had sorted everything into neat stacks and told him he needed boxes or a cabinet for the paper and ledger books and some new pencils. "All you've got here are stubs."

"You aren't going to be saving me any money," Levine said, but I could tell he liked what I had done. "Tomorrow you'll go shopping."

At the beginning, I was busy. I put away the old papers and made up a system for paying bills. I entered a whole year's business in a ledger, and I saw how Levine was doing, which was pretty good. He got rid of the door and bought a real desk that was so big we had to move the dividing crates back to make room for it. He was very proud of that desk, and after I polished it, you'd never know it was secondhand.

On days when buyers or suppliers came in, I stood behind Levine with a new pad and a sharp pencil to write orders: how many shirtwaists in which sizes by such-and-such a day, or how much thread in what colors to be delivered at such-and-such a price.

The men were impressed that Levine could afford a full-time girl, even though I was his sister-in-law and probably working cheap. Actually, I knew from doing his books that I was getting paid almost as much as his best stitchers, who were making some of the highest wages in the neighborhood. I also saw that he didn't fire people when they got sick and that when one of the men had a baby Levine gave him a whole day off for the bris and didn't even dock his pay.

Celia's husband wasn't such a ganef after all.

But after a few weeks, I didn't have enough to do and there were days I could have screamed from boredom. Why is it you get more tired from sitting and doing nothing than from running around doing too much?

But even a bad day at work was better than being at home. The best part of the week was going to the Saturday Club meetings, where I was a person who knew how to cook eggs over an open fire and play lawn tennis and do the turkey trot.

My mother never let me out of the house on Saturday night without making a stink. "Those women, they smile in your face but behind your back they're laughing at you and calling you a filthy Yid."

I didn't say anything back. We both knew that I was going to go — no matter what. Levine was paying me good money, which meant she could buy chicken every week and didn't have to do as much piecework sewing at home.

I kept enough to save for Rockport Lodge and even buy myself something now and then. The first thing I bought was a green felt cloche. You know what I'm talking about? A hat that's shaped like a bell and fits around your face.

In my whole life I never enjoyed buying anything more than that hat. It wasn't expensive but it was stylish and I felt like a movie star when I wore it. I loved that hat.

My mother took one look and said it made me look like a meeskeit, ugly. That hurt my feelings and made me so mad, I told her I wasn't going to talk to her unless she used English. And by the way, she knew enough to understand every piece of gossip she heard in the grocery store.

I said it was for her own good. "What if you had an emergency and I wasn't there?"

"So then I'll be dead and you'll be sorry," she said, in Yiddish, of course.

After that, when she suddenly needed me to run to the store or get my father at shul — always on a Saturday night — I shrugged and slammed the door on my way out. I was feeling my oats, as they used to say. What could she really do? Without what I earned, she would be back to sewing sheets ten hours a day and eating potatoes every night.

Money is power, right?

MAYBE I WOULDN'T BE A WALLFLOWER AFTER ALL.

I'm not sure how much you want to know about your grandmother's love life. Not that I had so many boyfriends.

My first kiss was that summer in Rockport when I was sixteen. There was a dance, and since there was a coast guard training camp in town, there were always more men than women, so all the Rockport Lodge girls knew they'd be dancing.

I had never been to a dance so Rose taught me the fox-trot and the waltz. She said I was a natural. "If anyone asks you to do anything fancy, just say you're out of breath and would he like to sit this one out with you."

Of all the girls, I really did not have anything to wear, but Filomena tucked and basted one of Helen's dresses so it looked like it had been made for me. Irene pomaded my hair and piled it on top of my head and Gussie pinched my cheeks for color.

When they were finished, I went to look at myself in the bathroom mirror. It was like one of those before-and-after pictures. When I looked in that mirror on the first day I was there, I saw a pale, scared girl with circles under her eyes. But here was a grown-up woman with a daisy behind her ear, smiling to beat the band.

My brown hair was lighter from the sun and with it pulled back and all fancied up, I could see that Celia wasn't the only Baum girl with an oval face and wide eyes. Maybe I wouldn't be a wallflower after all.

The dance was in an empty barn that smelled of bleach and horses. There was a Victrola in the corner playing a waltz, but the town girls were all bunched up in one corner, whispering and staring at the coast guard cadets in their sharp white uniforms, who were leaning against the opposite wall, smoking cigarettes.

"Elegant, ain't it?" Irene said.

When we walked in, the cadets straightened up, and right away Helen, Irene, and Filomena were out on the dance floor. Rose took me to the refreshment table, where a very tall cadet was standing near the punch bowl. "Allow me, ladies," he said and filled us each a cup.

He was so tall that I had to tilt my head up to look at him. His hair was as black as Filomena's but very fine and parted on the side. His eyes were dark blue — almost purple — with the kind of long eyelashes girls dream about. He looked me over and said, "Green suits you."

I was so nervous I almost said, "You, too."

He asked if I liked to dance.

Rose said, "Addie can really cut a rug. What about you?"

"I'm not bad, if I say so myself. My mother taught me. By the way, I am Harold George Weeks from Bath, Maine."

Rose shook his hand. "I'm Rose Reardon and this is Addie Baum. We're from Boston."

"Nice to meet you, Miss Reardon. First time in Rockport, Miss Baum?"

Just then the record changed and he grabbed my hand. "The turkey trot is a snap. Four steps in a box and then you hop."

Before I knew what was happening, we were on the dance floor and he had his hand on my back. He leaned down and whispered, "Don't think," and the next second, I was hopping and spinning around the room and having the time of my life. We were practically flying in circles but somehow I wasn't getting dizzy.

I was completely out of breath when the song ended but Harold didn't let go when a fox-trot started playing. I was counting the steps in my head, but I kept losing track and stumbling. Harold pulled me closer to him — he smelled like lemons and leather — and said, "You're thinking. Just follow me and you'll be fine." He really knew what he was doing, because the way he steered me around the floor made me look good.

When that song ended, he bowed and strutted over to the other cadets, who shook his hand and slapped him on the back. My friends ran over to me and Gussie said, "I thought you didn't know how to dance." Helen asked what his name was. Irene said he was the best-looking man in the room.

But Filomena made a face. "He knows it, too."

"How can you say that?" I said. "You didn't even talk to him."

"I know a wolf when I see one."

Rose pinched Filomena's cheek. "Oh, she's just jealous that he asked you instead of her."

I danced with a few other cadets, but they were flat-footed and clumsy compared to Harold Weeks. I kept hoping he'd come back but he was dancing with one of the local girls who knew how to tango and wore rolled stockings and a lot of rouge.

I'd given up on dancing with him again when he tapped me on the shoulder and said, "Can you spare a waltz?"

I didn't want to sound like I'd been dying for him to ask, so I said, "I could ask you the same question."

"Jealous, eh?"

I just smiled and tried to flirt like the other girls. I tilted my head to one side and opened my eyes really wide. Someone had told me that men like it when you let them talk about themselves, so I asked him why he joined the coast guard.

"I was supposed to take over from my father at the ironworks, but I hated the idea of building ships and never going to sea."

"What did he say when you enlisted?" I asked.

"I didn't tell him."

"You mean you ran away?" I was thrilled to think we had so much in common.

He said, "I told my mother so she wouldn't worry. I'm a lot like her and she has a mind of her own. You should have seen the looks in church when she walked in with her hair chopped off, like Irene Castle."

So much for having anything in common. When the song ended, I heard Miss Holbrooke calling me and the other lodge girls off the dance floor.

"I see I have to let you go," Harold said. He took my hand up to his lips and said, "Meet me outside on the porch at midnight. I'll be waiting for you."

And just like that, I had an *assignation*! I don't know how I knew that word but I knew it meant something romantic — maybe not so respectable but completely thrilling.

I told Filomena about it on the way back, but instead of being happy for me, she said, "Don't you dare. He thinks he can take advantage because you're so young."

"Maybe he likes my eyes," I said. "Maybe he thinks I'm a good listener."

"You think he's coming over in the middle of the night to talk to you? I thought you were smarter than that."

We went back and forth. She told me he was a skirt chaser and to wake up but I thought she was just being mean or maybe Rose was right and she was jealous.

Finally she gave up. "If I can't talk you out of it, swear that you'll stay on the porch or else I will go out there with you."

After I promised not to leave the porch, Filomena didn't say another word to me all night. She just turned off the light and pulled the pillow over her head. I hated that she was mad at me, but Harold was so handsome and no man had ever paid me that kind of attention. And when was I ever going to have another assignation?

I was lying on top of the bedspread, waiting for the first stroke of midnight, like Cinderella except I had both of my shoes on. I flew down those stairs and out the kitchen door, which they never locked.

It was very dark — no moon or stars — and I didn't see Harold anywhere. I waited and worried and was starting to give up when I saw his white uniform moving through the orchard.

He took my hands and kissed them really slowly, and not just on top but on the palms, too. It made me shiver. But when he tried to pull me toward the trees, I sat down on the step and tucked my skirt around my legs.

"Oh, so you are a good girl," he said and sat down with his leg right against mine. "Good girls don't usually dance like that."

I said, "Like what?" trying to act as if I'd had this kind of conversation a million times.

"Free. Willing to go along and let loose. We were special together, Addie. Didn't you feel it? I could have gone on dancing all night with you."

He sounded so much like a character in a magazine story that I giggled.

"What's so funny?"

"Nothing," I said. "I guess I'm not used to compliments."

"You should be." He put his arm around my waist, I leaned my head on his shoulder, and imagined how romantic we must look.

Then he turned my face up to his and kissed me on the mouth.

"Your first time?" he said.

"Oh, no. I'm not a baby, you know."

"Of, course not," he said. "I wouldn't do this to a baby." He kissed me again. He was as good a kisser as he was a dancer, and I followed him like I did with the fox-trot — without thinking.

It was very exciting and, well, let's just say that I didn't realize how far along things had gotten until I heard the church bell.

That's when I sat up and said I should go inside.

Harold had his arm around my waist and said we should go out to the hammock in the orchard where we could look at the stars. "It's so beautiful, Addie," he whispered.

I said no and that I had to go inside. When he didn't let go of me, I said it again.

A window upstairs opened and somebody coughed.

Harold let go of me. "I shouldn't have come." He sounded mad.

I said, "Don't be mad."

"Come with me and I won't be."

But I didn't move and the coughing got louder.

Harold stood up, lit a cigarette, and walked away. No goodbye. Nothing. It was awful.

Filomena pretended she was asleep when I got in bed, which was okay with me. I didn't want to talk about what had happened or how I was feeling and, boy oh boy, was I feeling things. I didn't know if that meant I was a floozy or if I was in love. And what was Harold Weeks feeling? Maybe he was a wolf after all or maybe I had done something wrong.

The last thing I wanted to hear from Filomena was "I told you so." Especially since I would have done anything to see him again and I was miserable because I knew that was never going to happen.

WE GOT A SUFFRAGETTE IN THE FAMILY.

Starting in September, Levine wouldn't stop talking about Thanksgiving. "The Americans say a prayer before they start eating," he said. "What do think, Mr. Baum?"

"By us it's not a holiday," Papa said.

"Why not? We live in America so we should celebrate like Americans. This week I filled out citizenship papers for Celia and me. My boys were born here so they don't have to worry. Not Addie, either. But the rest of us, we have to apply."

"For what?" Papa said. "So they can find us easier to throw us out? Or put boys into the army?"

"For voting," said Levine.

Betty sniffed. "So why should I bother if they don't let me?"

Levine clapped his hands. "We got a suffragette in the family. What do you think, Celia? Is Betty right? Should women vote like men? Celia?"

Like always, Celia was mending clothes and not paying attention. She had dark circles under her eyes and she'd gotten so thin that her clothes hung off her like they were pinned to a clothesline.

Levine said it again. "What do you think about votes for women?"

She looked lost, so I said, "Of course women should be able to vote. In Australia, they vote, and in Denmark." After a year in the Saturday Club, I'd heard a lot of lectures about suffrage and I was about to tell him all the states where women were already voting in America when Levine put his hands up.

"I'm not fighting with you. Mr. Louis Brandeis says that in Palestine women should vote; that's good enough for me."

"You are a modern man, Mr. L.," said Betty.

"I hope so. And I want you all to come to eat by us for Thanksgiving, like real Americans with turkey and apple pie!"

Celia did hear that. "You never said anything before." She looked terrified.

"Maybe you should have given her a vote," I said.

"It'll be fine, Celia," he said. "Addie will help you. I'll give her the whole day off from work — with pay."

Mameh made a face. She had tried to teach Celia to cook, but Celia burned everything she put on the stove and nicked her fingers whenever she picked up a knife. She couldn't boil water and chop carrots at the same time and whenever Mameh tried to correct her, she covered her face with a dishcloth. "Who would have thought a girl who sews with such golden hands would have trouble peeling a potato?"

Celia's apartment was a wreck: pots and dishes piled up in the kitchen, dust in the corners, and a sour smell of dirty clothes. Mameh got so disgusted, she stopped going.

But I missed Celia and went to see her a lot, though I wasn't sure Celia was always glad to see me. Instead of "hello" she would apologize for the mess and then try to clear the table so we could have tea, but first she had to wash the cups and then she couldn't find the tea. She never seemed to finish anything and she never sat down.

But the worst thing was how Levine's sons treated her. In the beginning, they were real monsters. Myron, who was six, was just plain nasty when Celia talked to him, and Jacob, the three-year-old, copied what his big brother did. Every time Celia gave the little one a bath, she got black-and-blue marks all over her arms.

But no matter what they did, she wouldn't let anyone say a word against them. "Imagine how they must feel to lose their real mother. Who am I? A stranger."

Things got a little better after Levine gave Myron a smack for talking back to her. But "better" meant that they just ignored her, which wasn't hard to do since she was getting quieter all the time.

The day after the big discussion about Thanksgiving, Levine was waiting for me at the door when I got to work. "Your sister says no turkey. No matter what I tell her, she won't have it in the house. It would be a nice thing for the whole family. I want you to talk to her. The boys would be so disappointed."

I thought Levine was the one who would be disappointed, but I understood how he felt. Every year in school we learned about the Pilgrims and how the Indians gave them turkey. I wanted to have Thanksgiving like the pictures in the newspaper, too, but not if it was going to make Celia miserable. I couldn't take his side against her.

I told him it would be better if he asked Betty to argue for the turkey, figuring she'd be able to talk Levine out of the whole thing. She was always telling Celia to stand

98

up for herself.

But it turned out that Betty agreed with Levine. "It's not such a big thing," she said. "He doesn't ask anything from us and we're all better off because of him, you most of all. You have to help me to talk Celia into it."

Betty hadn't been to Celia's apartment for a while and after being shocked at the mess, she took off her hat and gloves and started washing dishes like it was something she did all the time.

"You don't have to," said Celia.

"Of course not," Betty said. "Now go comb your hair."

After the sink was empty and the table was clean, Betty poured us tea.

"This is so nice," Celia said and smiled like I hadn't seen in months.

Betty patted her hand. "So what do I hear that you won't make your husband a turkey?"

Right away, the light went out of Celia's eyes.

"How can she cook a turkey in this place?" I said. "Do you see a pot big enough? Do you see an oven?"

"He's her husband," said Betty. "He pays the bills, he wants what he wants. I told Herman he could buy one of those cooked turkeys from the Italian butcher."

"Treif meat in my house?" Celia whispered, like she didn't want God to hear. She rubbed her hands up and down her cheeks. "No. If it has to be, you can come here to eat, but chicken from the kosher butcher." The tea went cold while Betty came up with one argument after another, but nothing changed Celia's mind. Finally she said, "Maybe you should go now. I have to make something to eat for him and the boys."

As soon as we got outside, I said, "Since when are you calling him Herman?"

"What are you mad about?" said Betty. "You're the one who told him to talk to me. He doesn't know what to do with her anymore. She's crying all the time, even in her sleep. So I told him how she didn't talk for a whole year when Papa brought us to America. At first, she cried so much she would make herself throw up. She walked in her sleep, too. She's not a strong person, our Celia. She is afraid of everything."

Betty lowered her voice. "And I mean everything. Since the wedding night she hasn't let him near her. I mean in the bed. Can you imagine? All these months? He could divorce her for that."

I tried to think where Levine and Betty could have talked about such a thing: across from each other in a restaurant where strangers could hear? In his office after I left? In Betty's room?

"I give him credit," Betty said. "He's doing his best with her. I told him, if worse comes to worst, I can bring the turkey from the Italians. Celia doesn't have to eat it."

But it never came to that.

Somehow, Celia won the turkey argument and Levine said we would have Thanksgiving chicken at five o'clock, which was a ridiculous hour since usually no one got off work until six. But Levine said that was when regular Americans ate, so we would, too.

Papa made fun of the goyishe simcha, the gentile party, but the week before the holiday he asked me to tell him the story about the Pilgrims and the Indians. Mameh decided that she would make a tsimmes of mashed carrots, "So at least there will be something to eat." Betty said she would help Celia clean the apartment and Papa went to the barber. I thought maybe it wouldn't be so bad after all.

I Thought I Was in Love.

You remember my cadet, Harold Weeks? Well, I did see him again.

I was on my way to Saturday Club when a man in a dark overcoat walked up to me and said, "Pretty hat on a pretty girl."

When I realized who it was, all I could say was "What are you doing here?"

He said, "Aren't you glad to see me?"

He'd gotten posted to Boston and "looked me up." He remembered that I'd said something about my Saturday-night meetings and did some snooping.

Who knew you could be too happy to speak? He had gone to all that trouble to find me when I was sure he'd forgotten all about me. It was like a dream.

He said he wanted to take me to dinner and I said yes.

He talked as we walked, though I was practically running to keep up with those long legs of his. He told me he didn't like

102

being in the coast guard anymore. He was bored all the time and his shipmates were stupid. He didn't sleep at all when they were at sea, and the Boston barracks were disgusting. His uniform didn't fit and he hadn't had a decent meal in weeks.

We went to a famous restaurant that I'd never heard of where everyone was eating things that didn't look like food to me: clams, oysters, lobsters. But I thought it all had to be good, because everything was so elegant. The tables were set with heavy silverware and wineglasses, and the waiters wore big white aprons and moved around the room like they were on roller skates.

The women were wearing beautiful dresses and gorgeous hats with big feathers. I thought I must look like a weed in a rose garden but Harold didn't seem to mind. He was excited about the menu and ordered a huge amount of food and a whole bottle of wine.

I tasted the lobster, which wasn't bad. But the clam was so slimy I swallowed half a glass of wine to wash the feeling out of my mouth. So then I was tipsy, another first for me.

I could hardly look at Harold eat the oysters. "You don't know what you're missing," he said.

He was better-looking than I remembered. His teeth were perfectly white, his finger-nails were perfectly clean, and in the gaslight his eyes were blue-black. When he talked, I could feel his voice vibrate inside my head, as if I were standing next to a big bell.

When the waiter brought coffee, Harold said, "I haven't shut up all night, have I? What about you? Are you still working at a shop?"

I couldn't remember what lie I'd told him and was trying to think of a way to change the subject when I recognized a man sitting across the room.

"See the old man by the potted plant?" I said. "The one with the white beard who looks like he's going to fall asleep in his soup? I heard him give a lecture about Longfellow once."

Harold took my hand under the table and moved his leg so it was touching mine. "Longfellow, eh? I didn't realize that you were such a highbrow."

I forgot all about time until we walked outside and I asked how late it was. If I got home past nine thirty, Mameh might send my father out to find me, and if he went to the settlement house, Miss Chevalier would think I had used the club as an excuse to do something I shouldn't. I hated the thought of disappointing her — never mind what would happen at home.

Harold said it wasn't even nine o'clock and his curfew wasn't until eleven.

When I told him I had to start for home right away, he stopped smiling. "After a meal like that, I figured we'd take a walk and have a little fun."

I said I was sorry but I couldn't be late.

He took off up the street with his shoulders bunched up around his ears and I really did have to run to catch up. Eventually he slowed down and put his arm around me. "I never stopped thinking about you, Addie," he said, and when he leaned down to kiss me, I kissed him right back.

"That's my girl," he said.

I was his girl! He pulled me into a doorway and we kissed some more.

I didn't have a telephone number to give him, so Harold and I decided to meet in front of the State House the next Saturday night.

Keeping that secret made me feel like I was living inside a novel. The week seemed like it would never end. I kept bumping into things at work and at home I was so touchy, Mameh said she was going to give me an enema, which was her cure for everything.

105

For our second date, Harold took me to a Charlie Chaplin picture. I loved Chaplin, but Harold seemed bored and after a few minutes he kissed me and then, well, he got fresh and I told him to stop it.

When we left the movie he asked if I was afraid of him.

I tried to make a joke out of it. "Should I be?"

He chucked me under the chin. "What do you think?"

It was still early, so we walked along Washington Street with all the other couples that were strolling along arm in arm. Harold said that on one of his walks around the city he had found a wood carving that looked exactly like the ships his family built. "It's on the door of a bank, so nobody notices it," he said. "It's one of my favorite things in Boston. How about if I show it to my favorite Boston girl?"

We left the crowds and walked to a street where all the big banks and lawyers' offices were. In the daytime it was crowded and noisy, but at night it was like a cemetery and I got a little nervous.

Harold knew a lot about the decorations on the sides of the buildings — what they stood for and when they were made. Then he stopped. "Here we are."

The door he wanted to show me was at the end of a long entryway, where it was so dark I couldn't see the carving at all. Harold took my hand and ran it over the outlines of the boats and the water. And of course, we started kissing.

Like I said, Harold was a really good kisser, and by then I was really getting the hang of it, so I closed my eyes and stopped thinking. But then he started getting rough. He bit my ear and pawed at my chest, and when I tried to push him away he pinned me against the wall. The next thing I knew, he had his leg between mine and was pumping against me hard, with his mouth clamped over mine so I couldn't tell him to stop. I could hardly breathe.

It didn't last long. When he pulled away he kissed my cheeks and my forehead, sweet as could be. Then he sort of growled, "Now I bet you'd like me to say that I love you."

Not very nice, is it? Not the kind of thing you tell your granddaughter. I don't think I ever told anyone about that particular experience. Who was I going to tell? Filomena would say not to see him again and I didn't want to hear that. I thought I was in love.

I must have mentioned something about

where I worked because that's where Harold sent the letter. It started "Darling," and was full of compliments. I was wonderful, I was smart, pretty, a good sport, and modern. He said he'd never met anyone like me — a real city girl but not hard. There was even a little pressed flower in the envelope.

He said he was going to Washington, D.C., for a few days, but I should pick a time and place for our next date and he would be there "or die trying." I thought that was very gallant.

I wrote back for him to meet me at nine o'clock in the morning on the State House steps on the Thursday that was Thanksgiving. I had the day off to help Celia, but I could still get to her house in plenty of time. And since it would be broad daylight, I wouldn't have to worry about him getting fresh.

I went a few minutes early but Harold was already there, waiting for me with a rose. It was the first time I'd ever seen him in the daytime and I was swept off my feet all over again. The brass buttons on his coat were gleaming and the sun made his black hair shine. He had grown a little moustache, which made him look dashing and older. "You look so handsome," I said.

He laughed. "For that, you're getting

breakfast at the Parker House."

I knew all about the Parker House. I asked if we could get some of their rolls.

He said I was adorable. "I don't think they let you out unless you eat one of those things."

There were Oriental rugs and a big chandelier in the lobby, which was as quiet as a library, but the restaurant was completely different — loud, and cloudy with cigar smoke from tables full of men wearing good suits. I was the only woman in the room except for a white-haired lady who was drinking tea and reading a newspaper.

A boy in a white jacket brought us coffee and a basket of those famous rolls, which were beautiful and warm.

Harold told me about all the important people he had met in Washington and how pretty the monuments were. "You have to see it sometime."

When he finished his bacon and eggs, Harold put his hand on the inside of my knee and said, "Look at you — taking everything in with those big green eyes of yours. It's just like the night I met you, I thought to myself, now, here's a girl who's on the lookout. You were free as a bird, Addie. The new woman."

I tried to move my chair back and said,

109

"How could you know all that about me from just a few dances?"

"I know talent." He squeezed my thigh. "That was a real lucky night for me. But then, I'm a lucky man."

Harold stopped the busboy from refilling my coffee cup and asked for the bill. "I've been assigned to the coast guard commander's office. My father may have had a hand in that. But I don't care; it's a way out of that damn barrack."

I told him that was wonderful.

"Of course, it means I'll be moving to Washington," he said, as if he were talking about a change in the weather. "I ship out tomorrow."

"Tomorrow?"

I felt as if I'd been knocked down — like when the tide had pulled my feet out from under me at the beach. Miss Holbrooke had said, "That's the undertow. A girl was dragged out to sea last month. They never found her body."

Harold said, "I didn't want to tell you until everything was settled. And I've got another surprise for you." He put his arm around me and walked me to the elevator. "I got us a room so we can have a proper goodbye."

That was the moment I couldn't fool

myself anymore. Filomena had been right and I had been an idiot.

I said, "You think I'd go to a hotel room with you? Is that what you think of me?"

A bell sounded and an old man in a red cap opened the elevator grate.

Harold leaned over me and whispered, "Don't give me that. You let me buy you fancy meals. You didn't squawk when I pawed you from one end to the other. You can't say I haven't been patient. So shut up and do as you're told."

I tried to pull away from him but he tightened his grip on my hand.

"You're hurting me," I said — and not in a whisper.

Harold looked around to see if anyone was listening and said, "Aw, sweetheart," to make it seem like we were having a lovers' quarrel. "Now, be a good girl."

He pushed me into the elevator, but I said, "Let me go," loud enough so the elevator man said, "What's going on?"

Harold had murder on his face. "Do you know what that room cost me, you little sheeny bitch?"

When he reached for the grate I bit him. I really sank my teeth into his hand.

He howled and made a fist. I started screaming, "Don't hit me, don't hit me."

When Harold saw the bellmen come toward us, he backed away from me, turned up the collar on his coat, and started to walk across the lobby — not in any big hurry — as if he were taking a stroll through the park. I watched him, feeling like that drowned girl in the undertow.

When the doorman opened the door for him and he disappeared, I realized that everyone was staring at me and I took off in the opposite direction from the door. I was running without knowing where. I guess I was looking for another way out, but all I found was a stairway going down, so that's where I went and ended up in the basement, where I was almost hit in the face by a big tray loaded with cups and saucers.

It stopped an inch from my nose and I heard "Jesus Christ!"

It was the busboy who had poured my coffee. He put down the tray and asked what I was doing in the basement and what happened to my sailor.

I started to cry.

He was so nice. He said, "It's okay. I didn't think you looked like the type."

I guess everyone in the restaurant thought I was a floozy, to put it nicely.

I walked back to the North End as fast as I

could. I kept my head down, thinking about how stupid I'd been.

I liked to think of myself as smarter than most girls, but I had talked myself into believing I was in love with a man who thought I was easy, who insulted me, who was ready to force me. So stupid.

The thing is, I should have known what kind of man he was from when we were on the dance floor. When Harold leaned down to tell me to meet him on the porch, he — I can't believe I'm saying this to you — he stuck his tongue in my ear. I was disgusted that anyone would do such a thing, but I was also thrilled — from one end to the other, if you know what I mean.

But even after that night in the doorway when I had bruises all over my back? Even then I kept fooling myself.

I'm still embarrassed and mad at myself. But after seventy years, I also feel sorry for the girl I used to be. She was awfully hard on herself.

It Was My Fault.

It was barely eleven o'clock when I got to Celia's house but the kitchen was already a disaster. There were pots and dishes on every surface and a hill of unpeeled potatoes on the table, where Celia was standing over some thick and sticky syrup that was dripping onto the floor. Jacob ran toward me, his hands and face smeared with the spill but Celia stared at me as if she wasn't sure why I was there.

And then she started to sink, as if her knees were letting go in slow motion, until she was sitting on the floor between the table and the stove. That must have been when I realized that the pool on the floor was blood because I screamed, which scared Jacob, who started crying.

Celia's hands were bleeding from cuts on her fingers and palms, all the way to her wrists. "What happened?" I said. "Does it hurt?"

She didn't seem to be in pain. She smiled at me and watched me try to wrap her hands with the dishcloths as if it had nothing to do with her.

Meanwhile, I was begging her to tell me what happened. She just shook her head.

I tried to lift her onto the chair, but even though she was nothing but skin and bones, for some reason I couldn't budge her. I kept saying, "Celia, stand up. Celia, please. Celia, talk to me."

By then, her eyes were closed and I'm not even sure she heard me.

Finally I propped her up so she was leaning against the stove. I picked up Jacob, who was sobbing, and told Celia I was going to get help.

That's when she opened her eyes and said, "I'm sorry to be so much trouble."

I said, "It's okay. Stay still. I'll be right back."

People were standing on the sidewalk to see what was going on with Jacob screaming and when they saw him and me covered with blood, someone hollered, "Murder!"

I tried to tell them about Celia but they were yelling "Call a cop! Get that kid away from her!"

A policeman pushed through and said, "Hand me the boy."

I told him Jacob wasn't hurt. "It's my sister. She cut herself but I can't carry her. She needs a doctor. Hurry."

He ran inside and I stood on the stoop with Jacob, who was whimpering and shivering in my arms. I could feel the blood starting to harden between my hands and his shirt.

The cop came flying out with Celia in his arms, her head folded against his chest like a sleeping baby. "Out of my way," he said, and ran to the saloon across the street. He kicked the door open and yelled, "Riley, I'm taking your beer cart!" He wrapped Celia in a horse blanket and set her down on the seat beside him. When I tried to climb in back, he said, "You get the little boy someplace safe and go fetch the husband." He sounded calm but I could see his hands were shaking; he wasn't much older than me.

As he was driving away, I yelled, "Where are you taking her?"

Someone behind me said, "He'll go to the Mass General on Fruit Street."

Someone else said, "No. Mount Sinai is closer."

"I don't think it matters. Did you see the color of her?"

A woman crossed herself and said, "Poor thing."

I ran home, handed Jacob to Mameh, said Celia had had an accident and I was going to get Levine.

I was still covered with blood when I walked into his office and before he could ask I said, "Jacob is fine. Celia cut herself."

"What are you saying? Where is she?"

"Mount Sinai, I think. I'm not sure. A policeman took her."

He told me to get Myron from school and wait for him at my house. But first, I went for Papa and I swear the lines on his face got deeper when I told him what happened.

When I got back with Myron, Jacob was wrapped in a towel, his hair wet from a bath, and my mother was feeding him carrots. Papa sat across from them with a prayer book in his hands, rocking back and forth.

I stood by the window to wait for Celia. I imagined the cop carrying her through the door but now her eyes would be open. Her hands would be covered with clean white bandages. Mameh would scold her for being so clumsy. Papa would take her face between his hands and kiss her forehead and I would become the sister that Celia deserved.

Celia wouldn't have let me apologize for

117

being late. She would have said, "An accident can happen anytime." Nobody could forgive like Celia. She was the only person in my family who ever kissed me.

I closed my eyes and prayed, "Come home now, come home now."

The afternoon dragged on and on. Jacob fell asleep on my bed. Myron went out to the stoop and no one tried to stop him. When it started to get dark, Papa turned on the light and stood in a corner with his prayer book while Mameh stared at the door, chewing her lips and wringing her hands. I heard the neighbors whispering on the landing, and as much as I wanted to go out there and chase them away, I was afraid to leave the window. I got it into my head that I had to stay there or Celia wouldn't come home.

The chatter on the other side of the door stopped and Levine walked in, red-eyed and stooped, followed by Betty, who looked scared and lost, still carrying a cake box for Thanksgiving. Then the policeman who had taken Celia to the hospital came in. The front of his uniform was black with blood but his arms were empty.

He took off his hat and walked over to Papa. "Sir, I'm sorry to bring such terrible news. The doctor said your daughter lost too much blood and there was nothing they could do."

"Sima!" Mameh fell on her knees. "My jewel!" she screamed. "She was like gold, that one. Pure gold."

"I'm sorry," said the policeman. "Maybe if I had gotten there sooner . . ."

"It was not your fault," Papa said. "My daughter said how fast you were to help. I want to thank you." Levine leaned his forehead against the wall and cried without making a sound. Betty held on to Papa.

I opened the door for the policeman, Michael Culkeen — I'll never forget his name. He said, "Can I have a minute, miss?"

He led me past the neighbors and we walked down the block until there was no one to hear us. He took off his hat again and sighed. "I feel real bad about this, but I have to ask if you saw what happened with your own eyes. The doc says I have to make a report because of the way she had those cuts across her wrists. He said it would take a while for a person to bleed like that."

I said it wouldn't have happened at all if I'd gotten there earlier. I said my sister could sew the wings on a butterfly, but in the kitchen she was always cutting her fingers. I couldn't stop talking; "She was the sweetest person you'd ever meet. This is all my fault." I told him he should arrest me.

Officer Culkeen sighed and said, "Don't you go blaming yourself." He had kind blue eyes and an Irish lilt that reminded me of Rose. "It was you that gave her a fighting chance." His next sigh turned into a groan. "I've been on the force just a year and I got to think it's like the priest says: God wants the good ones with him. I shouldn't have said anything. Your sister was such a little slip of a thing. Put me in mind of a cousin of mine," he said. "You go back inside now. You're shaking like a leaf."

Celia was buried in a cemetery in someplace called Woburn — way outside the city. Levine made arrangements for the plot, the coffin, and a hearse. He paid for a car to take the family to the burial, too, but I stayed home with Myron and Jacob.

I couldn't decide which was worse, watching them put Celia into the ground or not being there to see it. Either way, I was sure there was no punishment I didn't deserve.

It wouldn't have happened if I had been there.

That's what I thought about first thing in the morning and last thing at night. Celia would still be alive if I hadn't been with that horrible man, if I hadn't been such a fool.

It was my fault.

All week, neighbors and strangers walked in and out of the apartment. The men were quiet when they came for prayers before work and again in the evening. In between, women walked in and out with food and stayed to drink tea, wash dishes, and talk.

They never ran out of stupid things to say. All of them had a sister or a cousin who lost a child and never got over it. Mrs. Kampinsky had heard of a woman who dropped dead exactly one month after her son was hit by a car.

Mameh repeated the story of Celia's accident again and again: the plans for a big meal, the knife that slipped, the policeman, the funeral in a terrible ugly place too far away to ever visit. Then she would burst into tears and scream "Ai, ai, ai," and they would have to grab her hands to keep her from tearing her hair out. They said how sorry they were and then they raised their eyebrows behind her back. Whenever I heard my mother's version of what happened, I felt sick to my stomach.

On the last day of shiva, the men hung around afterward, eating and drinking, talking about layoffs, the price of coal, the weather — as if it didn't make any difference that Celia was under the ground.

I hated them.

Betty and Levine took the boys for a walk and Mameh went to lie down on my bed late in the afternoon after the last cup was washed and put away. Papa fell asleep, sitting up on the sofa.

I stood at the window without seeing the color of the sky or the people on the street. Celia was dead and I had no right to think about anything else. I would keep her in my mind forever. I would stop going to Saturday Club and get a second job. I would give my parents every nickel like Celia used to. I would be a better person. I would be a different girl.

Someone knocked on the door.

Papa woke up. "It must be Gilman," he said. "Addie, go tell him he'll get his rent next week."

But it wasn't the landlord.

Rose held out a little bouquet of violets. "It's from all the girls at the club," she said. Her fair skin was chapped from the wind. Gussie wore a checkered scarf wrapped all the way to her nose. Helen had a new red hat. Irene took my hand and wouldn't let go. Filomena kissed me on both cheeks.

I felt like I was seeing them for the first time and I couldn't believe how beautiful they were.

"Get your coat," Filomena said. "We're taking you out for some fresh air."

■ ■ ■ ■

1917–18

■ ■ ■ ■

IT WAS LIKE WAKING UP FROM A BAD DREAM.

If it hadn't been for Filomena I don't think I would have gone out of the house after work or on weekends all that winter. She dragged me to Saturday Club a few times, but I really wasn't ready to be in a room full of happy girls, so she took me to Sunday movie matinees instead. I only wanted to see sad pictures, which meant we saw a lot of people cough themselves to death; Filomena always picked a comedy. "Life is hard enough," she said.

She took me to the art museum, too. It was free admission in those days. I had never been, but Filomena knew where everything was. She knew something interesting about a lot of the paintings, and when no one was around, she ran her fingers over the sculptures. She said it let her see them better.

When it got to be spring, she said we should pick a week to go to Rockport

Lodge. I told her I wasn't going.

"If it's money, I'll help," she said.

When I said it wasn't the money, she said, "Is it Celia?"

The sound of her name made me flinch. I hadn't heard it in months. I think my parents were always bickering about stupid things — about nothing, really — because they were afraid of saying it. Levine and I talked only about work.

"Celia would want you to go with me," Filomena said.

Hearing her name wasn't any easier the second time and I snapped at her. "You don't know what Celia would want. Even I don't know. I never asked her how she was feeling or what her day was like. I treated her like she was . . . a chair."

She knew I felt responsible for Celia's death and I'm almost positive that she had figured out that I was late getting to her house that day. She might have suspected that I'd been with a man, because when she asked me where I'd been the two Saturdays that I had missed club meetings, I fumbled and muttered something and probably didn't look her in the eye. Maybe she even guessed it was Harold.

Filomena touched my hand and said, "You know that she loved you and she wanted you to be happy, right? No matter what you think you did."

I couldn't argue with that so I didn't answer.

"Addie, if you don't go, then I'm not going, and I'll be heartbroken. You wouldn't want that, would you?" Italians are just as good as Jews when it comes to guilt.

Eventually I gave in and Miss Chevalier put us down for July.

Levine said of course I could have a week off and for the first time since Celia's shiva, he came to the apartment and told Mameh and Papa that because I was such a good worker he was sending me on a vacation. Whatever else he was, my brother-in-law was a mensch.

I couldn't be one hundred percent happy about going to Rockport Lodge because of its connection to Harold Weeks and what happened because of him. But it would be good to get away from the disappointment on my parents' faces whenever the door opened and it was me who walked in and not Celia.

We took the train this time — cheaper than the boat. And the minute I stepped onto the Rockport station platform, smelled the air, and felt the sun on my face, it was like waking up from a bad dream.

We got to the lodge, and I loved how everything looked the same: the blue plates, the dust on the parlor chairs, the white curtains on all the windows. Mrs. Morse was just as wide as I remembered and there was still butter on the table for every meal.

Filomena and I had a room to ourselves again, which was wonderful. When we were putting our things away — this time I had extra clothes and even a valise — she said, "I want to ask you for a favor."

I said, "I'll think about it," as if I wouldn't have jumped off a cliff if she asked me.

Miss Green had given her a letter of introduction to an artist who had a summer place nearby. "I was thinking of going tomorrow when the others are at church. She lives on Old Garden Road."

That was the street with all the mansions. I said, "Try and stop me."

We walked up and down the block looking for the number on the envelope until Filomena lost her nerve. "Maybe it's the wrong address," she said. "It's probably too early to call, and anyway this woman probably went to some fancy New York art school and thinks I'm just someone who paints flowers on china plates like an old lady with no talent and nothing better to do."

But I found the house. It was hard to see from the road because you had to climb down a set of steep granite steps on the bluff facing the water. It was nothing like the fancy castles on the other side of the street. It was small and covered with unpainted gray wood shingles, which you only saw on fishing shacks in those days. The door was painted bright red — Filomena called it Chinese red — and it was wide open.

We could see inside all the way through to a wall made of windows, with a glass door and a little balcony that looked like it was floating over the water. The walls were bright yellow and there were wooden beams on the ceiling that a not-too-tall man could reach up and touch. Very *artistique.*

Filomena knocked a few times and when nobody answered, she said, "Let's go." But I was dying to see what kind of person lived in a place like that, so I hollered, "Anybody home?" A woman answered right back, "Come in, come in, come in," like she was singing a song.

I almost laughed when I saw her, because she was practically a cartoon of a flapper. Her eyes were smudged with kohl and her hair was short and wet, which made her look like a seal. Her toenails were painted a weird shade of orange and she was wearing

131

a man's sleeveless undershirt and a pair of trousers rolled up over her knees. I thought she might be about Filomena's age.

"Sorry I'm such a mess," she said. "But who are you?"

I said I was Addie Baum and this was Filomena Gallinelli.

"Filomena?" she said. "What a spectacular name. I'm Leslie Parker but I'm trying to get people to call me Lulu."

Filomena handed her the letter. "You met my teacher, Edith Green, in New York last summer and made her promise that I'd call on you when I was in Rockport."

Leslie wrinkled her nose. "Edith Green? Can't place her."

"You were talking about glazes."

She remembered: "Oh, the lady *potter*! But look at us standing around like a bunch of horses. Sit down, sit down." She waved us toward the couch and stared at us with smudgy raccoon eyes and asked me if I was a potter, too.

Filomena said no, that I was staying at the lodge with her.

"Did you bring her along for protection in case I was some kind of crank? And I suppose I am. But why don't you tell me all about yourselves: your work, your love life."

I had never seen Filomena act so stiff or

132

talk so formally. "I work with Miss Green in the Salem Street Pottery. Miss Green is an instructor at the Museum of Fine Arts school and a published illustrator of books for children."

"I remember her perfectly," Leslie cried. "She works in the style of William Morris, n'est-ce pas? Arts and Crafts. Very sweet, but I'm really crazy about African ceramics. The masks, and those figurines: shocking, don't you think?"

I could almost see smoke coming out of Filomena's ears — not that Leslie noticed. She was digging through a pile of magazines and papers on the coffee table. "Thank God," she said, holding up a pack of cigarettes. "Addie, dear, do you see my lighter anywhere?"

It was still unusual for women to smoke in those days, at least for any of the women I knew, so I asked if her family minded about the cigarettes.

Leslie answered as if being an orphan was a little detail, like losing her keys. "My parents died when I was a baby. My uncle has taken care of me ever since; wonderful man and devoted to me. He'll be back next week.

"But it's so perfect that you're here now. Uncle Martin bought a potting wheel and a kiln a few months ago. He lost interest after ten minutes, as usual, but the whole kit and caboodle is sitting out back, and I hope you don't mind, Filomena, dear, but would you give the studio a once-over? A friend is coming up this afternoon. Perhaps you've heard of him? Robert Morelli? He works mostly in bronze, but he mucks around with clay, too."

Filomena was on her feet. "I'd be glad to."

"It's out the side door through the kitchen, to the left," Leslie said. "Do you want me to show you the way?"

"We'll find it," said Filomena. "Come on, Addie."

When we got outside I said, "What a character."

Filomena was furious. "She's horrible. Did you hear how she talked about Miss Green? Who ever heard of Leslie Parker? And what a chatterbox. I thought she'd never shut up."

The "studio" was nothing but a shed, a ten-foot-square wooden box so stuffy and dusty that we both sneezed when Filomena opened the door. She peeked into barrels of clay and looked over the tools and dried sponges. "Most of these have never been used."

When she took the cover off the potter's wheel, she gasped. "It's brand-new." She pushed the stone disk and it started spinning. "Miss Green hires men to work the wheels and the kiln; I've never even touched one of these before."

Leslie poked her face through the door and asked, "What's the verdict?"

Filomena said, "I'd kill for the chance to work here."

"Exactly whom would you kill?" Leslie said. "Don't answer that. Do you think the place is up to snuff?"

"It seems fine, but you should make sure the lids on those barrels are tight; it would be a shame for all that clay to go to waste."

Leslie thanked Filomena and told her to use the place all she wanted. "Don't be a stranger."

When we were walking back to the lodge, I said, "Leslie really rubbed you the wrong way, didn't she?"

"Don't tell me that you liked her?"

I waved an imaginary cigarette and tried to imitate her voice. "You have to admit she was entertaining."

"She is so full of herself. And she has that whole house to herself while my sister is raising five kids in two rooms. Not to mention all that equipment going to waste. It's not fair!"

So I told her to go and use the studio.

"Don't be a stranger."

"I can't think of anyone stranger than her," she said. "Besides, I didn't believe a single word she said."

The next day was rainy and cool, which meant we were stuck inside. Filomena said, "I hope they won't make us play charades all day." She hated games.

At breakfast, Miss Case came to our table and handed Filomena a thick envelope. "This just arrived," she said quietly. "I hope it's not bad news." We ran upstairs to open it in private, but the only thing inside was a pencil sketch of a bird.

"What is that supposed to be?" I asked.

"It's a sketch of something I made yesterday when I was fooling around with a piece of clay. I meant to put it back in the barrel."

"Did Leslie do it?"

Filomena pointed at the initials in the corner: *R.M.*

"Let's go meet him," I said. "We're not going to do much in this weather and I promise to protect you from Leslie."

The front door was closed but it opened the second I knocked, as if someone had been waiting for us.

He needed a shave, there was powdery white dust all over his clothes, and his hair was starting to go gray. But he was the most beautiful man I'd ever seen in person.

He shook Filomena's hand and said, "You must be Filomena, daughter of light, virgin martyr, protector of all innocents." He smiled a movie-star smile. "Don't look so surprised. It was my grandmother's name."

He took my hand next. "You must be Addie. Leslie tells me you're very deep, which means she didn't let you get a word in edgewise so she has no idea who you are."

He introduced himself as Bob Morelli and said Leslie had gone to town for burnt sienna and bread and would be back soon. "But come to the shed in the meantime; I want to show you something."

The place had been aired out and every inch dusted and scrubbed. The tools were clean and laid out in a straight line, and a little sculpture of a bird — the one from the drawing — was on the window ledge, sitting on a nest made of fine clay threads.

Filomena picked it up. "No eggs?"

"You didn't make a papa bird," he said. "She's waiting for him."

She stared at him for a moment and shrugged.

"What's that?" she asked and pointed to the wet burlap bag sitting on the pottery wheel. Morelli lifted it and said, "Just don't tell me a six-year-old could have made it."

That's exactly what I would have said. It was a bowl, I guess, smooth and round at the bottom but square and off-kilter on top.

He ran his thumb around the edge. "It's supposed to look rustic. The Japanese don't always insist on symmetry. Sometimes they fire things so they look scorched."

Filomena seemed offended. "I am not familiar with Japanese art."

"Yes you are! Some of Edith Green's lines are very *japonais.* And they share a kind of serenity, I think."

She said, "I think what we do is beautiful."

"Of course it is," he said. "Leslie doesn't know her ass from her elbow when it comes to ceramics. She might turn out to be a decent painter someday — not great, but good. The kid's only twenty, after all. How old are you, if I may ask?"

"You're not supposed to ask," she said and then she told him she was "going to be twenty-one."

"*Miss* Gallinelli. Unwed, twenty years old, and traipsing around on your own, hmmm," he said. "That means your parents are dead and you don't have any brothers."

Filomena laughed. "I guess you really are Italian."

He said, "What can I say to make you like me?"

"I don't know," she said. "How old are you?"

"I'm going to be thirty-five. An old man."

"Still unmarried?"

"My wife and I no longer live together."

Filomena closed her hand around the little clay bird and crushed it.

He said, "Ouch."

I wasn't sure what was going on and tried to think of something to say. Luckily, Leslie barged in with a bunch of overstuffed string bags. "The gang's all here," she said. "Bob told me I was all wet about your pottery, Filomena. How did he put it? 'Will withstand the test of time.' Unlike my pitiful efforts — he didn't come right out and say that, but I know what he thinks."

A loaf of bread fell on the floor and Leslie spilled a bag of peaches as she went to pick them up. "I got us some lunch," she said. "But don't get your hopes up. I'll just be opening some cans, as usual."

"I'll help," Filomena said, but Morelli put his hand on her elbow. "Wouldn't you like a try at the wheel?"

"Come on, Addie," Leslie said. "Let's let them play in the mud. We'll make our own fun."

And I did have fun. Right off, Leslie talked me into trying on a pair of pants, which is all she seemed to own. It turned out to be much more than playing dress-up. When I put them on, my whole body felt different and I wanted to see what it could do. I took giant steps around the room and sat cross-legged and rolled around on the floor. I ended up in front of a mirror.

I never wanted to take them off, and it wasn't just the physical feeling. I told Leslie, "It makes me want to try riding a bicycle and ice skating and all kinds of things."

She asked what other kind of things. And do you know what popped out of my mouth? "I'd go to college."

She asked if I wanted to be a teacher or a nurse or something like that.

I said, "I'm not sure what I want to do."

"It doesn't matter. You'll figure it out when you're there," she said, as if going to college were as easy as walking into town.

When I told her I hadn't even finished high school, she said, "You know the Ayer School? Uncle Martin could put in a word if I asked."

Ayer was a girls' prep school in Boston. "I doubt they'd be interested in a Jewish girl."

She said, "Oh dear. I thought Baum was German. Not that it matters a bit to me. I have loads of friends who are . . . why, half of the instructors at the Art Institute in New York are . . .” she stopped. It wasn't polite to use the word *Jew* back then. So she said, “There must be other places.”

“There's Simmons College,” I said. “They even accept the Irish, if you can imagine.”

That got her back up. “Don't try to pin that kind of snobbery on me. There are lots of reasons women don't go to college — if they're Irish or Hottentot or whatever. Nobody gives a damn if a girl goes — in fact, it's easier not to. But that shouldn't stop someone who's prancing around in trousers and telling her innermost thoughts to a complete stranger.”

When Morelli and Filomena came in to wash up, she laughed at the sight of me in Leslie's pants. I said, “Leslie thinks someday all women are going to wear them.”

Morelli said, “The serious potters already do.”

Leslie brought out a tray with peaches, crackers, and boiled eggs, but Filomena was too excited to eat. “It was so hard at first,” she said. “I made some colossal messes, and one of them flew off the wheel and all the way across the room. I was ready to give up but Bob wouldn't let me. And then, just like that, I got the hang of it and he's going to fire the last little bowl I made."

He said, "She's a quick study."

She said, "He's a good teacher."

They seemed more relaxed with each other. He wasn't staring at her anymore and she couldn't stop talking about the feeling of clay spinning between her hands. Maybe I'd been wrong to think they'd been flirting. Besides, Filomena was too smart to fall for a married man.

Morelli stood up and walked to the balcony door. "I'm going out for a smoke."

Filomena picked at the clay under her fingernails, brushed the dust off her skirt, cleared her throat, and followed him outside.

"Love is in the air," said Leslie.

I said, "But he's married!"

She shrugged. "The wife is crazy as a bedbug — a real nightmare. They've been separated for years but he won't divorce her because of the little boy. Bob is the last of a dying breed — a true gentleman."

I couldn't believe she was talking about adultery as if it was no big deal. As if Filomena wouldn't get her heart broken — or worse.

When they came inside, I said it was time we got back to the lodge.

Instead of answering me, Filomena turned to Morelli, who looked at his watch and said, "I have to go into town to make the telephone call I told you about."

Then she said, "Okay, Addie, let's go."

Filomena was silent on the way back so I rattled on about what it was like wearing pants and my conversation with Leslie about college. "I know you don't like her," I said, "but she's not such a bad egg."

When we got to the porch, Filomena stopped before we went inside and said she was going back later. "And tomorrow, too. I don't need another hike through Dogtown."

But the next day wasn't a hike; it was a schooner sail around Cape Ann and we had talked about how much fun that would be.

Filomena just shrugged.

"He's married," I said.

"What does that have to do with me studying with him?"

I wanted to shake her and tell her not to be a fool and that it was going to end badly. I wanted to say, do you think he really cares about your pottery? Why can't you see he's a wolf, too, just like Harold Weeks?

But all of that stayed inside my head. What I said — and it came out sounding prudish and angry — was "What are you going to tell Miss Case?"

Her answer was just as chilly. "I am not going to miss the chance to learn from a master."

It was awful. We never talked to each other like that, so I tried to lighten things up. "I suppose it doesn't hurt that the teacher looks like Rudolph Valentino."

Filomena didn't think it was funny. "I know what I'm doing."

I didn't see much of her for the rest of the week. She left before breakfast and didn't get back until right before the door was locked. There was one night she didn't come back at all. I worried about her but mostly I was mad.

I had been looking forward to staying up late and talking — and so had she. We never ran out of conversation, and even when we talked about other people, it was never gossip. I always felt I understood myself better after we spent time together. And the way she laughed at my wisecracks and thanked me for my opinions made me think maybe I was as smart and funny as she said I was.

But she had chosen to be with Morelli instead of me.

I suppose I was more hurt than angry, but I walked around in such a foul mood, Irene handed me a bottle of Lydia Pinkham's and said, "I figure you're either constipated or you have cramps."

"You don't think this stuff works, do you?" I asked.

"Whatever's bothering you, there's enough spirits in there to cheer you up."

I decided not to waste the rest of my vacation stewing about Filomena and threw myself into everything: lawn tennis, croquet, cards, charades, you name it. The only thing I didn't do was go to the dance; I told everyone I had a terrible headache that night.

After Filomena disappeared, there was a lot of whispering and staring at our table. Gussie moved the empty chair — Filomena's — and we sat closer together and acted as if nothing had changed. Someone saw Filomena walking with Morelli on Main Street and Miss Case stopped talking to any of the Mixed Nuts, as if it was our fault.

We didn't talk about Filomena among ourselves until Friday morning, when Rose said, "Do you think there's a chance she'll show up for the banquet tonight?"

Gussie said, "I don't know if she has that much brass."

Irene said, "I bet she'd come if Addie asked her."

Helen chimed in. "Would you?"

They were all looking at me when Rose said, "You know, Helen is getting married this year, so it would be the last time with all of us together at the lodge."

I couldn't say no to that and the truth was, I was glad for an excuse to see her.

Leslie's door was open, so I walked in and found Filomena and Morelli sitting on one of the couches. Her head was on his shoulder and he was running his hand through her hair. He said, "Hello, Addie."

I had never seen Filomena's hair unbraided and loose like that, and it was as if she was naked. I kept my eyes on the wall behind her and asked if she was coming to the final banquet tonight. "The girls wanted me to ask you. Rose, especially."

I looked at Morelli. "There's a singing contest and skits."

"It sounds like fun," he said.

"It's childish, but we enjoy it," I said. "I'd better go; lots to do before tonight."

Filomena gathered her hair and stood up. "I'm coming with you."

She offered Morelli her hand. "Goodbye, Bob. I can't begin to thank you."

He drew her fingers to his lips and kissed them slowly, one at a time. I had never seen anything so sexy or so sad.

And then she ran out of there like she was

late for a train.

Filomena didn't touch her dinner and went upstairs before I read my poem. I didn't get back to the room until late and she was already asleep.

In the morning, I found a note on her pillow and I remember every word because I counted them — all fourteen.

Dear Addie,
I'm taking the early train. I'll see you soon.

Your friend,
Filomena

THE QUICK BROWN FOX JUMPS OVER THE LAZY DOG.

Levine changed his business from ladies' shirtwaists to men's shirts. Mostly he sold local but some of his customers were Jewish shopkeepers in the South. The day he got a typewritten order from a small town in Alabama, he decided that sending out handwritten bills made him look small-time. So he bought a secondhand typewriter to keep up and told me I should take a class so I could use it "professionally."

Typing was not what I had in mind for my first night school class, but it was a good thing to know and it meant a night out of the house without an argument. Even better, there was an English class that met right afterward.

The typing class was in a cramped room with a low ceiling on the basement floor of the high school I should have graduated from. All twenty seats were filled, and except for two American girls, the rest were daughters of immigrants like me.

The teacher was Miss Powder, a tall, skinny lady — I couldn't tell if she was twenty-five or forty-five. She stood up straight as a broomstick all the way to her hair, which was pulled into a tight little bun on top of her head.

Before we even touched the machines, she talked like she expected us to be a disappointment. "None of you will take this advice seriously, but there is nothing more important for the typist than hand position and posture." She said, "An erect spine translates into accuracy on the page. Slouching is slovenly. Also men will make certain *assumptions* about the kind of girl who slouches."

Miss Powder roamed around the room whenever we were practicing, slapping our hands if they weren't in exactly the right position and pinching back our shoulders. As soon as we knew the basics, she brought in a stopwatch and bell to time us for two minutes as we typed *The quick brown fox jumps over the lazy dog,* as fast as we could, as many times as we could.

The bell made everyone nervous except Maureen Blair, a dark Irish beauty who was the best in the class. I was second best and Miss Powder held us up as examples for the others. She always blamed their mistakes on posture, but I thought it probably had more to do with the fact that most of them could barely read.

One evening, Miss Powder showed up with her hair pulled so tight that she looked a little Chinese around the eyes. She was spitting mad. "You will notice an empty chair tonight," she said. "Miss Blair has informed me that as she is now engaged to be married, so she has no *need* to continue.

"I trust that none of you are considering doing anything so . . . so . . ." She couldn't think of a strong enough word. "When I think of the poor girls who were turned away in favor of someone like *that*." I don't think Miss Powder could have been any more outraged if Maureen Blair had murdered her own mother.

After typing class, I ran upstairs to the second floor and Shakespeare. I don't think I would have picked a whole class on just one writer, but it was my only choice and it turned out to be a good one. Strange, but good.

The teacher was Mr. Boyer, a short, chubby man with bright blue eyes and a thick white moustache. He had a deep voice and talked as if every other word started with a capital letter. "It is my Privilege to introduce you to the Greatest Writer in the History of the English Language," he said. "Have any of you had the Pleasure of seeing the Great Bard's Work on the Stage?"

Nobody had.

"A shame," he said. "In this class, at least, you will hear the Immortal Words of one of his Greatest Works, *The Tragedy of Romeo and Juliet.*"

And then he opened a book and started reading the play and didn't stop until the bell rang. He picked up where he left off in the next class and the one after that.

At first, I didn't understand half of what was going on; there were too many words I'd never heard before and I had trouble with all those names. But it was a little like listening to music — Mr. Boyer read with a lot of feeling — and somehow after a while it started making sense.

By the time he finished the play, there were only ten students left out of the twenty-five who started. A moment after he closed the book, Sally Blaustein wailed, "They both died? After all that?" I felt exactly the same way.

Mr. Boyer's face lit up. "Our first Question," he said, and then, without any explanation, he started reading the play all over again. But this time, he stopped after every scene and made us ask questions about what we'd heard.

I learned a lot from those questions — not just about the play but about the other people in the class, too. Iris Olshinsky asked Mr. Boyer for definitions of a lot of words — sometimes the simple ones, and usually more than once. He never got annoyed or impatient with her or with any of us. Actually, he seemed to be delighted when anyone asked anything at all.

Mario Romano didn't seem to like any of the characters except the Nurse. Sally Blaustein felt sorry for everyone but especially Paris, who also died for love. Ernie Goldman wanted to get the facts right: Who was a Capulet and who was a Montague? Was there really a drug that would make everyone think you were dead when you really weren't?

I asked about Juliet; in some scenes I thought she was wonderful but in others I thought she was an idiot.

Mr. Boyer timed it so that on the last day of class he read us the last scene, and even though we all knew what was going to happen, there were gasps when Romeo picked up the dagger and tears when Juliet woke up and found out he was dead. When he got to the last word of the play, I felt like a dishrag.

Mr. Boyer motioned to Ernie and handed him a pile of papers and announced, "Mr. Goldman will distribute these for your Final Examination."

He had never mentioned a final examination before. We must have looked scared to death.

"There is no cause for worry, my friends," he said. "All I ask is that you pose One Question that has most Intrigued or Confused you about the Play."

That seemed easy enough and everyone finished up in a few minutes. But when Ernie started to collect the papers Mr. Boyer stopped him and said — actually, he never just "said" anything. If he wasn't reading the play, he usually *pronounced* or *declared* — but this time he lowered his voice like he was telling us a secret.

"One more thing, my friends. Please be so kind as to answer your own question."

Everyone went right to work, but I froze. *"Was Juliet a great heroine or a foolish little girl?"* I couldn't just choose one or the other and I didn't see how I could say she was both at the same time like I did with Paul Revere.

Other people were turning in their papers

153

and I still hadn't written a word. I was starting to panic until out of the blue I remembered my father saying that Jews answered
questions with more questions. So that's
what I did.

*"Was Juliet a better poet than Romeo? If
Juliet found out about Rosaline, would she
still love Romeo? Should Juliet have given
Paris a chance? Why is love so dangerous for
Juliet? Why are Juliet's parents so blind? Was
the Nurse Juliet's friend or enemy? Would Juliet have killed herself if she had been twenty-
five years old instead of thirteen?"*

We sat and watched Mr. Boyer read our
papers. He nodded, he smiled, he shook his
head, he frowned, he laughed a little, and
he sighed a lot.

When he was finished he said, "Congratu-
lations to you, one and all, on Completing
the Course. Each of you will receive the
Highest Grade I am permitted to bestow.
And now, ladies and gentlemen, I send you
on your way. A Sweet Sorrow."

I waited to be the last one to leave the
room to tell him thank you and to ask what
he was teaching next term and if I could
take it.

"I am flattered," he said, but he was retir-
ing. I had taken the very last class he would
ever teach. "That explains my unorthodox

methods," he said. "I am now Beyond Reproach. But I would like to give you an assignment, if I may."

I said yes, of course.

He told me to go and see the play "on its feet." You know, onstage, in person. He said he was sure I would understand Juliet if I saw her walking and breathing and speaking her poetry. "You might even come to love her."

I've seen *Romeo and Juliet* maybe twenty times since then: movies, Broadway, even high school performances. Remember when I took you to see it in the Berkshires, under the trees? I do love Juliet now, but every single time I understand something different about her. That's probably why Shakespeare is a genius, right?

Stumbling into Mr. Boyer's class was one of the best accidents that ever happened to me. When I started teaching, I remembered how he talked to us, and you know what? If you treat every question like you've never heard it before, your students feel like you respect them and everyone learns a lot more. Including the teacher.

I Figure God Created
Margaret Sanger, Too.

The Saturday Club was changing. Younger girls joined, older ones married and disappeared, including Helen, who moved to Fall River, which was a real schlep in those days. Filomena was still working for Miss Green, but she had stopped coming to meetings. Gussie said that Morelli was teaching art in Boston; I don't know how she found out these things, but she did.

Irene and Rose were still Saturday Club regulars and best friends from Rockport Lodge. They shared a room in the South End and Rose got Irene a job as a switchboard operator at the telephone company where she worked. Irene always had some juicy stories about conversations she listened in on. "Rose never does it, but she's too good for this earth," Irene said. "If I didn't eavesdrop I'd die of boredom." Irene always made me laugh.

But one Saturday when I was on my way

to the meeting — it must have been in the spring because it was light outside — I saw Irene running toward me and I could see that something was wrong. My first thought was that Rose was sick. For such a big, strong girl, she always had a cold or a headache. But it wasn't Rose.

In one breath, Irene told me that Filomena had come to their room that afternoon, pale as the moon, and asked if she could rest there for a few hours. But after a little while, she started having terrible pains in her stomach.

I said, "Why didn't you get her sister Mimi? She'd want to know if Filomena was sick."

Irene cupped her hands around my ear and whispered, "She said not to go to any of them. She did something to herself so she wouldn't have a baby."

I'm not sure I ever heard anyone say the word *abortion,* but I knew exactly what Irene was talking about.

When a woman "lost" a baby, there were two different ways of talking about it. The first one was sad. People would say, "Poor thing," and tell stories about how it happened to their cousin or their best friend who had wanted a baby for years.

The other kind of "lost" made people

157

frown and bite their lips. "How is she?" they'd whisper, sometimes like they were worried, sometimes like she was the scum of the earth. When Mrs. Tepperman down the block died after she "lost" a baby, there was a rumor that they wouldn't let her be buried in the Jewish cemetery, as a punishment. That wasn't true but it shows you how people thought.

I said, "Maybe you should take her to the hospital."

"Do you know what they do to girls who come in like that?" Irene said. She was right. I'd heard of girls being tied to the bed when a priest or a cop tried to get them to confess. And there was a story going around about a girl who ran out of the hospital and jumped off a bridge after the doctor said he was going to tell her parents.

"Rose said we should ask Gussie what to do," said Irene, "but I worry about the mouth on her. I figured you'd want to know and maybe you'd have an idea of something we can do for her."

I said I didn't but that my sister might.

I never just showed up out of nowhere at Betty's rooming house, so when she saw me — and I must have looked pretty grim — she said, "Which one of them died?"

When I explained about Filomena, Betty

158

said, "Poor thing," with tears in her eyes. I could have kissed her. And she did know what to do.

She said, "You know the Florence Crittenton Home? There's a nurse there — Cécile or Céline, something French — I heard she helps girls in trouble. But stay away from the ladies who run the place; they don't understand about things like this." Then she said, "Why don't I go get the nurse? Tell me where to bring her." I did kiss her for that.

Filomena was sleeping when I got to Irene and Rose's room. She was shivering and sweating and her face was the same gray as Celia's had been when the policeman carried her down the steps so I thought she was dying for sure.

Rose was on the other bed with a rosary in her lap. She looked like a different person without a smile on her face.

Irene came in with a little bundle and said she'd been to see Mimi. "I told her that Miss Green twisted her ankle and asked Filomena to stay with her for a few days. She gave me some clothes for her."

There wasn't much we could do except wait for Betty. Rose patted Filomena's forehead with a damp cloth and Irene put drops of water between her lips. I held her

159

hand. The three of us were usually big talkers, but we didn't have anything to say.

Filomena cried when she woke up and saw me. I told her everything was going to be fine, a nurse was coming to help, and she had nothing to worry about. I didn't believe a word I was saying, but it seemed to calm her down.

She was asleep when Christiane got there. She was French Canadian and she looked like an angel in her white uniform, but she was all business. After she took Filomena's pulse, she had us help her to the bathroom and into the tub.

Christiane handed me a pile of small cotton cloths and said I should roll them as tight as I could. She mixed something inside a hot water bottle with a tube at the bottom. Then she looked Filomena in the eyes and said, "Try to relax, my friend. It won't take too long. Take breaths. Count to one hundred."

Filomena's face was like a mask, staring at the ceiling as the liquid went into her and blood gushed out. Christiane praised her and said she was doing great. It didn't take too long, just as she'd said. But we were all exhausted. And Filomena? I don't think she unclenched her jaw until she fell asleep.

After we got her into bed, Christiane took me, Rose, and Irene to the hall and told us we were to keep Filomena quiet, feed her soup and tea, and not to let her out of bed for two days.

"I think she used bleach," she said. "At least she didn't poke herself with an ice pick. Oh yes, I've seen that. When they poke, it is terrible. But I think your friend will be all right. It was good you found me so quick."

I got home very late. Papa was asleep so Mameh couldn't make a big scene and I snuck out of the house before sunrise to see how Filomena was doing. They were all asleep, Rose and Irene in one bed so Filomena could have the other.

She was pale but she was breathing normally. When she woke up, she held my hand and whispered, "The nurse was here a little while ago. She said I was lucky. I told her you were my luck, the three of you and your sister. I never even met Betty. I wouldn't be alive without her. Or you. Especially you, Addie."

I spent the whole day with her. Filomena had a lot of pain in the morning but by the afternoon she was better. While she was napping, Irene said, "You know there are ways to keep this from happening. I've got a pamphlet all about it."

Rose crossed herself. "God forgive you."

Irene said, "I figure God created Margaret Sanger, too. My own mother had five babies in six years and died giving birth to the last one who died, too. I am not having any more than two children. I'm going to loan the booklet to Filomena when she's back on her feet. You should read it, too, Addie."

"Don't worry about me," I said. Seeing what Filomena had gone through and after my *assignations* with Harold Weeks, I didn't think I'd ever have sex.

Filomena decided to move to Taos, New Mexico, with Bob Morelli. I tried to talk her into staying but she'd made up her mind. "I'm pretty sure Mimi figured out what happened with me, which means all my sisters know. They'll be relieved if I go away."

I didn't believe her but she said if she stayed, she couldn't be the invisible maiden aunt who disappears into the kitchen when company comes. "Something like this always comes out," she said. "It's better this way."

Not for me, it wasn't.

I made her promise to write, but artists are artists, not writers. She did send post-cards, though: a lot of postcards — sometimes four a month. I have two shoe boxes full of them: pictures of mountains and rivers, of Indian men on horses and women weaving blankets. Filomena wrote like she was sending telegrams. "Moved into small house." "Sold pottery. Bought silver bracelet."

She always ended the same way: "I miss you. Come visit."

YOU MAY KISS THE BRIDE.

My father believed that Celia would be alive if she hadn't married "that ganef." So when Betty announced *she* was going to marry Herman Levine, Papa called Levine every bad thing you can call a person. In Yiddish that's a lot. "He buries one daughter and he wants another one? Your sister's body isn't cold."

"It's a year," Betty said.

"I forbid it."

Betty lowered her head like she was a bull, which is what she did when she was really mad. "You can forbid all you want but Herman and are I getting married next Thursday afternoon at three o'clock. I would like you to be there, but if you're not, that's okay."

Then she stood up, put both of her hands on her belly, and raised her eyebrows.

Mameh's reaction was almost as shocking to me as the idea that Betty and Levine had

164

been, you know, shtupping. I was waiting for her to call Betty a whore and tell my father "I told you so," but all she said was, "We'll be there."

I had no problem with Levine anymore; he'd been like a brother to me in a lot of ways. But the marriage took me completely by surprise. He never let on and neither did she. Betty was always telling me about going out to dinner with one fellow or another, but when I stopped to think, I realized it had been a while since she'd mentioned anyone.

Betty said it happened "naturally." She had run into Levine on the street and found out that Jacob, the little one, had been having nightmares ever since Celia died. "But Herman was even more worried about Myron," Betty said. "He was doing terrible in school and getting sent home for fighting. I felt sorry for them." She took the boys out for ice cream a few times and cooked them a few meals. She said, "One thing led to another and I just became part of the family," as if there weren't any difference between making soup and getting pregnant.

"You're not going to give me any grief, are you?" she said. "He makes me happy." The next time I saw her with Levine, it was obvious that he loved her, too.

Betty's wedding was one hundred percent different from Celia's. First of all, it was in Temple Israel on Commonwealth Avenue, which meant we had to take a streetcar to get there. Levine was waiting for us in the foyer, which was twice the size of Papa's whole synagogue. We were a little early, so he showed us around.

The sanctuary was huge. There was a high dome ceiling and an arch of golden trumpets hanging over the pulpit; Levine said that was to make it look like Solomon's Temple. Mameh said it was beautiful. My father didn't say anything, but with all the tongue-clucking and snorting, he didn't have to.

The ceremony wasn't in the sanctuary, thank goodness; we would have felt like ants. It was in the rabbi's study, which wasn't a closet either, believe me. I remember a big vase of flowers and books up to the ceiling.

The rabbi was younger than the groom and he didn't wear a beard or a yarmulke. He shook all our hands and asked my father something in Hebrew, which changed the sour look on his face to complete confusion. I guess you should never judge Jewish books by their covers, either.

Betty came in from a side door wearing a

166

tan suit and a hat with a little veil that stopped just under her nose. She looked beautiful. Myron and Jacob were in matching suits she'd picked out for them and Jake carried the ring for the ceremony.

The wedding was quick and half in English, but there was no way to break a glass on the Oriental rug in that room, so it ended when the rabbi said, "You may kiss the bride."

A secretary brought in a tray with a decanter of wine and a sponge cake, the rabbi asked Papa to say the blessing, and seven months later, Leonard Levine was born.

He was a cute, good-natured baby, but I hardly ever got the chance to hold him because my parents wouldn't put him down. To them he was a miracle. Mameh lit up like a candle when she saw him and grabbed him out of Betty's arms the minute they came over. She covered his face with kisses and pretended to eat his fingers. "Look how delicious," she said. "Look how handsome! Has there ever been such a boy?"

My father couldn't get enough of his grandson, either, and even stopped going to shul in the evening in case Betty brought the baby to our house. Lenny was named after my father's brother, Laibel, and Papa called him "my Kaddish"; he didn't have a son to say the prayer for him after he died and that was ages before women could do it.

But Kaddish didn't have anything to do with the way my father played peekaboo with Lenny or laughed at every sneeze and yawn. Papa was a completely different person with him. It was the only time I ever heard him sing.

But not even Lenny could keep my mother and my sister from fighting. Mameh would start complaining about something — anything — until she got herself worked up about how bad America was.

Especially the food. Everything here was terrible: bread, eggs, cabbage: "The cabbages I grew were sweet like sugar," she said. "You can't get anything like that in this miserable country." She went on and on until Betty couldn't stand it anymore and grabbed Lenny. "I wouldn't trade cabbages for running water and toilets. I was the one who had to carry water in those filthy buckets. Remember when you brought the goat inside so she wouldn't freeze to death?

"What do you think, Papa? Is it better your grandson crawls on a dirt floor or grows up where he can go to school like a real person?"

My father smiled at Lenny. "According to that husband of yours, his sons will be doctors and professors in this country. Who knows?"

That would have been the nicest thing Papa ever said about Levine, but he couldn't leave it alone. "Even a broken clock is right twice every day."

You Know — Living Life.

We didn't call it the First World War when it was happening. When it started, almost everything I knew about it came from newsreels. We saw British soldiers marching in rows and explosions with dirt flying into the air, but the next moment soldiers were cleaning their guns or sitting up in hospital beds, with pretty nurses carrying trays. Then the movie started and it all melted together. None of it seemed real.

Some people in the neighborhood were worried about family in the old country, but we didn't have anyone left over there. My mother's only cousins had immigrated to Australia and South Africa. My father had an uncle who went to Palestine, but nobody had heard from him in so long he was probably dead.

For three years, most people weren't interested in the war. They were just working, trying to get ahead, have a good time.

170

You know — living life.

But not my brother-in-law. Levine read two newspapers every day and knew where the battles were and what the politicians were saying. He was sure that America was going to join the war sooner or later. "And when that happens, they're going to need a lot of shirts."

Levine got it in his head that the commander of the navy was Jewish and decided to go to Washington, D.C., and talk to him "man to man." It turned out that Josephus Daniels was a Christian and Levine didn't get anywhere near him, but he said the trip was a success because he'd met "people with connections" at the boardinghouse where he stayed. He was so sure of himself that he rented a much bigger space in the West End and borrowed money for sewing machines so he would be ready when the big orders came.

"Meshuggener," my father said. "Crazy."

Levine didn't look so crazy in 1917 when the navy and army started ordering uniforms. He had to keep the factory open eighteen hours a day and he couldn't find enough workers to keep up. After I finished up in the office, I pitched in and helped pack boxes.

The war was the only thing anyone talked

about. When the draft started taking boys from the neighborhood, a lot of the older Jews got scared and talked about how young men used to be kidnapped by the Russian army; most of them never came back. But the boys I knew weren't worried. They wanted to show how patriotic they were and went to enlist. In the beginning it seemed like a big adventure and everyone was singing "Over There." The war was supposed to be over in a few months.

Of course it wasn't. Coal got scarce and food prices went up. There were more beggars in the street and every week another business closed. One night, someone painted *Hun* on the door of Frankfurter's Delicatessen and broke all the windows. The place closed for good, which was even sadder if you knew that the owners were Polish Jews who picked the name because they thought it sounded American.

It was a strange feeling knowing that my family was doing fine because of the war. I think it made Levine uncomfortable, too. I was the only one who knew that he had a drawer full of pins and medallions from having bought so many war bonds.

We moved in 1918, right in middle of the war. It was Betty's doing. She found two apartments, first and second floor, in the

West End. They were close enough to the factory so Levine could have supper with his children and she could put in a few hours here and there while Mameh took care of Lenny.

Believe me, I wasn't the least bit sorry to leave that miserable tenement, even if it was the only place I'd ever lived. The new apartment had indoor plumbing and electricity, and I got my own room with a door I could close. It was worth walking a little farther on Saturday nights to see my friends.

I was still going to the Saturday Club again but the meetings weren't exactly fun. We rolled bandages and knitted socks and the lectures were about things like using cornmeal instead of flour and chicory instead of coffee. There was no money for punch and cookies and it was so cold in the settlement house we had to keep our coats on, but I didn't mind; I was there mostly to see Rose, Irene, and Gussie.

One night, Miss Chevalier told us that the Salem Street building was being sold and we would get together in the library instead. She tried to make it sound like it was all for the best, but I knew it killed her.

The library was crowded and stuffy but the girls and I kept rolling and knitting, doing our bit for the war effort — even if it wasn't much. It was dull, except for the night Miss Chevalier brought a friend who had been an ambulance driver in France.

Her first name was Olive and she must have been as old as Miss Chevalier, but with her uniform and cap and the way she said things like "A-1" and "fed up," she seemed more our age. She had signed up for the English ambulance service when she found out they let girls drive. "I learned how to change a tire in the trenches and all the boys had to admit I was as good as any of them."

After she told us about driving through terrible weather and stories about the other women drivers, one of the girls raised her hand and asked if they were still looking for volunteers. "I'd do anything to get behind the wheel of a car."

"Would you really do anything?" Olive said it with so much bitterness, I swear the temperature in the room dropped twenty degrees. She glared at the girl who had asked the question and said, "Would you hold an eighteen-year-old boy in your arms while he died? A boy with a hole in his belly, who had soiled his trousers and was screaming for his mother? Would you do that?"

She went on like that until Miss Chevalier stopped her. Though not before the girl who'd raised her hand ran out of the room, sobbing.

After that night I found myself counting gold star flags hanging in windows — one for each son lost in the war. The next time I saw a picture of Mary Pickford selling Liberty bonds, I wondered which of the handsome soldiers around her were dead. And when I passed a man with an empty shirtsleeve pinned to his shoulder, I shuddered to think he might have been wearing one of our shirts when his arm was blown off.

How Do You
Go on After That?

Today, nobody bats an eye when you hear someone has the flu. It can still be dangerous for older people, but even most of them get well. In 1918, it was nearly always fatal, and it went after young people. More soldiers and sailors died from flu than from the war.

It happened fast. First a handful of sailors were sick, five days later two hundred men were down with it, another few weeks and thousands were dying. When it spread to the city there weren't enough doctors and nurses to take care of all the sick people, partly because the doctors were dying, too. Not that there was much anyone could do. There was no medicine. Getting well was luck, pure and simple. Or God's will, if you believe in a God who kills children and babies.

The flu was fast, too. Someone would leave the factory with a headache and two days later Levine would see the worker's name in the list of flu deaths in the newspaper. There were weeks when that list had five hundred names on it.

The city sent out wagons to pick up the bodies but after a while the drivers were afraid to go inside anyplace where there was sickness, so people left corpses out on the porches and even on the sidewalk. A lot of the dead were buried in unmarked graves. It was a real plague and not so long ago.

The health department closed the movie houses and concert halls and told people to stay away from crowds. Nobody should have been out dancing, but a lot of people ignored all the warnings. My friend Rose was one of them.

Betty took Myron and Jacob out of school even before the health department closed them and she kept them inside. My mother put a red string on all the doorknobs to keep out the evil eye.

It didn't help. One morning Myron said he had a terrible headache and couldn't get out of bed. Levine said he would take care of him and told Betty to take Lenny and Jacob downstairs and stay there. But she left them with my mother and ran back to be with Myron, too.

We weren't allowed near him, but I went

up and left them food in the kitchen — trying to hear what was going on in the back bedroom. When I went back later, nobody had touched a crumb and I heard them in the bathroom with Myron, trying to cool him down in the bathtub. At night, I heard Myron coughing and moaning and Levine begging him to hang on.

Downstairs, Jacob was frantic and kept asking where was Mommy and Daddy, where was Myron. Lenny was quiet. Even though he was barely a year old, he knew something was wrong. No one was paying attention to him, not even my father, but he didn't make a fuss; he just watched us with big eyes.

Papa couldn't sit anymore and went out to find a doctor, even though there weren't any. He was only gone an hour, but when he got back we had to tell him that Myron was gone. He was nine years old.

A few hours after Myron died, Betty came downstairs. All she wanted was to see the boys. Jacob ran to her and hugged her and wouldn't let go. Betty picked him up and whispered, "How's my Jakey? How's my Jake?"

Mameh said, "They both ate a good dinner but Lenny was a little cranky so I put him to sleep in my bed."

Betty dropped Jake and ran to the other room. She screamed, "He's blue."

She took Lenny upstairs and Jacob tried to follow her but I caught him and held him tight while he screamed and sobbed and finally cried himself to sleep.

Mameh, Papa, and I sat up at the table most of the night, not talking or looking at each other, listening for sounds from upstairs. When I brought hot tea upstairs, Levine met me in the kitchen and said, "He seems a little better. He took some water and smiled."

I fell asleep with my clothes on and woke up before it was light. Lying in bed, I listened to the footsteps overhead, back and forth, from one end of the apartment to the other. They took turns. Betty walked faster than Levine, but they followed the same path, back and forth, steady as a heartbeat. It went on like that until the afternoon.

When the footsteps stopped, we all looked at the ceiling. Papa said a blessing. Mameh threw a dish towel over her head and wailed. Jake put his head on my lap.

After a little while, I tiptoed upstairs and walked through Betty's apartment. In her house, it was always immaculate, nothing out of place. But with the natural order of things all upside down — children dying before parents — everything she did to keep things in order looked wasted and pathetic.

I stopped at the doorway to the boys' room. A breeze from the open window ruffled the sheet covering Myron's body. In the other bedroom, Betty was curled up on the bed, facing the wall. Levine sat with his back to her, staring at the cradle, which was covered with a blanket. He looked at me with dead eyes and I could feel the sadness coming off him, like cold air on my face.

They had lost two children in two days. How do you go on after that?

Coffins and hearses were impossible to come by, but somehow my father managed to get both and the next day we went to the cemetery; me, Papa, and Levine. The city went by in a blur but we slowed down when we passed through a little town where people were pushing baby carriages under red and yellow leaves, as if it were just another nice day in October.

It seemed like we'd been driving for hours when the driver turned down a dirt road and through a field of weeds to a stand of scrawny trees that marked the cemetery — the saddest, the most forlorn place I'd ever seen. Two men with shovels were waiting for us, and two big mounds of dirt.

■ ■ ■ ■

Myron had turned into a nice kid. Betty hadn't let him get away with anything, but she also hugged him a lot. She called him Mike, he called her Ma, and did his chores without being asked. He was good in arithmetic. His top front tooth was a little crooked. He had a nice singing voice. That was Myron.

We followed his coffin from the hearse to the grave, where the men lowered the half-sized casket into the ground and waited for Levine to pick up the spade. But he didn't move. He couldn't. So Papa stepped forward and shoveled a little bit of dirt into the hole, but so gently, it sounded like rain on the coffin. When he was finished, Levine and my father said Kaddish.

The driver came back carrying something that, from the distance, looked like a hatbox. When Levine saw it, he made a noise like a wild animal caught in a trap.

Lenny had been born with a head of silky brown hair. He smiled at everyone and Betty joked that he was going to be a politician when he grew up. He liked peas and his first word was *ball*. That was Lenny.

He and Myron were like silhouette portraits cut out of black paper — like shadows of the people they might have been if they'd grown up.

Papa tried to force the shovel into Levine's hands to bury the baby. I couldn't watch anymore and went looking for Celia's grave.

I had a stone for her in my pocket. I'd found it on the beach in Rockport and carried it around with me ever since. It was white and smooth, almost as round as a pearl. I put it on top of her gravestone and said, "I'm sorry."

Papa came and put a plain brown pebble next to mine. He traced Celia's name with his finger. "Your mother said Celia shouldn't come to America with me. She thought she was too delicate. But Mameh had another baby on the way and her mother was sick, too. I thought it would be easier for her if I took both girls." He wiped his eyes. "She would still be alive if I'd left her there."

Levine walked over to us. Papa put an arm around his shoulder for a moment before he started back to the car.

Levine hadn't shaved or combed his hair for four days and his face was swollen. He put a third stone on Celia's headstone and whispered, "She would be alive if I hadn't married her."

"It wasn't your fault," I said. Like it wasn't

my father's fault. And for the first time since she died, I thought maybe it wasn't all my fault, either.

■ ■ ■ ■ ■

1919–20

■ ■ ■ ■ ■

I Was Still Gun-Shy About Men.

Nobody talked about the epidemic when it was over, but everyone was carrying around their own load of heartache, acting as if no one had died. I felt like I was skating on a pond that wasn't frozen all the way through and if anyone asked me, "How's the family?" the ice would break.

People kept saying, "Life goes on." Sometimes that sounded like a wish and sometimes it felt like an order. I wanted to scream, "Life goes on? Not for everyone, it doesn't."

But when Betty said she was pregnant again, "life goes on" became a fact and I found myself looking forward to the new baby in a whole different way. She had another boy, Eddy, a blue-eyed blond who laughed, I swear, from the day he was born, and I finally understood why people got so silly about infants.

From the beginning he seemed to like me,

too. I was the only one who could settle him down when he got fussy. Betty got a kick out of that. "Auntie Addie to the rescue." My mother was thrilled with the new baby, but my father would hardly look at him. Papa was never the same after Lenny died.

I was spending more and more time upstairs with Betty. I don't know where she learned how to be such a good mother. She was strict about manners and school but she would get down on the floor and play with her boys, let them climb all over her, anything for fun. And Levine thought she walked on water.

I finally forgave Betty for being happy in the life that had been a disaster for Celia. I had stopped hating Levine a long time ago, but for some reason I could never get myself to call him Herman.

When the war ended, the big orders stopped coming and Levine had to lay off half his workers. He slipped each of them a twenty-dollar bill, which was a lot then, but he felt so bad about firing people that he started losing weight. Betty wasn't going to stand for that. She told him to get out of the shmatte business and go into real estate.

Levine said he'd give it a try, but the first building he bought looked like a big mistake. It was a wreck of a house on a run-down street but it was cheap and close to downtown. "Location, location, location," right? He sold it a few months later for three times what he paid.

Levine went around telling people, "I made a killing and I didn't hurt anyone." So he sold the shirt factory and started over in a one-room office downtown.

The business was just the two of us and he was mostly out, walking around the city, talking to people, getting to know the neighborhoods, and figuring out where to buy property he could sell at a higher price later. My job was to wait for the phone to ring and look through the newspapers for stories about fires and foreclosures — anything that might mean someone was selling. Of course I looked at the obituaries, but I read everything else too, down to the sports pages; once in a while a player would have to sell a house in a hurry.

With all that reading, I got to be an expert on Boston politics, the social set, and the Red Sox. I could also tell you anything you wanted to know about Fatty Arbuckle's drinking problem, the League of Nations, and the fight over Prohibition. I got in the habit of reading a newspaper even when I wasn't at work because it made me feel like I was living in a bigger world. I never stopped, not even during the Depression. I just read them a day late.

One time, I saw a story about three brothers who were suing each other over their family's fish store in Roxbury, a place Jews were starting to move to. From what I could tell, none of the brothers wanted to run the business, so I told Levine to see if they'd sell it to him and split the money. He took my advice, bought and sold the store, and made a bundle. For that he gave me a nice raise and a "promotion" to executive secretary.

I was going to Saturday Club, but the girls I knew were getting married and having children. Even the younger members were "dropping like flies," as Gussie put it.

Gussie was a real career woman by then. After a few years at Simmons, she went to the Portia School of Law, which was women only, and passed the bar on her first try. When no one would hire a lady lawyer, she went out on her own. Her first client was a woman who wanted to open a hat store but didn't know anything about banks or leases. Soon Gussie had a "specialty" as the lawyer for women who wanted to start their own businesses and for a long time, she never had to pay for cake, dresses, or flowers.

Irene, Gussie, and I all liked our jobs and

didn't talk about men all the time, so Gussie started calling us the Three Musketeers. But work didn't mean the same thing for Irene and me as it did for her. Gussie was a lawyer with every fiber of her being.

Irene was a supervisor at the telephone company with thirty girls under her, but it was still just a job and she didn't want to do it for the rest of her life. And although Irene didn't talk about it in front of Gussie, she did go out with men. After she bobbed her hair — like everyone except me at that point — her green eyes looked twice as big and pretty. But the moment any man told her what she should or shouldn't do, he was finished. As for me, I would have preferred not working for Levine, but how could I complain about a job where I got to read most of the day?

I was still gun-shy about men because of the coast guard schmuck, but I was still as romantically inclined as any twenty-year-old girl who went to the movies. And by then I knew not all marriages were as bad as my parents'. Betty and Levine were happy, and I liked Helen's husband, Charlie, who was a sucker for their little girl, Rosie. They named her after our friend Rose, who died of the flu. And you want to hear something strange? The baby was born with red hair. Nobody in either family had red hair and they had picked out the name when Helen was still pregnant, but Rosie came out a redhead.

Every now and then Betty would try to get me to go out on a date. "There's nothing wrong with books, but you could also go out with a fellow once in a while, have a nice meal. Why not?"

The one time I made the mistake of saying "I suppose you have someone in mind," she was ready for me, and two days later I was eating steak with a man who sold children's shoes. The next morning, before I was even out of bed, Betty came to my room asking about my rendezvous.

I said it was very educational and did she know that Boston was the center of the children's shoe business and that you can sell more pairs of shoes to girls but you can charge more for boys, and that shoemakers in Massachusetts were going to put themselves out of business if they kept raising their prices?

Betty said, "Okay, so he didn't sweep you off your feet, so what? You got out of the house and the food was good, so it wasn't a complete waste." She also said I had to kiss a lot of frogs before I found a prince and lined me up with a high school teacher. He sounded interesting but turned out to be a nudnik, too. Almost the first thing he said when we sat down was that he'd been cheated out of a promotion to be principal, "and the only reason is because I'm Jewish." Meanwhile, he yelled at the waiter for forgetting the ketchup, for bringing him coffee without cream, and for being slow with the bill. I told Betty they probably didn't give him the job because he was a jerk.

The next one was a good-looking man who was in dental school. He took me to a beautiful white-tablecloth restaurant, but by the time I'd finished my lamb chop, I knew I was there only as a favor to one of Levine's business friends.

At least the dentist was honest. He said he needed a wife with connections. "I know that sounds bad, but it's the only way I'll be able to set myself up in practice. And it's not like money would be the only condition."

I said, "I guess you'd also want two arms and two legs." For spite I ordered the most expensive dessert on the menu, the one with the cherries that they light on fire. You know the saying about how revenge tastes better cold? Well, it tastes just as good warm.

Betty was ready with a nice quiet book-keeper, but I said I didn't want to meet any more frogs. "So what are you going to do?" she said. "Sit around the house and listen to Mameh call you an old maid and say 'I told you so,' and that you're 'too smart for your own good'?" Betty kept hocking me about going out again until I said, "Would you leave me alone if I go back to night school?"

She said that would be okay but that she wasn't going to stop nagging me until I signed up and started class. It was annoying how she treated me like I was one of her children and not a grown woman. But it was a good thing, too.

I Thought He Was Sweet and That I Was Sweet on Him.

I ran into Ernie Goldman on the trolley but I wouldn't have recognized him if he hadn't introduced himself. He looked ten years older than the last time I'd seen him, which was only a few years earlier in the Shakespeare class. He was so pale and skinny, I thought he'd been sick, but then I saw the cane, which meant he'd probably been overseas in the war.

I asked what he was doing and he said he was working in his father's scrap metal business. When I told him I was on my way to a class at Simmons, he said, "I figured you for a college girl. You always asked the best questions."

When I said that was one of the nicest compliments I ever had, all the lines around his mouth relaxed and his whole face rearranged itself into a smile that reached up into his eyes. When a shy person smiles, it's like the sun coming out.

We got to my stop and said goodbye and honestly I didn't give him a second thought. But the next morning, there was a bouquet of roses on my desk. The note said *May I take you to dinner on Saturday? Ernie Goldman.*

Five minutes later, the phone rang and Betty said, "Herman says you got roses from Ernie Goldman? Who is he? Do I know him?"

He asked me to pick the restaurant. Betty said the Marliave was nice but when we got there, I was mortified; the dining room was lit with candles and all the tables were full of couples holding hands and whispering. There was even a violin player walking around playing schmaltzy music. I was afraid Ernie would think I was being pushy, but he didn't seem to take it that way. He held out my chair and said he liked how quiet the place was.

I knew Ernie was shy, so I'd thought up some questions to get him talking, but he managed to turn them all around and I wound up doing most of the talking while he leaned forward and watched my face as if he was afraid of missing something. It was very flattering, and when I got him to smile I felt like I'd won the lottery. By the end of the evening, I thought he was sweet and that

I was sweet on him.

We saw each other once a week after that, and when he found out that I usually went to Saturday Club, he asked if I would prefer we go out on Sundays instead. He was thoughtful that way, nothing like the blow-hards I'd been fixed up with, and the complete opposite of you-know-who.

Ernie was formal, even a little stiff, but I didn't hold it against him. I was pretty sure it had something to do with his being wounded, but when I asked where he'd been in the war he shook his head. "The doctors said I should put it all behind me." I didn't ask again.

When I think back, I get mad at what they did to those poor men. Ernie must have had PTSD — they called it shell shock — and the doctors told him to keep it all bottled up inside. They didn't know any better, but it was like treating syphilis with candy bars.

A few weeks after we started going out, I finally got up the nerve to get my hair cut. The barber said I was lucky; my hair was so thick and wavy, it looked like I'd had it mar-celled. Of course, what I wanted was straight hair with big spit curls on each side, but that would have taken a pound of pomade. No girl is ever happy with her own hair, is she?

197

But I did look good, if I say so myself. On the way home, a stranger actually stopped me on the street and asked if I was single.

When Ernie didn't notice my haircut at all, I was hurt. Betty just shrugged and told me not to worry about it. "Typical man."

But I was starting to wonder about Ernie. It's not like I wanted him to make a pass at me, but after three months he hadn't even kissed me on the cheek. Once when we were at the movies and he had his hand on the armrest, I put my hand on top of his. He didn't pull away, but he didn't take it, either, and I felt like an idiot.

And then there was the day at the art museum. I'd gotten two postcards in one day from Filomena, so I told Ernie I'd rather go look at the paintings than go to a matinee. He said okay, like he did to everything I suggested, but when we got off the trolley I saw he was limping more than usual. I asked if he wanted to sit down and rest and he snapped, and I mean like one of those turtles that bite. "Don't talk to me like that."

I pointed out some of the paintings Filomena had shown me but Ernie didn't seem interested in anything, so after a little while I said we should leave.

We were on our way out when he stopped

and stared at a big painting of a young man floating in the sea. Right next to him was a huge shark with its mouth wide open, like he was getting ready to bite the man's head off. Some men in a boat were trying to rescue him but it looked like they were too late. His skin was gray and his eyes were glassy. It was gruesome.

One look was enough for me but Ernie couldn't take his eyes off it.

"It's from a true story," he said. "Do you see the blood in the water, there? Do you see that his foot is missing?"

"What an awful way to die," I said.

"But he didn't die." Ernie limped across the gallery to a bench facing the painting and I sat down with him. He was still staring at the painting. "This was the first place my nurse took me when I got out of the wheelchair. She said if Watson could be the mayor of London without a foot, there was no reason I couldn't get myself up and out of the house."

"And you did," I said.

Ernie put elbows on his knees and held his head in his hands and sat like that for a long time. He didn't answer me when I said we should go, and eventually one of the guards came over to see if something was wrong. Ernie didn't say another word all day.

That night, I decided to break it off. I felt guilty — like I was abandoning a puppy I had adopted. And there was even something unpatriotic about walking away from a veteran of the war. But Ernie had been getting moodier and quieter, and then there was the physical element, or the complete lack of it.

The next morning, Ernie called me at work and said how much he enjoyed our time at the museum, as if nothing had happened. He asked if I'd go to the movies with him on Sunday, but I said I couldn't because I was going to Revere Beach with Betty and the family. He told me he didn't like going to the shore so I thought I was off the hook.

But later that day I got a bunch of daisies and the note said, "Maybe you could teach me how to like the beach." It was so sweet, I thought, Okay, one more chance. But by the weekend I was praying it would rain so I wouldn't have to see him again.

No such luck. Sunday was sunny and hot and Ernie met me with a daisy in his hand. "You look pretty," he said, and I could see how hard he was trying. "Your hair is pretty, too."

There wasn't room in Levine's car for us

to ride with them, but I wanted to take the trolley anyway. With everyone going to the beach, it was like a party. There were hampers in the aisles and children running around and strangers debating where to get the best ice cream. I thought it was fun, but Ernie pulled his hat low on his forehead to shut it all out.

I told him it would be better once we got off, but it wasn't. The boardwalk was mobbed like downtown at Christmas, only with the roller coaster roaring overhead. The beach was even worse. It was like an obstacle course of blankets and people. It was hard for him to walk on sand and the cane didn't help at all.

When we found Betty and Levine, Eddy shrieked and held out his arms for me to pick him up. Jake was jumping up and down. "Aunt Addie, tell Pop to let me go to the arcade. I'll win a toy for Eddy. Tell him I'm big enough to go by myself."

Betty said, "Take him to the arcade, Herman. I have company now so you don't have to worry about me." She was very pregnant and trying to cool off with a big straw fan. "The baby makes me even hotter than usual. At least I don't have swollen ankles like when I was pregnant before. Herman thinks it means I'm having a girl, which is what he wants." She patted her belly. "This one is moving around just as much as my other boys. But no matter what comes out, this is the last one."

I could see that Ernie was mortified by the way she was talking about her body; he didn't know where to look and was sweating through his jacket. I asked Betty if she'd be okay for a few minutes if we walked to the water to find a breeze.

It wasn't any cooler there and we ended up near a bunch of boys who were setting off firecrackers left over from the Fourth of July. The popping made Ernie nervous so we started back and that's when the first rocket exploded over our heads. Ernie jumped and tried to walk faster.

The next blast was so strong, I could feel it in my chest, and babies started crying. Ernie threw himself down on the sand face-first, his hands around the back of his head. I crouched over him and said it was just kids making noise, but then a whole string of loud explosions went off, echoing up and down the beach.

Ernie pulled himself up and ran, dragging his bad leg behind him. He was running blind, with his head down and his hands over his ears, so he had no idea that he'd knocked a little boy to the ground or that the boy's father was chasing him. He was a short man with muscular legs and it took him no time to catch up to poor lame Ernie in his shoes full of sand. He tackled Ernie, who curled up in a ball and started making those terrible choking noises men make when they cry.

The man stood over him for a moment, but then he kneeled down and started patting Ernie on the back, saying things like "It's all right now, soldier. I know. I was there, too, but it's all right now. You're home."

When he noticed me holding Ernie's hat and cane, he said, "Are you the wife?"

"Friend of the family," I said, ashamed of how fast I'd answered so no one would think I was married to this poor lunatic. "What should I do?"

"Let's get him out of here," he said and hoisted Ernie up by the armpits and dragged him toward the boardwalk. A man with an empty sleeve met us and said, "There's a police car down by the carousel."

I said I'd go and ran down the street as fast as I could. When the cops heard that Ernie was a veteran, they turned on the siren. They were very kind to him as they got him into backseat — they must have been in the war, too.

I never saw Ernie again. His parents sent him to a sanitarium in Colorado. I heard that they sold everything and moved out there to be with him.

Betty said, "I hope you aren't taking this too hard. I never thought he was right for you."

"I should have ended it a long time ago," I said. "I was going out with him for something to do. God, that sounds so awful."

"Don't be so hard on yourself. He wasn't in love with you, either."

That didn't make me feel any better, and it was a long time before I even thought about going out again. First Harold, then Ernie? It was pretty clear I didn't have any talent at picking men.

■ ■ ■ ■ ■

1922–24

■ ■ ■ ■ ■

If I Wasn't So Busy, I Would Have Felt Sorry for Myself.

Levine went into business with Morris Silverman, who was a much bigger fish in Boston real estate and also a very nice guy. Everybody liked Mo Silverman. The only problem was that he already had three girls in his office and there wasn't enough work for four secretaries. Betty wanted him to fire one of his girls. "I'm sure you're a better typist."

But to me, it wasn't a problem at all. I had wanted to change jobs for a long time. I hadn't done anything about it because no one was going to pay me as much as Levine and also it would have made a big stink at home.

So this was a good thing. Gussie was always saying she could get me a job with a judge or one of her businesswomen. And Miss Chevalier was working for the Boston Public Library, so I could ask her to recommend me for a job there. When Silverman said he wanted to talk to me about "the situation," I was ready to tell him there were no hard feelings.

But instead of letting me go, he asked if I could just wait a few months. One of his girls was getting married and leaving in September but he didn't want to let her go sooner because she was paying for the wedding herself. "She's an orphan," he said, and he offered to pay me a little something on the side. It would be our little secret and I would start again in the fall. That was a mensch, even if he did ruin my escape plan.

Betty thought it was perfect timing. She said I could spend the summer at home with her and the boys. "It will be good practice for when you have your own children." She needed the help with the twins, who were two years old at the time — I guess they would have been your second cousins — Richie and Carl. Eddy was still a little kid, too. Jake was ten by then. I think he was Betty's favorite and I don't think anybody in the neighborhood ever knew that he wasn't her natural son.

But spending three months with them — and around my mother — would have given me a nervous breakdown. Mameh never let up: I read too many books, I had too many friends, I dressed like a floozy, it was selfish to waste money on movies, and I was an ingrate because I wouldn't answer her in Yiddish like Betty. Mameh didn't call her Betty-the-whore anymore, although behind her back it was "Betty-the-climber" and "Betty-who-thinks-she's-better-than-you-and-me."

Once, as a kind of peace offering, I asked her in Yiddish if she needed anything from the store, and all she did was make fun of my pronunciation. Betty let that kind of thing roll off her back, but it always got my heart racing like I was being chased, and if she started in at night, I couldn't fall asleep.

There was nothing I could do to please my mother, never mind that I was paying most of the rent.

When I told Gussie what was going on and that I might get stuck babysitting for Betty until September, she said, "You could go to Rockport Lodge for the summer."

I thought she was joking. I hadn't been to Rockport since the summer Filomena fell in love with her sculptor. Gussie not only went every year, she knew half the women on the lodge's board of directors, which is how she knew that the girl who had been hired to make the beds and sweep the halls had quit at the last minute. "It's not a great job and the pay is lousy but it might be better than staying home and changing diapers. By the time you get back, I'll have something better for you."

It sounded too good to be true: room and board, living away from home for the summer in the most beautiful place I'd ever seen? Gussie made a phone call and I was hired.

I told my parents I had a job as the assistant to the director at Rockport Lodge, which was sort of true and sounded better than "cleaning lady." My father had no opinion but of course my mother thought it was terrible. Why would I do such a thing when my sister needed me? Who would be watching me? She used two Yiddish words for "tramp" I'd never heard before.

Betty told me to go. "You're only young once. Never mind what I said; you don't need to practice on my kids; they already love you to pieces." But because Betty was Betty she also said, "Of course, they'd like to have some cousins already."

I started crossing off days on the calendar. I got a valise and repacked it a hundred times. Buying that train ticket made me feel like a world traveler.

The director of Rockport Lodge that summer was Miss Gloria Lettis — not a youngster, that one. She had tiny eyes and the biggest bosom I'd ever seen. She was also very full of herself. Before I could put down my suitcase she said, "Come along," and showed me to a closet full of buckets and mops — some for the bathroom only, some for the stairs and hallways. I was still carrying my bag when we went to see the linen cabinet, which I had to keep in the same exact order at all times, and then outside to the garbage bins, where I would empty wastebaskets every morning. I had never seen the annex, which was a new one-story building behind the main house, like a long cabin with unpainted rooms for twenty or thirty more girls. That's when I started to realize how much work I was in for.

In the kitchen, Miss Lettis handed me over to Mrs. Morse, who hadn't changed at all. She took one look at me and sighed. "Not very strong, are you? I just hope you don't run away after the first week like the last girl."

I promised I'd be there all summer but I could tell she didn't believe me. She showed me my "room," which was the old pantry and only big enough for a cot, a stool, and a few pegs for my clothes. And it was right next to the stove, so when the oven was on

I had to get out of there or I would bake, too.

After a week, I thought I might have been better off with four boys than sixty girls who never picked up their magazines and were always losing their socks and hankies. I didn't understand how they could get the bathrooms so dirty or how they managed to track in pounds — and I'm not exaggerating — of sand. I never stopped sweeping. If I wasn't so busy, I would have felt sorry for myself.

But it wasn't until the first Saturday changeover that I understood why that other girl had run away. As soon as the group that was leaving brought their suitcases downstairs, I started stripping and making beds, dusting and mopping floors, and carrying out heaps of trash. I lugged baskets and baskets of dirty linen to the laundry shed, where a tall African-American lady with white hair was boiling a huge pot of water. I barely finished before the next group arrived. I was so pooped that I ended up sleeping straight through supper.

Mrs. Morse was offended that someone could be too tired to eat her food, so she told Miss Lettis that either she get me some help on Saturdays or she would not be back the next summer. "And I will tell the board that you were the reason why."

Lucy Miller showed up the very next week. I couldn't imagine how a bony thirteen-year-old kid with blond pigtails would be much help, but she'd been cleaning up after six brothers her whole life, so she could strip and make a bed in half the time it took me. Thanks to her I never missed a Saturday lunch out of tiredness again. And believe me, that was a meal I didn't want to miss.

The food in the kitchen was better than what they got in the dining room — especially Saturday lunch. When we finished eating, Hannah, the washerwoman, tipped her chair back on two legs and said, "That was a real Sunday dinner we had, even if it is only Saturday."

I had never sat down with a black person before and I was a little shy of her at first. I had read *Uncle Tom's Cabin,* so what was I going to say to someone whose grandmother had probably been a slave? But Hannah was easy to be around and a great storyteller. She even got Mrs. Morse to laugh about the summer people in the big houses in town; they seemed to think that the locals were deaf, blind, and too stupid to see that Father was drunk every night or young Miss was doing more than just talking to the gardener.

After a few weeks, my arms and legs were stronger and I wasn't dead tired at the end of the day, so one evening when the girls were playing charades, I changed clothes and went to join in. There were a lot of puzzled faces when I walked into the parlor, but once they figured out that I was the girl who washed the toilets, nobody would look me in the eye.

I don't think they were being mean. If the cleaning girl had shown up for charades when I was a guest at Rockport Lodge, I probably would have done the same thing — more out of embarrassment than snobbery, I hope. There must have been someone doing the cleaning when I was there on vacation, but I can't remember seeing her. To this day whenever I lay eyes on a chambermaid, I smile and say hello.

After that night, if there was music or a lecture I wanted to hear, I pulled up a chair on the porch and listened through the window. On quiet nights when it was really dark, Mrs. Morse gave me an oil lamp so I could sit out where it was cool and read a book.

A Girl Should Always Have Her Own Money.

Where I grew up, it would have been bad manners to sit in a woman's kitchen without asking about her children and her parents, her opinion of the neighbors — even her digestion. Mrs. Morse and I talked about the weather and what was on tomorrow's menu and that was it.

But on Friday nights, when she stayed late to get ahead on the weekend baking, I watched her make bread, rolls, cakes, and cookies and she'd tell me how she came up with her recipes and why she used butter for some things and lard for others. She kept her eyes on the dough or the batter and chatted away like a different person — a happier person.

Mrs. Morse made pie for the girls the first week, but Miss Lettis decided it wasn't fancy enough for the dining room, so she baked them just for us in the kitchen. I told Mrs. Morse I'd eat her pie three times a day if I could. She said, "Too much of a good thing can make you bilious." But after that, she always gave me the biggest slice.

I knew Mrs. Morse liked me, even if she didn't say so. She told me to get out of the lodge in the evening sometimes: "Go into town, have an ice cream, look in the shops. Lucy can show you around." But Lucy was too young and silly and I told Mrs. Morse that I was saving my money.

She approved. "A girl should always have her own money so she's never beholden to anyone."

I said that was very modern of her, but she didn't think so. "As far as I can tell, common sense hasn't been in fashion for a long time."

What I knew about Mrs. Morse — and it wasn't much — came from Lucy, whose grandmother was a second cousin or something. I think everyone in Rockport was related to each other.

Her first name was Margaret and her husband had died when she was young. She had a son named George, who was a "disappointment." But Lucy forgot to mention that Mrs. Morse had a sister named Elizabeth, who I met when she stopped by one Sunday afternoon after church.

I saw the resemblance right away: high

foreheads, close-set gray eyes, and thick iron-gray hair. But Margaret Morse was round and mild, where Elizabeth Styles was thin and suspicious. She looked right over my head when I said, "Nice to meet you."

I went outside so the two of them could talk in private, but Mrs. Styles was so deaf, I might as well have been sitting at the table with them.

She shouted, "I can't believe you're back here again."

Mrs. Morse said, "It suits me," and that she couldn't afford to stop working.

Mrs. Styles thought she could do better in one of the big summer kitchens out on Eastern Point. But Mrs. Morse liked being in charge of her own kitchen and going home to her own bed at night. "And don't worry about the money. I'm doing just fine."

Mrs. Styles said, "I still don't know how you stand it around here. All those foreigners would give me the willies."

Mrs. Morse lowered her voice a little. "At first, I thought the Italians would steal. I was sure the Irish would smell bad, and I was a little afraid of the Jews. But, after all these years, I tell you some of them are nicer than Americans."

"These days, they're all trying to be flippers."

"Flappers," Mrs. Morse said. "Our mother would have fainted dead away to see all the leg they're showing."

Mrs. Styles said, "Mother would have taken a stick to them. Things were better back then."

Mrs. Morse said she thought some things were better nowadays, but Mrs. Styles didn't see it. Summer people had ruined the town and it was taking your life in your hands to cross the street what with all the automobiles. "And those bathing costumes? You can see all the way up to you-know-where. It's terrible."

Mrs. Morse said, "Well, there's nothing you can do about it so why don't I cut you a nice piece of chocolate cake?" She could fix almost anything with a piece of cake — or pie.

IT'S NOT YOUR PROBLEM, ADDIE.

On the hottest nights, when my room was stifling, I took my pillow and blanket to the porch and made a bed out of chairs and little tables. When you're young you can sleep anywhere. One night when I was out there, the sound of the kitchen door woke me up. We never locked it and I figured that one of the upstairs girls had been gallivanting. But when I went inside for a glass of water, Mrs. Morse was holding on to the back of a chair, shaking all over, and there was blood on her mouth.

I made her sit down and ran a washcloth under cold water for her face. I asked if she wanted me to get Mrs. Lettis or her sister, but she shook her head. After we both calmed down, I did a pretty good imitation of Betty and ordered her to stay over and sleep in my bed. I took the biggest knife I could find and went back to the porch to keep watch.

I didn't have to ask who had hurt her. Hannah said that Mrs. Morse's son was mixed up with the rum-running going on all over Cape Ann. Canadian boats full of liquor would unload onto smaller boats off the coast, and the locals who ferried the stuff in made good money delivering booze to hoodlums who came up from Boston. Men like George Morse skimmed bottles to sell to the rich summer people, who never gave up their cocktails during Prohibition, but if too much went missing, well, those suppliers were very tough characters.

Mrs. Morse stayed in the kitchen the next day and kept her head down, so I was the only one who saw her swollen lip and the bruise on her jaw. She went home after supper but she was back with a valise after lights-out. She said she was going to sleep on the porch, but I knew she couldn't risk Miss Lettis finding her. That woman was like a one-woman vice squad. The summer before, a girl had been sent home for drinking and another had eloped from the lodge so she was taking extra care to protect our reputation. No hanky-panky of any kind would be tolerated, which was the reason I could talk Mrs. Morse into staying in my room.

I camped out on the porch and when I

heard someone walking toward the house, I ran inside. Mrs. Morse was waiting at the door and I begged her to go upstairs. She wasn't having that. "You go. I'm going to take care of this." I wasn't going to win that argument so I went, but only as far as the dining room, where I could keep an eye on her.

She let him in when he started kicking the door. George Morse was an inch or two taller than his mother and broad in the shoulders, with big meaty hands that he clenched and unclenched like he was getting ready to punch someone. I could smell the booze on him from the other room.

They argued in whispers for a few minutes and then Mrs. Morse sank into a chair with her face turned away from George, who hung over her. "You know they're going to kill me if I don't get them the money. What do you need it for anyway? I know about your goddamn nest egg, so don't tell me you don't have any. You're just a stingy old woman with one foot in the grave anyway. What kind of mother won't save her son? Do you want to see me dead? Is that it? If you don't give me that money, I'm going to burn down the house."

When he grabbed her wrist, I ran into the kitchen and said, "Leave her alone."

He looked me up and down and got a sickening look on his face. "Who is this little dish?"

I told him to get out or I'd call the police. He just laughed. "You're not bad-looking. Maybe if you come outside and play patty-cake with me, I'll let it go for tonight."

Mrs. Morse said, "Let her be, George."

He let go of her wrist and came toward me. "Come on, missy. I've got a little rum left. Or maybe you like wine? I can get that, too. I'm not a bad guy. Just got myself into a little jam."

He was right up against me, breathing into my face. "Tell her, Ma. Tell her I'm a nice guy."

But Mrs. Morse had gotten a knife and was behind him, jabbing him in the back. When he tried to turn around, she poked him hard enough to make him yelp. "I'll run you through if I have to," she whispered, using the knife to get him to the door. Before he left he said, "Next time I'll bring my own knife and I won't be so polite with your little friend."

I didn't realize how scared I was until he was gone. My voice squeaked when I said we should call the police but Mrs. Morse said it wouldn't help; the rum runners and the cops were in cahoots.

I said, "So what are we going to do?"

She patted my hand. "It's not your problem, Addie. Go to sleep now. I'm going to sit here a while."

There was no sleeping that night. I kept hearing the awful things George had said to me and to his mother. I could still see the ugly look on his face and the bruise on Mrs. Morse's jaw and it made me remember a woman from Levine's factory who came to work every Monday morning with a black eye or a swollen lip. Everyone pretended not to see it and no one said a word, including me.

What could I say? "Call the police"? If they did come, they were gone after a few minutes. "Leave the bum"? How could she feed her children on her own?

But with my own eyes I had seen George hurt Mrs. Morse. I knew I couldn't let it happen again, but I had no idea how to stop it.

On Saturday, I met Bess Sparber, who knew Gussie from the courthouse. She was staying at the lodge that week and wanted to say hello and see how I was doing. She was a short blonde with a handshake like a longshoreman's. She had a little space between her front teeth, which I always think makes a person look honest. I was desperate to talk to someone and told her what was happening to Mrs. Morse.

She said, "This happens all the time. I hear things in court that would make you sick to your stomach: a woman who lost an eye to a beating, a little boy who had maggots in the strap marks on his back. 'Home sweet home'? Don't make me laugh."

She said she'd help in any way she could and that she'd get others to pitch in, too. That gave me the idea to find out who was staying in the room right over the kitchen.

George hadn't shown his face for a few days but I knew he'd be back, so I locked the kitchen door at night to have some warning and kept a knife and a broom handy.

The moment I heard his footsteps, I tapped the ceiling with the broom handle, then waited to open the door until George started hollering. As soon as he came in, a dozen girls holding croquet mallets and tennis rackets surrounded him. Girls kept coming, quiet as mice, until they filled the room. The only sounds were his breathing and Bess smacking a baseball bat across the palm of her hand.

When George spotted Mrs. Morse standing at the door, he lunged at her, butting his shoulder into the girl next to him like a football player. It must have hurt but she didn't budge and the others closed in until he was trapped.

Mrs. Morse told him to get out. George called her an old bitch and worse and kept throwing himself toward her. But the girls didn't give and eventually they pushed him back out the door.

After the lock clicked, there was a big sigh of relief. Bess and I wanted to get everyone out of there as quickly as possible, but Mrs. Morse had to shake hands with each and every girl first.

In the morning, Bess came to the kitchen and said, "That was terrific, but now what are you going to do?" We might try to pull the same stunt for a few nights, but then a whole new group of girls would arrive and they might not be so willing. Or someone might let the cat out of the bag and get Mrs. Morse in trouble. Or George could bring a gun.

I had to get help from someone local and the only people I knew to trust aside from Mrs. Morse were Hannah and Lucy. Hannah laughed when I told her how we got George out of the kitchen. She said, "Wish I could have seen his face," and said I should talk to Lucy because she knew everyone in town.

Lucy got very quiet when I told her what was going on. "George Morse is a shit-heel," she said. "He grabbed me between the legs when I was ten years old and I still feel dirty from it. You tell Mrs. Morse not to worry anymore."

I'm not exactly sure what happened but Lucy talked to her uncle Ned, a temperance man who wasn't shy about using axes, and not just on whiskey barrels. Ned's drunken father had broken his nose when he was a boy, so he saw it as his calling to protect the weak — by whatever means necessary.

A week went by without a visit from George. Mrs. Morse stopped jumping up every time the door opened and went back to sleeping in her own house.

Another week passed and it seemed that George Morse had vanished from the face of the earth, but since nobody wanted to see him, nobody went looking for him. There was a rumor about a body washing up on Long Beach but I didn't see anything about it in the newspaper. Besides, he could have gone to Salem or Boston or anywhere.

Mrs. Morse never mentioned her son again in my hearing. But I had pie for breakfast every day for the rest of the summer.

By Addie Baum.

Remember when you were little and I let you stay up late so we could watch *Upstairs, Downstairs*? That show always made me think about Mrs. Morse's troubles with George and how Miss Lettis never found out. It wasn't because she was stupid or because we were so smart. She was just busy with "upstairs" dramas, like the girl who got appendicitis. But she went into a full panic when she was told to expect a newspaper reporter who was coming to do a story about Rockport Lodge.

It might not sound like a big deal, but publicity like that had never been welcome by the women who started Rockport Lodge; they grew up thinking that a lady's name should only appear in the paper when she got married and when she died. But that had changed and those women — and their daughters — read the society pages whether they admitted it or not, especially in the

Boston Evening Transcript, which ran a genealogy column every week and reported on the kinds of women's clubs attended by Boston's "First Families." I'm talking about the Lowells and the Cabots and that set. The *Transcript* was like *People* magazine for Beacon Hill types, and the rest of us, too.

Miss Lettis got a phone call from the chairman of the Lodge board and was told to expect a certain "Miss Smith" and to make sure she left with a delightful impression. Everything had to look its best, which meant I polished the banister twice and dusted every damn book in the house. The night before the big visit Miss Lettis sat down in the kitchen — something she never did — and went over the lunch menu with Mrs. Morse.

She was nervous as a cat, folding and unfolding her hands, and telling us more than she was probably supposed to. She said our visitor was the most popular society writer in Boston so we had to put our best face forward or the whole world would hear about it.

Miss Lettis came from Pittsfield, so she didn't know that "Miss Smith" had to be "Serena," who wrote a column called Out and About. Everyone read it, not only because she had the juiciest gossip but also because sometimes she poked fun at the people she wrote about, like the time she said Beacon Hill ladies were such penny-pinchers they wore their shoes until the soles were thin as communion wafers.

Nobody knew Serena's real name. There was a rumor that she was from a First Family herself, which would have made her a traitor to her class and even more fascinating. Some people argued that "she" had to be a man because a woman couldn't be that witty. When the car pulled up in front of the lodge, I felt like a detective solving the mystery of Serena's true identity. Reading all those newspapers paid off because the minute I laid eyes on her I knew it turned out that she was Mrs. Charles Thorndike. Case closed!

When a Brahmin like Tessa Cooper marries a Brahmin like Charles Thorndike, there was always an announcement in the paper and sometimes a picture of the bride. Miss Cooper had sent every editor in town a photo that showed off a bare shoulder. Very racy.

Miss Lettis had put on her best "welcome" face, but when she saw three cameras hanging from the driver's neck, she gasped, "I didn't get permission for pictures," and ran inside to call Boston for instructions, leaving Miss Smith high and dry.

She perched on the porch railing and lit a cigarette.

The portrait didn't do justice to her heart-shaped face and her big eyes. Her dark hair was almost as short as a man's and parted on the side — a style you might have seen in a fashion magazine but much too much for Boston.

I must have been feeling very brave that morning because I went right out there and said, "Would you like something cold to drink, Mrs. Thorndike?"

She looked surprised at hearing her name, but then she smiled and shrugged. "You read the papers, do you? I could do with a drink but I don't suppose you have a gin fizz handy."

I didn't know what to say: it was eleven o'clock in the morning and the middle of Prohibition.

She laughed. "Relax, child. I'm joking. Are you here from one of the girls' clubs?"

I wasn't about to tell her I was the maid, so I said I was a member of the Saturday Club, which was true.

She knew who we were. "Mother's missionary society bought all their Christmas presents from your little shop a few years ago. Are you one of those adorable pottery girls?"

"Adorable"? She was getting on my nerves. I said no, that I was a secretary in a real estate office and taking classes at Simmons College. "That makes you a real go-getter as well as a fan of the gossip columns."

That rubbed me the wrong way, too, so I said the society pages were a big waste of time, "except for Serena." Then I looked her right in the eye and said, "I get a kick out of the way you poke fun at Boston's high and mighty."

That wiped the smug little smile off her face.

Miss Lettis reappeared, calmer now that she had her marching orders. There would be no pictures inside the lodge and no pictures of the girls.

"Doesn't leave much, does it?" said Mrs. Thorndike. She stood up and flicked her cigarette out on the lawn. It must have taken all of Lettis's self-control not to run over and pick it up. "Let's get this over with."

They went off on a grand tour that had been carefully laid out. They stopped at the tennis court, where it just so happened that the two best players were in the middle of a game, and from there paid a visit to a group of well-groomed girls who were reading poetry to each other. Another bunch was crocheting handbags — all of it phony as a three-dollar bill.

Tessa Thorndike didn't seem all that interested. She didn't talk to any of the girls or write down a word of what Miss Lettis told her about the history of Rockport Lodge or what happened there. Instead of eating lunch in the dining room with everyone else, she had her lunch on a tray in the parlor, by herself.

The lodge emptied out in the afternoon for a sailboat ride out of Rockport Harbor. Miss Lettis took the photographer to take pictures of the grounds and the house and Mrs. Thorndike went back to the porch to smoke.

I wandered out there with a book under my arm.

"No sailing?" she said.

I said I got seasick and asked if she was having a good time.

She sighed. "Not really. I'm on a tight leash; no funny business allowed." She sounded discouraged and less snooty. "The only reason I'm here is that Charles's mother gives money to this place and told the publisher she wanted something *nice*. If I were to be even a little bit clever, she would not be pleased."

I asked if her mother-in-law suspected that she was Serena.

"Mother Thorndike would make her son divorce me. She finds Serena vulgar, but Charlie thinks she's funny."

"He's right," I said.

"Why, thank you," she said and asked my name.

She said, "Addie Baum. That would make a good byline."

And just like that, I could see it in my head, *by Addie Baum,* in black-and-white. That's what I wanted to do with myself: I would write for the newspapers.

I had goose bumps, but I pulled myself together and said, "I don't think I could remember things as well as you do."

"You mean because I don't take things down? That's only because I'm lazy and nobody really cares what I write as long as I get the names straight, and they have someone else check to make sure that I do."

I said that she was a good writer but she shrugged off the compliment. "I send over a few pages or call the editor and read what I've got over the phone. But I'm always late and he's always mad. I've often thought what I need is an assistant to help with actually getting the things on paper and seeing they're in on time. It's all I can do to remember who was at which party — especially after a highball or two."

I said I took dictation and typed.

"Do you?" She looked me over and said what wouldn't she give for some of my curves. I would have given anything to be able to wear her dress, which fell in a straight line from her shoulders to her knees.

"You'd have to be at the house a lot," she said. "If we were in New York, I could tell people you were my social secretary, but that's not *done* in Boston. And I can't say you're a friend because everyone knows all my friends."

I said, "Couldn't we have met at Barnard?" Something else I knew about her from her wedding announcement.

She said, "You have the memory of an elephant. But since they all went to Smith or Wellesley, I suppose I could introduce you as a college chum."

The photographer was putting his cameras in the car and waved for her to get in. I gave her my telephone number at work. She shook my hand and said she'd call me in September.

I watched them drive away and started planning the rest of my life: I wouldn't have to be Levine's secretary forever, but I would

234

have to learn all about Barnard College and New York City if I was going to pretend to be her "college chum." What would I call her: Mrs. Thorndike or Tessa? I could imagine how proud Miss Chevalier would be to see *by Addie Baum* in the paper.

I couldn't wait.

My Jaw Hurt from Keeping Quiet.

Instead of dreading going back to work for my brother-in-law, I couldn't wait to get to the office in case Tessa called. By then I was calling her Tessa in my head. I went in early and left late so I wouldn't miss her. I even decided not to sign up for night school so I'd be free — night or day — to do whatever she needed. The minute I heard from her, I was going to quit my job and start a whole new life.

After a month without a word from her, I was going crazy. Maybe she'd forgotten me or maybe she'd decided it was crazy to hire a complete stranger or maybe someone told her that I was the maid.

I read the newspapers like a maniac, right down to the box scores and the classifieds, thinking that eventually I'd find something about Mrs. Thorndike. I knew she liked having her name in the columns. Finally I saw an item in the *Herald* about how the Charles

Thorndikes were enjoying their stay in London, where Mr. Thorndike was doing business. After that, they were planning to spend a few weeks in Paris before returning to their Back Bay home.

That explained why I hadn't heard from her. Either she had forgotten me or had forgotten that she was going on a trip to Europe when we talked. I wondered if there was still a chance that she'd call when she got back. I felt like a fly stuck on a piece of flypaper and wasted a lot of time feeling sorry for myself. Irene started talking about dosing me with Lydia Pinkham's again and Betty said no sourpusses at her party.

In December, Betty gave herself a birthday party. Mameh thought making a fuss about birthdays wasn't just a waste of money, it was like waving a flag at the Angel of Death.

It wasn't a big party: just the family, a cake with candles, and a bottle of homemade schnapps. Betty had bought herself a new outfit, which was an occasion in itself. She hadn't gotten anything new since the twins were born because she'd been trying to lose the baby weight. Betty had never been skinny and she was never really fat. She still had a nice shape, but it was well upholstered now and her new dress made the best of it.

But the real reason Betty wanted us all

together was to make an announcement. "You'll never guess what Herman got me for my birthday," she said. "A house!"

She could hardly get the words out fast enough to tell us about how many bedrooms there were and how many trees in the backyard. Herman was buying bicycles for the boys and a washing machine for her. Levine gave her a kiss on the cheek and said the house was too good a deal to pass up.

My parents were stunned.

Betty laughed. "Look at them! Don't worry. You're coming with us. Mameh can grow cabbages and Papa won't have to work anymore. No rent to pay. It's a two-family. We have the top two floors, and you'll be downstairs. Just like here."

Levine said there was a grocery store around the corner, and a kosher butcher.

"They have Jews there?" Mameh asked.

"In Roxbury?" he said. "Are you kidding?"

Betty said Mrs. Kampinsky from the old apartment building was living there already with her son and daughter-in-law. "She said to tell you hello and to visit as soon as you can."

Papa's face was like a mask. "You talk like it's all settled. Like I'm too old and sick to work. Like I am not still the head of my own house."

"Of course you are," Levine said. "If you want to keep working, I understand. There's even a trolley near us."

Betty started talking about how much quieter it was in Roxbury and how there were better schools for the boys. Levine said the neighborhood was coming up. My mother asked if there was a fish store close enough to walk to.

And then, boom, Papa slammed his fist on the table. "We are not going anywhere."

It was like the clock stopped. My father never did things like that. Even Betty was speechless.

Mameh said, "What do you mean we aren't going? I am going. Without me your grandsons would grow up like wild animals. You do whatever you want. Stay here and starve."

He said, "Addie will keep house for me."

"She can't even boil water." Mameh threw up her hands. "Ach, what do I care? You can both starve."

They went around and around for a long time: Levine explained, Betty argued, and Mameh yelled until finally my father stood up. "You can talk until the Messiah comes but I am not going anywhere." On the way out, he slammed the door so hard the cups on the table jumped.

Levine turned to me. "What's going on? I thought this would make him happy."

Happy was not a word I would put together with my father or my mother. But I told him that the problem was my father's synagogue.

After Lenny died, my father had gotten more religious. He started working the night shift so he could pray in the morning on his way home and ate an early supper so he could pray before he punched in. He made his schedule so he didn't work on Saturdays and spent most of it at shul.

Papa was a different person when he was there. At home he was quiet — aloof even. But when he walked in there, men would run over to shake his hand and he would smile and say things that made them laugh. He was an important man there — a scholar.

Levine apologized to Papa. They should have asked him first and of course if Papa wanted to stay put, he could always move later if he wanted. But if he did come, there was a synagogue a few blocks from the new house. It had a big library with a whole Talmud and electric lights so you could read at night. The rabbi had a long white beard.

"He's not American?" Papa asked.

Levine said, "I think he's from Germany."

"Even worse."

Levine gave up. There was no way he could change Papa's mind, but it turned out that he didn't have to because the landlord kicked my father's synagogue out of the storefront and Avrum, the caretaker, was moving to Roxbury. Avrum told Papa that he'd been to Levine's temple and said that the library was pretty good, which was like an A-plus. He also said that the rabbi wasn't bad for a German, which was high praise coming from a Hungarian.

So, in the end, Papa moved to Roxbury with everyone else. But I did not.

I didn't say anything about my plans until the day they were moving. Just as the truck pulled up I told my parents that I had taken a room in Mrs. Kay's boardinghouse on Tremont Street. It was a very respectable place and Betty told me to mention that it was mostly Jewish ladies who lived there, as if that would make any difference.

My father made a sour face but he didn't look surprised, which made me think that Betty had told him in advance. My mother was a different story. She gave me a look like I was a worm. "I should be glad you're going to a *Jewish* whorehouse?"

And that was just the beginning. I was

241

disobedient and stubborn. I was disrespect-
ful. I never told her what I was doing or
where I was going. I was a disappointment,
a fool. I had a big head.

The longer she went on, the madder she
got.

Finally, she said, "You'll be sorry. And
don't come back when you're in the gutter."

My jaw hurt from keeping quiet. I had
promised myself I wouldn't fight, but inside
my head I was screaming, *Don't call me a
whore. Why does reading books give me a
big head? Why don't you ever ask what I'm
reading? The gutter? Who's been paying your
rent?*

"You don't even look at me when I talk to
you!" Mameh screamed. "Get out of here,
go. I'm finished with you."

Betty said, "Don't be ridiculous."

"Look who's talking? The big shot! I
blame you for this — you and that husband
of yours. All you care about is money and
making a big impression. I know you think
I'm a nothing, a greenhorn. But you two
are peasants, climbers. I only hope your
children treat you the way you treat me."

Betty told me, "Don't pay attention."
Levine slipped me five dollars and said,
"She doesn't mean it."

242

I used to dream about how wonderful it would be on the day I went to live on my own but what I remember about that day is running to the curb and throwing up.

The boardinghouse was cheap and clean but my room was dark and smelled like mothballs. Actually, the whole building smelled like that, even the dining room. I was the youngest person there by thirty years and the only one who went to work. The rest were spinsters or widows living on pensions and all of them were lonely.

If I took a book into the parlor, one of them would sit down by me and complain about the landlady, or an ungrateful niece who never visited, or how awful the other women's table manners were.

They all agreed that things were better in the old days. Some of them were sad about it and some were bitter, but it was always "Nothing is as good as it used to be."

I swore I would never talk like that and you know what? Now that I'm an old lady myself, I think that most things are better than they used to be. Look at the computers. Look at your sister, the cardiologist, and you, graduating from Harvard. Don't talk to me about the good old days. What was so good?

Even with the old ladies and the moth-balls, I loved not having to explain where I was going or where I'd been. It was like being on a vacation from my family. I talked to Betty a lot. She and Levine got a telephone for the house and the two of them talked at least three times a day. She called me, too, and asked what I was up to and when was I coming for dinner, which I didn't do too often.

I knew I should have been looking for another job, but I couldn't stop hoping that Tessa Thorndike would rescue me when she came back to Boston. From the society pages I found out she was home. Mrs. Thorndike had been seen at a tea wearing a strange black dress, "very French for New England," which meant that everyone hated it.

A week after that, Serena's column returned to the *Evening Transcript* with a note about Mrs. Thorndike's recent appearance in a *très chic* Parisian *ensemble* by the world-famous designer Coco Chanel. Not that anyone in Boston was familiar with Chanel or even knew how to pronounce her name.

You had to admire the chutzpah of how she praised herself, but I finally realized that she was never going to call me. If I wanted a change, I'd have to do it myself.

For months, Irene and Gussie had listened to me talk about Serena and how she was going to hire me, a little too much, I guess. Because when I said I wasn't waiting around anymore, Irene said, "It's about time." Gussie said she'd make some calls and told me to start looking at the Help Wanteds. There were a lot of openings for typists and some of them looked interesting. I wanted to apply at Wellesley College, but it would have taken hours on the trolley. I inquired about working in a doctor's office — that would get me into a whole different world — but when I called the job had already been filled.

Irene said she'd keep her ears open, too, which meant listening in on calls she thought might lead to something. Not entirely kosher, I know, but Irene said nobody was going to give girls like us anything, so we had to take our chances wherever we found them.

She didn't even say hello when I picked up the phone. "The typist in the *Transcript* newsroom just quit. Put on your coat and get over there now."

IT MADE ME FEEL LIKE A REAL BOSTON GIRL.

It was already four in the afternoon when Irene called so I didn't get to the *Transcript* building until after five. The lobby was almost deserted, but I thought, What the heck, I'm here, so I asked a man about where I'd go about a typing job in the newsroom. He said go to the second floor and see if Mr. Morton was still around but not to bother if I couldn't type fast. Then he winked. "It won't matter to him how pretty you are."

I was always surprised when people told me I was pretty. I couldn't see it then, but when I look at old pictures of me, I have to say I was kind of cute. After I lost the baby fat on my face and cut my hair, my eyes seemed bigger and my nose looked smaller. And I was very lucky with my teeth.

When I look at my eighty-five-year-old face in the mirror today, I think, "You're never going to look better than you do today, honey, so smile." Whoever said a smile is the best face-lift was one smart woman.

Anyway, the man saying I was pretty made me smile and I went upstairs feeling a little less nervous.

I walked into a big room that looked like a hurricane had been through it. There was paper all over the floor. The trash cans and ashtrays were overflowing and it smelled of cigar smoke. It looked like the newsrooms you see in the movies — only with cockroaches.

Nobody was there. The *Transcript* was an evening paper, which meant that everyone would be long gone. In my head I was saying, Damn, damn, damn, but one of those damns must have come out of my mouth because I heard a voice say, "Ha!"

A fat man with a hat pushed back on his head walked out from behind a glass door at the far end of the room. I said I was looking for Mr. Morton about a job. He gave out another "Ha," and said, "You're looking for me."

"I'm here about a job," I said.

"The typing job, right? Don't tell me you think you're the next Nelly Bly."

I had no idea who that was. I just said that I could type.

"Fast?"

"Very fast. And I'm good at dictation."

He told me to hold out my hands and I silently thanked Miss Powder for her rule about short nails.

"You would have to answer the telephone."

I said I had lots of experience at that.

"What would you do if it was some crackpot called in hollering about the Bolsheviks in the police department, like it was your fault."

"Why would anyone call about that?" I said. "The police strike was five years ago."

He had a double chin and a heavy five-o'clock shadow, but he grinned like a little boy when he said the next "Ha!"

I thought he was laughing at me but I found out that "Ha" could mean anything, from "What a jerk" to "Good morning" or even "You're hired." That particular "Ha" meant I was hired.

My first month there was a blur. I never worked so hard, not even cleaning at Rockport Lodge, because I was trying to do everything perfectly and also because I was doing everything. I ran upstairs to the business office, downstairs to the pressroom, and back up to the advertising office. I went out for cigarettes and bottles in brown paper bags from the pharmacist. I answered the phone and listened to a lot of crackpots who complained about everything — their neighbor's dog, women drivers, broken streetlights, President Coolidge's collars.

Mort — he said he'd fire me if I ever called him Mr. Morton — said that the telephone was a curse except when you needed it, like when a reporter didn't have time to get back to the office to file a story. There were days I went home with a terrible stiff neck from taking dictation with the receiver between my ear and my shoulder. You have no idea how heavy those things used to be.

I did all the typing for the older reporters who refused to learn how. The younger ones used two fingers but they were fast. The guy who covered the courts was faster than me but he was also a terrible drunk. Sometimes he'd come in an hour before deadline, type his story, and pass out at his desk. I couldn't believe that anyone that pie-eyed could write so well.

But one day he was just too far gone and turned in a real mess. Mort told me to clean it up as well as I could and he'd finish it. Let me tell you, I slaved over those two pages and I was a nervous wreck when I turned them in. Mort moved my ending to the beginning, took out all the adjectives, cut the whole thing in half, and made it one hundred percent better.

"That's how it's done," he said. Best writing lesson I ever had.

Not that he wanted me to be a reporter. God forbid! Mort disliked women reporters. "They always stick themselves in the middle of the story. The stunt girls show off how brave they are, pretending to be a lunatic or a housemaid, and the sob sisters tell you too much about the murderer's clothes and nothing about the gun."

He didn't have such a great opinion of men reporters, either, and there were plenty of bad examples in that newsroom: not just drinkers but married men who kept asking me out to dinner. Mort said if he saw me with any of them he'd fire me on the spot. "Not that I expect you to be here very long," he said. "The smart ones leave fast and the good-looking ones go even faster, so I figure I've got you for six months, tops." Then he asked if I'd met Sam Gold in sales. "Nice boy, not married, one of your tribe. You could do worse."

"Don't be such a yenta," I said.

"I've been called worse things than a matchmaker."

That time I said, "Ha!" Obviously, I

wasn't Mort's first Jew.

He and I had what you would call a mutual admiration society, which is why he kept me away from the women's pages, or, as Mort called it, "The goddamn ladies' room." He hated the stories about clothes, cooking, makeup, parties and teas, women's clubs and charity events. "Fluff and nonsense." But it was popular with readers, and the society types followed that genealogy column the way my nephews read about the Red Sox.

Except for the columns, the whole section was written by two middle-aged women who never took off their hats. Miss Flora, who was tall and fat, and Miss Katherine, who was tall and skinny, could turn out copy faster than anyone in the newsroom, which was a good thing, since the women's pages kept growing. The soap companies and department stores wanted their advertisements to run next to stories their customers would probably read. Mort used to mutter, "Pretty soon they're going to have to change the name of the paper to the *Goddamn Ladies' Home Journal.*"

But nobody hated the section more than its editor, Ian Cornish. His nickname was The Bantam because he had red hair and a voice like a trumpet. I once saw him stand on top of his desk and holler, "I am in hell."

He was about thirty years old with nice green eyes and a cleft chin like Cary Grant's, but I've never cared for pale men with red hair. I think they look like shrimp that have been boiled and peeled.

Cornish had been sent to "the hen coop," as he called it, as punishment for a fistfight he'd had with someone upstairs. He figured he'd be called back to the news desk after a few weeks, but when he realized he was stuck with the ladies he started coming in late and never spent more than two or three hours in the office. Flora and Katherine were so good at their jobs it didn't make much difference, but when two more pages got added to the section, Cornish had to produce something, too.

Serena hadn't turned anything in for months, so he started a new column about women's clubs, parlor lectures, and private salons. Those were like book clubs today, but more formal. The toniest ones competed with each other for famous guest speakers.

Cornish called his column Seen and Heard, under the name "Henrietta Cavendish," and he didn't write one single word. It was all copied straight out of the morning papers, which he cut up and left all over his desk as if he was daring someone to catch him. He got away with it for so long, it was clear that none of the higher-ups were reading his column. Not even Mort.

I didn't have anything to do with the women's section. Flora and Katherine didn't need help and Cornish could type, or he could until the day he showed up with his right hand in a sling from punching someone who called him Mary, because of where he worked.

Mort wasn't happy about sending me over there. He had four daughters and he treated me as if I were his fifth. He thought Cornish was a weasel and warned him to be a gentleman or he'd break the other hand.

But Cornish was all business. He handed me copy to type without a "please" and took it back without a "thank you" and never looked me in the eye.

The first time he said two words to me was the day he gave me a piece of fancy stationery, holding it between his thumb and forefinger as if it were a dirty handkerchief. "Type this right away," he said. "Her Highness, Serena, has decided to grace us with her wit and we've got twenty minutes to rip up the section and fit it in."

I said, "Well, she is the best writer in the section."

He seemed surprised that I could talk.

"You may be right, but she's a royal pain in the ass. She writes whenever she pleases and I have to put up with it because the public likes her and so does the publisher. It's a damn shame she's rich because if she was hungry she might be a real spitfire."

That column wasn't one of Serena's best. Most of it was about the engagement party of a young woman who was probably a friend since it didn't contain a single sly or snappy word. Katherine or Flora could have knocked it off in five minutes.

I know it's not nice to enjoy someone else's failure, but Tessa Thorndike never called me, and I took more than a little pleasure in how mediocre her writing was. Not very nice of me, but you won't hold that against your dear old grandma, will you?

After a few weeks on the women's pages, I had to agree with Mort that it was a big waste of time: freckle-removal recipes, tips on sweet-smelling breath, hemline "news," and society drivel.

Cornish's column was the worst: a stolen list of "intimate" events with a roll call of the women who went to "lovely" teas and listened to "intriguing" lectures in "charming" homes. It didn't matter. Seen and Heard was almost as popular as the genealogy column and for the same reason: people like seeing their names in the paper.

Cornish's hand healed fast, thank goodness, but a few days after I went back to my regular job, Mort called me to his office. He was holding the telephone and said that Cornish was calling in sick and Katherine was at home with a dying mother, which meant I would be spending the whole day in the hen coop with Flora.

"He wants to talk to you."

When I picked up the phone he said, "Is this Baum?" That was the first time Cornish had ever used my name. "You're going to write my column today."

"Me?"

He said, "Why not? You're smarter than a monkey," and told me to go to the newsstand on the corner and ask for his copies of the *Herald,* the *Globe,* the *Advertiser,* and the *American.* "Write about any gathering of respectable females and look at the pictures. Sometimes you can get an item out of a caption. Just make sure you spell the names right."

That was my first newspaper assignment. It wasn't exactly a stop-the-presses moment, but I was excited. As I started to put it together, I realized that there was a strict pecking order to the lists of names. You always began with the very First of the First Families: Adamses, Cabots, Lodges, Winthrops, and such, followed by other well-known names, then club officers, married women, unmarried socialites, and at the bottom of the heap, spinsters of a certain age such as — and there she was — Miss Edith Chevalier.

I felt a shiver go up my spine when I saw her name and finally understood why people were so keen on reading those columns. Knowing Miss Chevalier meant that I was somehow connected to important goings-on in the city. It made me feel like a real Boston girl.

I made sure I got everybody spelled right and turned it in before the deadline, but Flora handed it back without even looking at what I'd written. Some big advertisements had just come in and they had to add a whole page to the section. "I don't suppose you could possibly give me six more inches in the next half hour?" She obviously didn't think I could, so I said it wouldn't be a problem.

The first thing I did was add the names of all the lecturers and what they talked about. In my opinion, it made the whole column much more interesting. The president of the League of Women Voters talked about "Why

Aren't Women Voting?" An English professor from Smith College explained "The Waste Land" by T. S. Eliot. A lady doctor spoke about Sigmund Freud's sex theory. Miss Chevalier had been at a gathering where a retired schoolteacher talked about her trip to Egypt, "with magic lantern illustrations."

But even with all that, I was still short and there was nothing left to steal. I was not about to go back to Miss Flora with my tail between my legs, so I came up with what I thought was a brilliant idea. I picked up the telephone and asked to be connected with the main branch of the Boston Public Library.

Miss Chevalier was surprised to hear from me. When I told her I was writing about her club meeting for the *Boston Evening Transcript,* she sounded delighted and was glad to tell me about the lecture.

She said she'd been "transported." The speaker was a seventy-five-year-old woman who had traveled all over the world by herself. Egypt was her most recent adventure. "I wish you could see the pictures of that spry old lady sitting on a camel in front of the Great Pyramids."

I had been taking down everything she said and asked if I could put some of her comments into my story. I said I didn't have to use her name. It could say, "According to one of the ladies in attendance . . ." But Miss Chevalier didn't mind if I quoted her as long as I included her full title: Supervisor for Circulation at the Central Branch of the Boston Public Library.

After I was done that day, I stood at the back door of the *Transcript* building and stopped the first paperboy who walked out with a stack of newspapers, which were, honest to goodness, "hot off the press."

I tore open a copy and found my story just the way I had written it, including Miss Chevalier's comments, word for word, right there in Seen and Heard by *Miss Henrietta Cavendish.*

I must have known I wouldn't get credit. It couldn't have come as a surprise. But I still remember feeling like a little girl whose lollipop had just been snatched out of her hands.

■ ■ ■ ■

1925–26

■ ■ ■ ■

Nice Turn of Phrase.

I didn't expect anyone but a few friends and Miss Chevalier to notice she'd been mentioned in the column, but I was wrong. The next morning there were at least a dozen phone calls from women wanting to know why Mrs. Taylor's book group had gotten special treatment. Mrs. Taylor herself called to ask why Miss Cavendish had spoken to "that librarian," when she'd had a Miss Saltonstall in her parlor.

The publisher was happy about the attention and told Mort to keep up the good work, which meant more work for Cornish. The other papers weren't running quotations, but they started a few weeks after us.

Cornish was not pleased. "I'm not going to talk to those damned bluestockings and you don't want me to. Do I sound anything like Miss Henrietta Goddamn Cavendish?"

Mort told Cornish to get Flora or Katherine to do the interviews, but for the first time anyone could remember, they said no. Miss Katherine said either he was joking or he was playing with fire. Miss Flora said this was the straw that would break the camel's back. They were masters of the cliché, those two.

And that's how I became Henrietta Cavendish. Cornish saw his chance and handed me not just the interviews but responsibility for the whole column. "You're a bright kid," he said. "You understand how this works. Just keep the publisher happy and everyone leaves us alone."

Cornish was right when he'd said a smart monkey could put the column together. It wasn't hard. If Cornish was in the building when I turned it in, he'd give my pages a quick once-over and Katherine did a final edit. It didn't occur to me how much I'd bitten off with writing a column twice a week on top of the typing and errands and phone calls. It didn't occur to me to ask for a raise.

I was over the moon.

I spent every spare moment — and not just when I was at work — trying to make the column as interesting as I could. Clubwomen started sending biographies of their speakers and lists of their guests in advance; sometimes they included the menu and I even got a few engraved invitations. Well, Miss Cavendish got them.

There were days I felt like I was in over my head, like when there were too many invitations and every lecture was about flower arranging. If Flora and Katherine hadn't helped me sift and sort, I would have been sunk. But they appreciated hard work and they knew I had no one else to turn to.

I wouldn't ask Cornish for the time of day. He treated the three of us like we were servants or children and only talked to me if word came down from upstairs that the publisher wanted a particular friend or relative mentioned.

Sometimes that meant I had to write about the stupidest things you can imagine. The worst was "The Scientific Evidence That Fairies Exist." I am not making that up.

I had been writing the column for a month when Miss Cavendish got a note directly from the publisher telling her to attend the next meeting of Harvard faculty wives, which was being hosted by his sister-in-law.

"Doesn't he know that there is no Miss Cavendish?" I asked Cornish.

"Kiddo, I'd bet a week's salary that he's never even looked at our chicken scratches."

Then he told me to tell the sister-in-law

that Henrietta was coming down with a terrible cold and she was sending me, her secretary, to take notes for her. To me, it sounded like a great adventure. I couldn't wait.

The meeting was on a Friday afternoon in a part of Cambridge I'd never been to, and I felt like a tourist. The mansions on Brattle Street were just as big as the ones in Rockport, but older.

The home I ended up at wasn't the biggest one on the street but very elegant inside. A maid wearing a uniform and a cap answered the door, took my coat, and asked for my name. For a girl who grew up in a cold-water flat it was like walking into a dream or a movie.

It was chilly outside but it felt like a June afternoon in that room, and not just because of the fireplace. The place was covered with roses: on the sofa, the rug, and the curtains, even on the china — pink roses.

The maid introduced me as Miss Abby Brown. That brought me down to earth. I couldn't be Addie Baum even when I was pretending to be the imaginary secretary of an imaginary columnist.

Most of the women at the meeting were old but the hostess couldn't have been more than thirty and very fashionable, which was

264

rare in Cambridge those days. It still is, don't you think?

I don't remember her name but when I explained why I was there instead of Miss Cavendish, she sent me to the back of the room so I wouldn't disturb anyone with my note taking. She was perfectly polite about it but I still felt as insulted and embarrassed as that night I tried to play charades at Rockport Lodge.

I stopped feeling sorry for myself the moment the speaker walked in. She was a black woman with gray hair and a short string of pearls around her neck. Mrs. Mary Holland — that's a name I never forgot — was there to talk about the anti-lynching crusade.

Mrs. Holland was a grandmotherly type with a kind face but her message was about as far from grandmotherly as you can get. She was there to shock and rally those women to her cause.

She started with a story about a sober, churchgoing Negro man who was lynched because he opened a grocery across the street from a white man's store. Her eyes filled with tears as she talked about a sweet twelve-year-old boy who had been murdered for smiling at a white girl. There were thousands of stories like that, she said, and a hundred about white women who had been lynched for speaking out against the murders.

She was ferbrennt — you know that word? Like she was on fire. She had those women on the edge of their seats. By the end of the speech, every last one of them agreed to sign a national petition and give money to make lynching a federal crime.

Mrs. Holland said she knew it was hard to believe that such horrors were happening in America in the twentieth century. She pulled a big envelope out of her bag and said she had the proof, but warned us not to look at the photographs "unless you have the stomach to face the evil men can do."

I thought I should look at the pictures to see if there was something I could use in the column. I didn't get past the first one. Two black men were hanging by their necks on a post — like one you'd hang a sign on. Their hands had been tied behind them; their feet were just a few inches off the ground. On either side of the bodies, dozens of white men were lined up and looking straight at the camera; some of them were leaning forward to make sure they got into the picture.

And as if that wasn't horrible enough, the picture was printed on a postcard. What kind of person would put a stamp on a thing like that, and who on earth would he send it to?

I went back to my room feeling sick about the whole human race and spent the weekend trying to squeeze as much of what I'd seen and heard into a few paragraphs. I was sure that Cornish would cut the whole thing, but I was going to try. Didn't a story about women trying to right a terrible wrong belong on the women's page?

When Cornish read it he practically ran into Mort's office and closed the door. They were in there for what seemed like a very long time and when they came out, Mort marched out of the newsroom with his head down and my story in his hand. Cornish said he was taking it to the publisher, who would make the call.

I started to wonder if I was going to get fired. But believe it or not, they ran the story. The sister-in-law had already telephoned the publisher to make sure that her meeting was mentioned in the paper. The secretary upstairs told me there had been a lot of phone calls that morning and a visit from the publisher's wife, who was a big supporter of the anti-lynching campaign.

They took out what I wrote about the postcards and they did not print the names of the women who had been there. They also buried it. Seen and Heard was usually featured on the women's page, but this time it started on the bottom, and most of it jumped to the back of the classified section.

People found it anyway and some of them called to cancel their subscriptions. One man said that his wife had fainted when she read the gruesome details and threatened to sue the newspaper. Believe me, there was nothing gruesome in that article, but there were a lot of disgusting phone calls. It was the first time I heard the word *nigger*, and I heard it a lot.

On the other hand, Miss Cavendish got a lovely note from an important Unitarian minister who thanked her for paying attention to such a national disgrace. The president of Wellesley College and a state senator sent compliments, too.

Mort said it would all be forgotten by the next day and I guess it was, but in my little corner of the world it was a big event. Miss Chevalier called to find out if I had written the piece. She said it was magnificent. "I only wish your name had been on it."

Betty got five copies of the newspaper and sent "my" story to the president of the National Council of Jewish Women. She told me they came out against lynching even before Leo Frank was lynched in Georgia, back in 1915. I hadn't known that, or even that my sister was a member.

The most surprising thing was how much Ian Cornish loved the commotion. He sat on the edge of my desk and talked to me like we were old friends. "It's good to ruffle the feathers on those silly hats."

I said it was a shame that so much had been cut out of the story and he gave me a lecture about how nobody but the writer ever knows what's missing. He said it happens to everyone. "Even me."

It took me a minute to realize that the man was flirting with me. "You need thick skin to do this job, which is why the ladies don't last long. Especially not young ladies with skin as lovely as yours." And then he asked me out to dinner.

I said no, but he didn't give up. He went on a flattery campaign. He liked how I had changed the part in my hair. He said my red scarf was "smart." He complimented something I'd written. "Nice turn of phrase."

I think I might have said yes to a cup of coffee except for his breath. Some men in the newsroom slurred and staggered in after drinking their way through lunch. Cornish held his liquor better than most, but I knew better than to go near a drunk, even for coffee.

He kept asking me out and I kept saying no until the day he showed me an invitation to the big opening-night party for the Metropolitan Theatre. It was going to be a dress ball, the most extravagant party ever seen in Boston. Serena would have been the natural choice to write it up, but she had disappeared and I knew why: Tessa Thorndike was expecting a baby.

Cornish said that he was thinking of turning the whole page over to a Seen and Heard report on the gala. "I could send you, but you've never done anything this big before. I'd be sticking my neck out."

I thought he was telling me I was going to cover the party, so I started thanking him, promised I'd do a good job and wouldn't let him down.

He stopped me. "Just a minute, kiddo." I would have to get the story without tipping anyone off why I was there, so no taking notes. I would have to bone up on who's who and what's what. He said, "We can go over it at dinner."

I didn't have the assignment. Cornish had me over a barrel. "Don't worry," he said. "It's just business. But since we have to eat, I know where to get the best steaks in town."

That didn't sound like business to me. Buying a girl a steak dinner was an expensive proposition and a lot of men expected something in return. But I really wanted to do that story and I wasn't a gullible kid anymore. I knew to keep my guard up.

So I said I'd meet him.

The address he gave me turned out to be a Chinese laundry, which meant we were going to a speakeasy. If Cornish hadn't already been waiting for me, I probably would have snuck off, but he grabbed my arm and walked me into my first saloon.

Glamorous, it was not. There was no music or dancing. The tables were bare and none of the cups matched. I'd never been anywhere so shabby, but even on a Thursday night it was packed to the rafters.

Cornish ordered us tea, which was whiskey and disgusting. "Maybe you'd prefer wine," he said and told the waiter to bring me a glass of grape juice, which tasted pretty much the same as the tea. I didn't drink that, either, but he didn't let it go to waste and ordered two steak dinners, rare. "I want them bleeding" is how he put it. And another round of "tea."

I tried to talk about the gala. I asked what time I should get there and what to do if I didn't recognize someone. He only wanted to talk about himself and his career: his first big assignment covering the mayor's race in Manchester, murder stories from the crime desk in Worcester, a juicy scandal in Providence. The *Transcript* was just another stop on his way to New York. "The big time."

By the time they brought dinner, Cornish was too drunk to cut his meat, so I started to put my coat on.

"Don't give me the fish-eye," he said. "I only drink because I'm stuck in that damned hen coop. Once I'm out of there, I'll be a goddamn choirboy."

One of the waiters came over and told him to pipe down or he'd throw us out. Cornish pretended to lock his mouth with a little key.

I said I was leaving, but he said, "I thought you wanted to talk about how you're going to make a big name for yourself at that swell party." That set him off about how women didn't belong in the newsroom. Old prunes like Flora and Katherine were okay. "But you're too pretty," he said, and if I wanted to write, I should go home and write sonnets about bluebirds or a romantic story for the *Saturday Evening Post*.

"But for God's sake, don't do any more 'poor Negro' stories. It makes you look dumb. Colored people don't feel things the

272

same as you and me. It's a scientific fact they have smaller brains than us.

"Besides, all these 'campaigns' are run by the communists, and that means the goddamn Jews are behind it. Those people will destroy the country if we let them."

I could hear my mother's voice: "They smile in your face but if you scratch a little they'll try to cut your throat."

That was it. I started for the door. Cornish got himself out of his chair and stumbled after me but I had to help him through the door and then prop him up against a lamppost. He leaned over to kiss me, and if I hadn't caught him, he would have fallen on his face. "If you get me a cup of coffee, I'll make a real pass at you."

I told him to go to hell.

A taxi pulled over and unloaded a bunch of college boys and I jumped in. It was my first taxi ride and I'm glad I did it, but oh my God, was it expensive. I didn't eat lunch for a week.

The next morning, Cornish was back on the edge of my desk and said, "You'll forgive me if I was a little fresh, won't you, kiddo? I should never mix wine and whiskey."

I didn't answer him and from then on he got nothing but the cold shoulder from me.

Finally he went back to acting like I didn't exist, which was a relief.

NEVER APOLOGIZE
FOR BEING SMART.

I didn't see much of Miss Chevalier. She didn't have a lot to do with the Saturday Club anymore and neither did I. Gussie was still a gung-ho member, but after Irene got married I sort of lost interest.

So when I ran into Miss Chevalier on the street after work, it was like seeing a rainbow. Except for a little gray in her hair and a few lines on her face, she hadn't changed much in ten years. She was still wearing the same sensible tie-up shoes and her smile still made me feel like I'd won a prize. I asked about the library and Miss Green. She asked about my family and how I liked my job.

I don't know why, but instead of saying what you're supposed to say, which is, "It's fine," I went off about how the men in the office treated me like I was a servant and that I hated writing about how Mrs. Porridge served pink petits fours in honor of

Mrs. Pudding, or who won the dahlia competition. I said, "I'm glad my name isn't on that damn column." It just spilled out of me.

Miss Chevalier said, "Oh dear."

I was still writing Seen and Heard, but with strict orders to stay away from Cambridge and anything "controversial." I also had to stick to the top of the Social Register and talk only to hostesses or chairladies, which meant that every program was "enlightening" and every speaker "distinguished."

There were a lot of times I wanted to change "distinguished" to "over the hill," but I didn't want to lose my job. It wasn't perfect, but in a newsroom at least you're never bored, what with the crackpots on the telephone, the reporters' tantrums, and the excitement when a story comes in late and a whole section has to be changed at the last minute.

But why was I kvetching to the woman who was my . . . what should I call her? My mentor? My guardian angel?

I said I was sorry.

"Never apologize for being smart," Miss Chevalier said. "Why don't you come to my house on Sunday afternoon. I'm hosting a few friends and I promise there won't be

276

any petits fours. I'm sure you'll enjoy the conversation."

I went, of course. I was curious to see where she lived and I wanted to say hello to Miss Green. Even though we had never had much to do with each other, she was the only person I knew who cared as much about Filomena as I did. I was missing Filomena a lot. She sent me a postcard every month, so I knew she was thinking of me, but it wasn't much comfort when I was feeling blue.

The Ediths were living in an old brownstone in the South End — the kind where you go up a flight of stairs to get to the front door and all the rooms have high ceilings and tall windows. It was on one of those wonderful blocks with a strip of grass and trees in the middle of the street. There was an elegant marble fireplace in the living room, but the paint was peeling on the woodwork and the rug was a little threadbare. Shabby-genteel, if you know what I mean.

There were no tea cakes or even tea, just as Miss Chevalier promised. She served sandwiches and coffee, which seemed much more modern to me.

I was sorry that Miss Green was under the weather and didn't come downstairs.

But when I saw her paintings on the walls, in my mind I started writing a letter to tell Filomena about how her teacher's purple skies and yellow hills reminded me of the tinted postcards she sent from New Mexico. I could imagine Filomena reading that and smiling.

Miss Chevalier introduced me to her friends, and what an impressive bunch. I met the president of the Women's Educational and Industrial Union, the director of the Boston school lunch program, a history professor from Wellesley College, and a lady doctor with a thick German accent.

The room was buzzing with conversations about politics and books — I didn't hear a single word about dahlias or summering in Manchester. I remember thinking how nice it was that these old ladies had such good friends.

Ha! Those "old ladies" were probably in their fifties. Being eight-five gives you perspective. It also gives you arthritis. Maybe you should stitch these pearls of wisdom on a sampler. Do you even know what a sampler is?

Not everyone was "old." There were a few girls like me, in their twenties, and they were interesting, too: a social worker for the city health department, a librarian, a high school teacher, and a law student.

When I found out that Rita Metsky, the law student, was going to Portia Law School, I said I knew someone who had graduated from there. "Do you know Gussie Frommer?"

She smiled. "Everybody knows Gussie." We traded stories about my outgoing friend, but Rita kept looking at the clock on the mantel and frowning. "My brother is supposed to give a talk and he should have been here by now. I told him I'd kill him if he kept these women waiting."

When he did arrive — out of breath and carrying a suitcase — he said the train from Washington was late and apologized like he had nearly missed his own wedding. Miss Chevalier told him to take a minute and have a cup of coffee. He winked at Rita. "My sister would tell you I don't deserve it."

You couldn't miss the resemblance between Rita and Aaron Metsky. They were both about four inches taller than me, with dark brown eyes; thick, almost black hair; and thin, straight noses, except that his was a little bit flattened on the end, like a hawk — but handsome.

He was a lawyer for the National Child Labor Committee and he'd been traveling around the country trying to pass the amendment against child labor. Aaron Metsky wasn't there to convince Miss Chevalier's friends about the need; those women supported everything they thought would help poor people, and keeping girls out of factories and sweatshops was one of their regular causes. He was there to report about how the campaign was going, but the news wasn't good.

He had just gotten back from two weeks in the South, where states had been voting the amendment down one after another. They saw it as a plot by northerners to keep them poor and weak. He said, "They're still fighting the Civil War down there."

But even in the North, farmers, the Catholic Church, and even the anti-Prohibition people were all siding with the mill owners. They kept saying that the law was a communist plot to take children away from their parents.

Aaron shook his head. "When people find out where I come from, they say if Massachusetts voted this down, what makes you think it's going to happen in Alabama or Mississippi? To tell you the truth, I don't have a good answer for them."

The social worker behind me jumped up and shook her finger at him. "I'll give you your answer: Bert Forster, a fourteen-year-old boy who lost all the fingers on his right hand from working in the Connecticut tobacco fields. Or Selma Trudeau over at the Florence Crittenton Home, who had a baby at fifteen because some man promised to marry her and take her away from the Lawrence mills."

The German doctor said that child labor could cause great harm later in life, too: deafness from loud machines, lung diseases from cotton dust, and nervous exhaustion that could lead to insanity and even suicide.

They were talking about my sisters. Betty was probably twelve when she came to America, Celia was maybe ten, and they went to work right off the boat. They got jobs wherever Papa went, which meant they worked in a candy factory and a shoe factory. When he became a presser, they learned how to use a sewing machine and worked in one sweatshop after another. Levine's was better than most because there was a bathroom and he didn't lock them in all day, but I remember how unbearable it was in the summer.

I wondered, did working as a little girl kill whatever strength Celia had been born with?

Betty was made out of stronger stuff, but she got away from factory work as soon as she could, and I knew she'd sooner cut off her arm than let any of her children work like she had. Betty and Levine wouldn't even let Jake sell newspapers after school. "Let him play with a ball," Betty said. "Let him be a little boy."

It was different by the time I was born. Pretty much all the children in my neighborhood went to school at least until they were thirteen or fourteen, and a lot graduated from high school. Some of the bigger boys sold newspapers and I'm sure lots of little kids worked nights and weekends making paper flowers or sewing piecework at home, but it wasn't as bad as factory work.

The discussion around me heated up. Miss Chevalier was standing up, pounding her fist on the palm of her hand. "The arguments against this law are outrageous. You hear things like 'A mother could be arrested for asking her seventeen-year-old daughter to wash the dishes.'

"How in God's name is protecting the young anything but just?"

Aaron didn't seem to be listening; he was staring at Rita, who was sitting next to me. She poked me in the ribs and whispered, "My brother can't keep his eyes off you."

I looked again and realized that she was

right; he was looking at me. When he saw that I was looking back, he smiled. Then I smiled. How could I not? He was smart. He had a nice way with words. He was Jewish. And he was good-looking.

Aaron seemed so perfect, I giggled. But then I remembered what rotten luck I had with men and went to get myself another cup of coffee.

After Aaron finished his speech, everyone rushed up to him with questions and advice. I waited for a while to see if he would come talk to me but I lost my nerve and left. I was halfway down the block and sorry I hadn't been a little more patient — or brave — when I heard someone call my name.

Aaron was running with his suitcase in one hand, his coat in the other, and a dopey smile on his face. "It's Addie, right? Rita didn't get your last name. I'm Aaron Metsky, her brother."

I said, "It's Baum."

"What is?"

"My name."

"Baum?" he said.

I laughed, he laughed. Then he asked if he could take me to supper, but only if I was hungry, or maybe I was already busy. Or was someone waiting for me? A fiancé? Or did I think it was too early to eat? Did I know what time it was?

He was adorable. But he kept on talking and talking, so I put out my hand and said, "Nice to meet you."

His hand was warm and he didn't let go of mine. We stood there grinning at each other like we'd hit the jackpot. Finally, I said, "Where do you want to eat?"

He asked if I liked Chinese food.

I said I'd give it a try. Did you know there was a time before all Jews loved Chinese food?

It was quite a long walk to the restaurant, but it went by in a flash. I had never had a conversation like that with a man. Not that it was profound or personal; it was just easy. We went from one topic to another, we interrupted each other, and we laughed.

Aaron used to tell people he fell in love with me at first sight, which sounded ridiculous the first hundred times I heard him say it.

When he said, "Here we are," I thought he was joking. "Here" looked like an empty brick factory. When he led me down a stinky alley, there was one second I wondered if I was doing something stupid.

But I knew I wasn't. Not with him.

He opened a big metal door and I felt like Alice in Wonderland, but with chopsticks.

The room was huge. It must have been a metal shop or some kind of factory. The machines were gone but you could see the wear on the wood floors. It was full of people — mostly Chinese — sitting at long tables on benches, putting food on each other's plates, and talking loud. Louder than my own family, which is saying something.

Aaron said there weren't any menus. You pointed to what was on a plate near you or let the waiter choose. But he had been there before and ordered some Chinese dumplings — like kreplach, but much better — and two plates piled with chopped vegetables, meat, and rice.

I couldn't believe how delicious it all was. Maybe it's something genetic, the Jewish Chinese food thing.

I asked Aaron if he knew what we were eating. "I don't know but I'm sure it's not cat."

"Cat?"

He said there was a nasty rumor that the Chinese killed stray dogs and cats for meat. "It can't be true, because I've eaten a lot of Chinese food and I never wanted to chase mice afterward."

Aaron was getting more adorable by the minute, and the way he looked at me made me feel like I was floating.

He started walking me back to my boardinghouse but I didn't want the evening to end, so I said I knew where to get the best coffee in Boston — if he wanted.

Of course he wanted, so we went to Filomena's favorite café in the North End, which was another long walk. The waiter sat us in a back corner where it was dark and quiet — as if he knew we wanted to be alone.

I asked Aaron if he liked his work. He said yes but also no. They had made a big mistake by writing the law to apply to everyone under the age of eighteen when all the state child labor laws were for fifteen- or sixteen-year-olds and younger.

"But I won't give up yet. My parents think I should leave Washington, move back to Boston, and go into my brother's law practice. It would be Metsky and Metsky until Rita passes the bar and then we'll change it to Metsky, Metsky, and Metsky."

He smacked himself on the forehead. "If Rita were here she'd tell me to shut up and let you talk." He took my hand and said, "Tell me something."

By that time, I was so comfortable with your grandfather that I talked about my sisters. I told him they had been child laborers when they came to America, and that after listening to what the German doctor said about how mental problems could show up years later, I understood Celia in a different way.

Aaron touched my cheek. He said the reason he'd gone to work for the child labor committee was his mother, who had worked in a cotton mill as a little girl. "There's a famous picture of a barefoot girl standing next to a big loom. Her eyes look old and hollow, the same as my mother's before she died. It was her lungs. The doctor said it was probably from the cotton dust."

Aaron was fifteen when he lost his mother. I was sixteen when Celia died.

Oh, Ava, there is so much sadness in this life.

It was a Sunday night and so quiet we could hear our own footsteps down Commonwealth Avenue. I didn't feel cold but under the streetlights I could see Aaron's breath in the air and I wondered if he was going to kiss me good night.

There was no kiss. Not then anyway.

It turned out that we were so late, my landlady had turned off the porch light. That meant the door was locked, and I didn't have a key. None of us did. It was the rule in a respectable house like Mrs.

Kay's: no late nights. She could throw me out for this.

I said, "Maybe I can take the trolley to my sister's house in Roxbury."

"The trains stopped running a while ago," said Aaron. "But my cousin Ruth has her own place in the Fenway. I'm sure she'll let you stay over."

He said it was a good thing we had drunk all that coffee to stay awake, but it also made me need to go to the bathroom — not that I told him that. We did not take our time on *that* walk, let me tell you.

A girl in a robe opened the door. "What the hell is going on, Aaron? It's almost one o'clock in the morning."

He explained what happened. "Tell Addie I've never done this before."

Ruth gave me the once-over and pinched Aaron's cheek. "It's true. As far as I know, he's a straight shooter."

I followed Ruth up to her flat, which smelled like cigarettes and spices. She gave me a nightgown, threw a blanket on the couch, and said good night.

I thought I'd never fall asleep, but I was gone the minute I closed my eyes. I guess falling in love makes you tired. Or maybe it was all that walking.

Ruth was still sleeping when I got up and

tiptoed out of the apartment. The sun was just coming up but Aaron was already there, sitting on the steps with his suitcase. He hadn't shaved and he was holding a bunch of daffodils he must have stolen from someone's yard. He said, "God, you're beautiful." So I kissed him.

LUCK. I'M TELLING YOU.

You know how people say that everything happens for a reason and that fate brings together people who are meant for each other? I don't buy that.

Luck, on the other hand, I believe in. And it was pure luck that I met your grandfather.

Aaron was living in Washington and the only reason he happened to be at Miss Chevalier's house that Sunday afternoon was because Rita went into a coffee shop and ran into one of her law professors who was sitting with Miss Chevalier who was interested to hear about her brother's work and asked if he would be willing to speak to some friends. It so happened that he was going to be in Boston at the end of March for Passover . . .

Luck. I'm telling you.

The night after we met was the first Seder, so he was in Brookline with his family and I was in Roxbury with mine. For most of the meal my mother was in the kitchen telling Betty what she was doing wrong, my father had his face in the Haggadah, and Levine was trying to make his sons sit still. I was thinking about Aaron and how we were planning to have breakfast before I went to work in the morning, but I must have been yawning a lot because Betty said that if I was so tired, I should sleep there. "You can take the trolley to work from here in the morning."

I said "No!" so fast that she gave me a look like *What's going on?*

I made up a story about having to be at work earlier than usual and asked Levine if he would drive me home. I was out of there before Betty could ask me anything else.

That week we were together as much as we could be. Thank God I didn't live at home, where I'd have to explain where I'd been and where I was going. Aaron told his parents that he had a lot of meetings at the State House, but he thought Rita probably suspected what was going on.

We went to cafés and restaurants in out-of-the-way places. We took long walks and talked and kissed. The kissing was very nice. We were compatible that way, if you know what I mean.

One night it rained and we went to a movie. We held hands the whole time and sat with our knees touching. I was glad we were in the dark so I could smile without having to explain why.

When we walked past Symphony Hall, Aaron told me how his mother used to take him there when he was a boy. She wanted all of her children to love music.

I said I wanted to go to a concert one day — I'd never been. I didn't mean it as a hint or anything, but he went inside and bought tickets for the next night. We got there early and watched the chauffeurs open limousine doors for the kinds of people who were always being mentioned in Serena's Out and About column. It was a sea of white hair and black coats except for one woman wearing a green velvet cloak and waving at someone across the lobby, with bright red nails.

I grabbed Aaron's arm. "Do you see that woman? That's Tessa Thorndike. She's the other reason we met."

Aaron asked if I wanted to say hello.

I said, "She wouldn't know me from a hole in the wall. I hope we're not going to sit next to her."

He laughed. "Don't worry."

When it was time to go in, the swells like

Tessa went downstairs and Aaron and I headed to the balcony with the regular people: students, shopgirls, clerks. I even saw some laborers' hands on the banisters as we climbed the stairs. I heard people talking Yiddish, Italian, German, and French. Everyone seemed to be in a good mood.

Our seats were in the last row of the highest balcony. Aaron held out his hands like he was handing me Symphony Hall on a platter and told me who the statues were and how many lightbulbs were in the chandeliers.

A man in a black suit walked out to the podium and stretched his arms wide, like one of the black seabirds in Rockport that hold their wings out to dry in the breeze. Aaron whispered, "Koussevitzky."

The music was different from anything I'd heard on the radio or from the piano at the movies. Some of the slow parts made me feel like crying, but when it got faster and the violinists were sawing away, my heart pounded like I was watching a horse race. I was listening not just with my ears but with my hands and my heart, too. I can't describe it. It's like trying to explain what chocolate tastes like; you just have to try it for yourself.

When the music ended I clapped until my

hands hurt. Aaron said, "I'm glad you like Mozart, too."

Taking me to the symphony turned out to be part of his plan to make me a real Boston girl. He said it was too chilly for a Red Sox game, but he took me to Harvard Yard and the Bunker Hill Monument. He even stayed in Boston an extra day for the opening of the swan boats at the Public Garden. We were on the very first boat of 1926.

I took your mother and aunt to the opening day of the swan boats every year when they were girls, just like I took you and your sister when you were little.

Aaron got the night train to Washington and I went back to my room and cried myself to sleep. When I went to work the next morning, Katherine said I looked like death warmed over and sent me home. I knew I wasn't going to feel better in my dark little room, so I went to see Irene.

She had married Joe Riley the year before, and they were living in a little apartment in the North End. They had met at work, where he was an electrician. It had taken him months to get her out on a date — she was off Irishmen at the time — but he finally got her to agree by getting down on one knee and singing "Let Me Call You Sweetheart" in front of God and everyone.

Irene admitted that he had a nice voice but said, "I had to put a stop to it."

She was nine months pregnant at the time, so I knew I'd find her at home.

I told her about Aaron and started crying about how awful it was that he had to leave. But instead of holding my hand and telling me, "There, there," she grinned. "It's about time you took a shine to a nice fellow, and this one sounds grand. I like the sound of his name, too. If I have a boy, maybe I'll call him Aaron. Would you mind?"

That wasn't what I wanted to hear. I was blubbering, "But he's gone. He left me."

Irene crossed her arms. "Didn't you just tell me he's coming back to see you next month? If you think he was lying, then you're better off without him and good riddance."

That set me off. Aaron was the most honest and decent man I ever met and how could she say such a thing?

Irene laughed. "All right then," she said. "So let's talk about what I should cook when you bring him over to meet us. I'll try to make something that won't make us all sick. I could send him an invitation, or maybe a warning would be better."

I Say So.

I read Aaron's first letter a thousand times. He made a list of everything he missed about me: my hazel eyes, my lovely hands, and my red shoes. He said to send him a list of novels he should read so he wouldn't feel stupid when I talked about books and writers he'd never heard of. As if he was stupid. A college man. A lawyer!

We sent each other two or three letters a week. He wrote about what was going on at work and what it was like to live in Washington. I didn't have anything interesting to say about my job, so I introduced him to my friends. Gussie was making so much money she bought herself a big house in Brookline and was renting rooms to Simmons girls who needed a cheap, decent place to live.

Irene was so bored at home, she spent the whole day talking to her belly and when she ran out of things to say she read out loud from the newspaper. She said the kid was going to come out of her wearing a Red Sox rosette.

I wrote to Aaron about the postcards Filomena sent from New Mexico and Betty's love affair with her electric mixer and how my sister was already planning Jake's bar mitzvah, which wasn't for months.

I started checking off days on the calendar until his visit, but then he wrote that the other lawyer in his office had quit and unless someone else got hired, he might not be in Boston for another month or maybe more. He said he was sorry three or four times and that he felt terrible.

He felt terrible? I was holding my breath until I saw him again and now I didn't even know when that was going to happen.

I started wondering if maybe Aaron wasn't so honest after all. Look at how stupid I'd been about Harold and Ernie. What did I really know about him? Who knows? Maybe he'd met someone else in Washington.

I wrote back, very polite, and said thank you for letting me know. I think I made some crack about how I hoped he'd enjoy the cherry blossoms and that I looked forward to his next letter.

Well, Aaron got the message and his next letter was three pages long about how much he missed me and how he hated being away from me and how bad he felt about keeping me waiting. He said he'd started working late every night and told his boss that he had to take a few days off to take care of some family business.

He ended with a cute little P.S. *I was glad that you ordered pancakes when we had breakfast together. Pancakes are the only things I know how to cook and I will make them for you every day for the rest of your life — if you say so.*

I don't know how many times I read that P.S. before what he was saying sunk in. My letter back to him had only three words. *I SAY SO.*

Maybe a week later, when I got home from work, my landlady was waiting for me at the door. She waved a piece of paper in my face and blamed me for almost giving her a heart attack. In those days the main reason people sent telegrams was to say that someone had died.

"I only opened it to see if I should get out smelling salts for you," she said. "Some people waste money like it was water."

Aaron's telegram said *Tell Irene I will be there on Friday.*

The four of us had a great time at dinner. Irene cooked a delicious meal. For dessert she went to the bakery and bought an apple pie. I said it was almost as good as Mrs. Morse's.

"Oh no," Irene said. "Once she gets started about those pies, there's no stopping her."

"But I want to hear what Addie has to say about pie," Aaron said.

Joe winked at me. "He's got it bad."

Aaron said, "Guilty as charged."

He had to go back to Washington on Sunday morning, so we really only had one day together.

I wanted to go to Rockport but it would have taken too long, so we got off the train at Nahant and walked on the beach for a couple of hours. We talked about where we might get married and how many children we wanted and we decided not to tell our families until Aaron moved to Boston. His plan was to be back by the Fourth of July or sooner if they could find someone to replace him.

That was the day he gave me the gold locket I always wear. Inside it's engraved, March 29, 1926. The day we met.

You know, if one of my daughters had told me she was going to marry a man she'd only known for a week I would have locked her in her room. But we weren't kids. I was twenty-five and he was twenty-nine. We were completely sure. And obviously we were right.

Aaron didn't tell his parents he was in town that weekend. Only Ruth knew. He slept on her couch Friday night, and Saturday night she stayed with a girlfriend so we could be alone, just the two of us, for the whole night.

I'll leave it at that.

AT LEAST SHE DIDN'T SUFFER.

I was counting the days until the Fourth of July and thinking about the best way to introduce Aaron to my family. When should I tell Betty, and would it be better to have her tell Mameh that there would be company for a Friday dinner or should I just have him come to the house on a Sunday afternoon?

He wasn't writing as many letters, but I didn't mind. I knew he was working extra hours so he could leave his job knowing he'd taken care of everything he could.

Things were moving along nicely until the middle of June, when my landlady died in her sleep.

"At least she didn't suffer."

That's what everyone said — in fact, that was all anyone said. Nobody disliked her; actually, nobody knew anything about her, including boarders who had lived in her house for ten years. She was a widow who didn't have children — that was it.

It was the fastest funeral I've ever been to. The only people there were the boarders and two nephews. There wasn't even a eulogy. After the service, the nephews asked us to meet them in the parlor that afternoon.

We all went. There wasn't a cup of coffee or a cookie anywhere, but it turned out that we weren't there for a shiva. It was a business meeting to tell us that they were selling the building and we had ten days to get out.

One of the old ladies fainted and the rest of them looked like they might keel over, too. There weren't a lot of boardinghouses left for women in Boston; rents were high and what could you find in a week, anyway?

Some of the women had relatives to turn to, but there were five who seemed to be completely alone in the world. They had probably planned to leave the boarding-house the same way as the landlady: feet first. I could hear them crying in their rooms.

My next-door neighbor stopped me in the hallway and begged me to help her. She said, "I don't have anyone else to ask."

I had no idea how to help but I figured that Miss Chevalier would, and by the time we had to move out, she'd gotten five beds at the YWCA on Berkeley Street.

I was embarrassed at the way they kept thanking me. I told Miss Chevalier, "You're the one who saved the day. I didn't do anything."

She said of course they should thank me. "You took pity on them and you knew whom to ask. That's more than half the battle, and you won it for them."

It wasn't a hardship for me. Aaron and I were planning to get married in the fall, so I'd only have to put up with my family for a few months. And I can't say I was sorry to be leaving that dark, smelly house.

On the day I moved out, I was sitting on the steps waiting for Levine to pick me up with his car. The idea of living under the same roof as my mother made me feel like I was fifteen again — in other words, miserable. But then the mailman came and handed me a letter from Aaron. It was like one of those silly coincidences that only happen in novels. I kissed the envelope. I nearly kissed the mailman. I was on top of the world until I opened it.

Dear Addie,
I hope you won't be too upset but . . .

Aaron was on a train to Minnesota to see if he could help get the amendment passed in St. Paul. Only four states had ratified so far and they badly needed a win. He said it would only be a few weeks, maybe a month. The rest of what he wrote was apologies: *Forgive me. I love you. We'll be together soon. I'm sorry. Don't be mad.*

I wasn't just mad, I was spitting nails mad. Hadn't he said it was a lost cause? Wasn't I more important than a lost cause? Who knew how long he'd really be gone and how long I'd be stuck in Roxbury with my mother breathing down my neck?

I wrote him an angry letter and tore it up. I wrote him a whiny, woe-is-me letter with tear stains all over it and tore that up, too. In the end I sent a postcard to the hotel where he was staying. *Dear Mr. Metsky. Please send mail for Miss A. Baum to Miss Henrietta Cavendish at the* Boston Evening Transcript. It wasn't nice but it could have been worse.

Moving into the house in Roxbury felt like I'd gone backward in time. Betty was upstairs with her family and I was on the first floor with my parents. It seemed as if nothing had changed, even though nothing was the same.

The boys had changed the most; all of them were taller, smarter, and louder. My mother called them wild animals — vilde chayas — and said Betty wasn't strict enough. But Jake, Eddy, Richie, and Carl were just healthy kids who got good grades and did whatever their mother asked. They were always glad to see Auntie Addie when I visited — especially Eddy. But after I told them how big they were getting and after they told me what they were doing in school, we didn't have much to say to each other. I was like a friendly moon circling around their busy little planet.

And even though he lived downstairs, my father was even more distant. I'm not sure he even knew which grandson was which. He never fell in love with any of them the way he had with Lenny. And he didn't see much of them, since he was in the house only to eat and sleep.

After Papa got laid off from his job, he did exactly what Levine had suggested and spent his days in the synagogue library with Avrum and a bunch of old men. We called them alter kockers. Today they would be "retirees."

The rabbi studied with them sometimes, and one day he asked if Papa would be interested in teaching boys to get ready for their bar mitzvahs. The parents would even pay something for his trouble.

I think that was my father's dream come true. He went to the barber and asked Betty to help him choose a new suit, "because a man who teaches Torah can't go around looking like a peasant." He didn't act much different at home, but he held himself taller. You could almost say he was happy.

Mameh had changed the least. She cleaned and cooked and complained. She wouldn't touch Betty's washing machine; she said it ruined the clothes and didn't get them as clean as she got them with her washboard, and then she groaned about how doing the laundry was killing her back. She grew cabbages in the backyard — bitter and hard like baseballs. No one would eat them but Mameh, who said at least they were fresh and what did we know.

My mother did go out of the house more since they moved to Roxbury. Maybe because there were no neighbors in the same building, or maybe it was because there were fewer cars. At first she did some of the shopping, but the greengrocer kicked her out of his store when she accused him of putting his thumb on the scale. She gave the butcher such a hard time about how much fat he left on the meat that he wouldn't let her in his shop, either.

Eventually, the only place Mameh could

go was the fish market, where she was friends with the owner's wife, who was as quiet as a fish herself. She had an unmarried nephew and the two of them decided he was perfect for me. Mameh said he was from a good family and he made a nice living. "He's thirty-nine years old and ready to settle down."

Betty said, "He's two hundred pounds and not very smart. Leave Addie alone, Ma."

"With ankles like that, she's not such a catch herself," she said, as if I wasn't in the room.

They still didn't know about Aaron. I wasn't worried about introducing him in person: a Jewish man with a good profession, from a nice family? What's not to like? But until he was standing next to me, I didn't think I could have said his name out loud without crying like a baby.

I HAVE NO CHOICE, ADDIE.

At least I still liked my job, which was never boring.

Miss Flora announced that she was leaving to be the editor of the women's page of the *Cincinnati Enquirer.* I was stunned. I always thought she was as Bostonian as the statue of George Washington in the Public Garden. And just as permanent.

If Flora had been a man, I'm sure Cornish would have understood why she'd want to run her own section, but he said good riddance and it just proved that women were fickle and didn't belong in the newsroom. The morning after she left I found him passed out under his desk. When he sobered up, he told Katherine that she'd have to take over Flora's work in addition to her own.

Katherine marched into Mort's office and said she would stay on only if she got a promotion and a raise, and if I came on as her full-time assistant. Cornish called that "uppity" and thought she should be fired, but Mort gave her everything she asked for.

I hadn't known much about Katherine or Flora. We didn't pal around after hours like the men did. Katherine was a hard worker but Flora had been the bigger talker. Until she took over, I didn't know how much Katherine had on the ball.

She told everyone to call her Miss Walters and to call me Miss Baum. "You and I can be familiar with each other," she said, "but why should they call us by our Christian names if we can't do the same to them? We're not their maids." She was right, but nobody in the newsroom was ever going to call me Miss Baum. When you start out somewhere as "the girl," you never grow up.

Katherine — Miss Walters — told me I would still be writing Seen and Heard, but she wanted more about the younger set, especially what they were wearing. She brought in a stack of *Vogue* magazines and I learned a whole new language: organza, peplum, bias cut, pinafore.

All that reading made me take a new look at what Katherine was wearing. Maybe I hadn't noticed because she was always in black, but now I realized that she wore whatever was the latest "silhouette," one of my new words, and that her drop-waist dresses were perfect for a woman of her height.

No one would ever call Katherine Walters a pretty woman: her face was strangely flat and one eye was a tiny bit higher than the other. After Flora left, she took off her hat, cut her bangs, and was suddenly striking and stylish, which is actually much better than pretty.

Katherine said I could also go back to writing about interesting lecture topics in Seen and Heard, but "nothing as upsetting as that piece about the Negroes." She said there was a place for stories like that, but not on the women's pages. She suggested I look into the work of the Women's Educational and Industrial Union and the ladies who sat on the symphony board of trustees. "You'll enjoy that."

I did. But I also had to write the "how to" stories that had been Flora's specialty: how to lose weight, clean the icebox, make homemade hand lotion, set the table for an afternoon of bridge or mahjongg, mend stockings so it didn't show. It wasn't hard, but it was a lot to learn about things that didn't interest me at all.

Katherine kept everything running smoothly so Cornish could go on as he did before: coming in late, reading the papers, joking with the reporters, and leaving early. Katherine kept her distance from him but she read him the riot act when she saw me delivering his morning coffee.

"Miss Baum's new responsibilities are such that she no longer has time to act as your personal servant. Please remember that."

He was too surprised, or maybe too hungover, to come up with a snappy comeback. But if looks could kill . . .

Cornish didn't speak to her at all after that. If there was something he absolutely had to tell her he dropped a crumpled-up note on her desk or sent a message through me. "Tell that blasted beanpole she's got to cut ten inches today."

I must have smiled at "beanpole," which set him off making up funny names for Katherine: Miss Maypole, the Giraffe, the Boston Colossus. He started announcing them loud enough so everyone in the newsroom could hear. The reporters got a kick out of this until the day he called her the Monumental Bitch.

You could have heard a pin drop. It's not as if those guys didn't use that word and plenty worse, but there were rules about where and when you were supposed to say them. Katherine had been ignoring Cornish's game but this time she said, in the sweetest, most ladylike voice, "My goodness, Ian. Do you kiss your mother with that mouth?"

That got a big laugh, and the police reporter, who was as foulmouthed as the rest of them, said, "Want me to get you a bar of soap to wash it out, Miss Walters?"

Work became a minefield for me after that. Katherine said she would let me go if I did any more favors for "that man." But the minute she stepped out of the room, Cornish would send me out for a magazine or a bottle of aspirin and threaten to fire me if I didn't do it.

To make things even worse, the weather was miserably hot and muggy. The newsroom only had three windows facing the street and when the sun hit them in the afternoon I bet it was ninety degrees in there. There was one fan, no water cooler, and those men didn't shower every day.

Aaron's letters became the bright spots in my life. They always started: *My dear Miss Cavendish, I hope this letter finds you and your staff in the best of health.*

The first one didn't mention my snippy postcard, which was big of him, but he didn't apologize for being so far away, either. He wrote about the trip west and his assignment, which was to talk to any state legislator who seemed to be leaning in favor of the amendment. He said he had eaten the best pancakes he'd ever tasted in his St. Paul hotel and was going to bribe the cook to give him the recipe.

He always ended his letters, *Sincerely and forever yours, A. Metsky.*

After a few weeks, his letters got to be less cheerful. It was as hot in St. Paul as it was in Boston, his hotel room was suffocating, most of the food was tasteless, and he felt invisible.

Going to Minnesota in the summer had been a big mistake; the state legislature wasn't in session and the representatives were back at their farms, which were all over the state.

Aaron was riding milk trains to talk to possible supporters, but all he got was splinters on his backside from sitting on wooden crates and bites from mosquitoes he claimed were the size of bumblebees.

He wired his boss to say that he might as well come back, but he was told to stay, find some stories about local child laborers, and get invited to speak at women's self-improvement societies and church auxiliaries. Aaron said that if you can move a roomful of mothers to tears, you could raise an army for a cause.

There were plenty of stories. For sixty years, children had been sent to Minnesota on "orphan trains." It was a well-intentioned idea, a way to give abandoned children a better life with wholesome farm families. Being out in the country had to be better than the misery of crowded orphanages, right?

Some of those children must have been well taken care of and loved, but it wasn't hard finding kids who were not. Aaron struck up a conversation with a young man at a café who said he'd been put on the train from Baltimore when he was twelve and his younger brother, Frank, was five. He remembered being lined up on a platform where the women would pick out little children with blue eyes and good teeth — like his brother — and the men chose bigger boys who could go to work right away. He was told to forget about his old family and start over, but he didn't forget his brother and tried running away to find him. He got a good hiding when he was caught.

There were plenty of orphan train children still living with families that had taken them in, but it wasn't easy to talk to them.

Aaron ran into a girl named Martha when

he was getting off the train at a stop just outside St. Paul. She was unloading sacks of flour and sugar as if they were full of feathers even though she wasn't any bigger than me.

Martha was sixteen. She had been eight when the nuns put her on the train and the Olsens took her in. She didn't pine for her family in New York; after her mother walked out, her father brought her to an orphanage. "He kept my brothers," she said. "He told them he didn't know what to do with a girl."

When Aaron asked if she was happy with her Minnesota family, Martha said the Olsens were not her family. They weren't as bad as some she knew about. They never hit her and she got plenty to eat and new boots when the old ones wore out. She said they even sent for the doctor once when she was sick. But they made Martha stop going to school when she was ten and they talked about her as "the girl."

"Tell the girl to pass the milk."

He said they treated her like something between a prize farm animal and a daughter.

Martha worked in the cookhouse, where she put out three meals a day for farmhands. In the winter, her hands bled from washing dishes.

She had taken to sleeping with a knife under her pillow in case one of the workers got any ideas, but she was really afraid of her "big brother," who wouldn't leave her alone. Martha said that Mrs. Olsen wouldn't believe anything bad about her son.

Those were hard letters to read, but they were love letters, too. Aaron was showing me who he was, what was in his heart. The more I knew him, the more I loved him. And he opened my eyes to what was going on around me. I started to notice boys and girls who should have been in school selling newspapers, shining shoes, scrubbing stoops, and carrying baskets of laundry. It made me proud of what Aaron was doing.

I couldn't leave his letters at home. My mother was always in my room, rehanging my clothes, rearranging my books, even refolding the clothes in my drawers. Once I asked if she was looking for something in my underwear. She said she didn't like a mess in her house and that I wouldn't care unless I had something to hide.

I kept Aaron's letters in a big envelope under a stack of magazines in the bottom drawer of my desk at work. I was the first one in the newsroom every morning, so I could get the mail for Miss Cavendish and check for new letters. Sometimes I pulled the drawer open just to see his handwriting.

One day when I opened the drawer, the envelope was gone. I made a beeline for Cornish's desk, since he was the only one I could imagine who would want them. He could use them to get me in trouble or blackmail me into going out with him again. He might even burn them out of pure spite.

Luckily, Katherine caught me before anyone else came in, "I've got them," she said.

She had seen Cornish sniffing around my desk after I left. "He must have noticed the way you were always leaning over that drawer and sighing. I asked if I could help him find something. It's convenient that he still isn't talking to me."

Katherine had taken the envelope home for safekeeping and told me to come to her apartment after work. "I'll fix dinner and you can tell me all about Mr. Metsky."

She had a tiny apartment in the Fenway, not far from where Aaron's cousin Ruth lived. But Katherine's place was like a jewelry box inside: a dark red rug on the floor, bright colored fabrics hanging on the walls, scarves hung over the lampshades.

"It's mostly from Morocco," she said. "I got them on my honeymoon."

I said I didn't know she was married. "Aren't you *Miss* Walters?"

"I'm widowed. He died in the war." She was quiet for a moment. "I don't like talking about him to strangers."

You should always be kind to people, Ava. You never know what sorrows they're carrying around.

It was a very exotic supper of things I'd never heard of: hummus, pita bread, olives with pits, and a kind of chopped salad. Katherine was pretty exotic herself: a Buddhist, a socialist, and a feminist. She graduated from Smith College, was a vegetarian, and did yoga. She was planning to visit all forty-eight states and had been to twelve so far, including New Mexico.

When I told her about Filomena in Taos, she said it was one of her favorite places. "You must see it. You and Aaron."

Katherine apologized for reading the letters. "At first I was just looking to see what Cornish was after, but I couldn't stop. It's been so long since I read anything so sincere or tender. You're a lucky girl.

"But poor Martha! What an awful story. Have you thought of writing about her?"

Katherine had read my mind. Martha was like a heroine in one of the short stories they printed in women's magazines; a sad, brave girl in trouble through no fault of her own. But when I said I was thinking of changing it to fiction, she said I should write it as a reporter.

"It will have more power that way. Lewis Hine changed a lot of minds with his photographs of factory girls. Martha's story might do the same thing."

We talked about it for a long time. She said the local newspapers wouldn't print anything like it, but there were magazines that would. The next day I was in the library reading *La Follette's, The Atlantic Monthly,* and *The Nation.* I wrote to Aaron and asked what he thought about my telling Martha's story but in a way she wouldn't be recognized. I can't tell you how relieved I was to get his okay, because I'd already read up on the orphan trains and written a first draft.

I was totally consumed by Martha's story and the idea that I was helping Aaron to save children from mistreatment. I rewrote that story I don't know how many times before I let Katherine see it. She said "well done" and made me rewrite it two more times before she said it was ready.

She let me keep my original title, though: "The Human Face of the 20th Amendment."

I took it to *The Atlantic Monthly* magazine

first, because why not start at the top and also the office was in Boston. The girl at the front desk was very stuck up. "We don't publish pieces by unknowns," she said.

After all the work I'd done, I wanted to say, who the hell do you think you are? But I was polite. I told her what my article was about and how it put a face on child labor and I hadn't seen anything like it anywhere else.

It pays to be nice. She took the story and said her mother started working when she was eleven years old. "She still gets sad when she talks about leaving school. I'll put it on the editor's desk myself."

When I went back a week later, the same girl handed it back to me. She said she was sorry. "I told you they don't publish unknowns."

Katherine said rejection was part of the business and to try *The Nation,* where she knew one of the editors. It was published two weeks later. I opened and closed that magazine over and over for the thrill of seeing my name on that page:

By Addie Baum.

I'd never been prouder of anything.

I sent a copy to Aaron — special delivery, no less. Irene and Joe were very impressed and asked what I was going to write next.

Gussie bought a dozen copies and said she always knew I had it in me.

Katherine took me out for dinner to celebrate and Miss Chevalier called to ask if I would speak at one of her Sunday afternoon gatherings. "I seem to remember that you can be very effective in front of an audience."

I wanted to show it to my family. Betty would have made a huge fuss and told everyone in the neighborhood and all of her clubs and organizations. Even my parents might have been impressed. Maybe. But since I didn't know how to explain how I knew about Martha without mentioning Aaron, I decided to wait.

I was walking on air all week and I guess I didn't hide my feelings very well because Betty asked if I'd met someone, Eddy told me I looked pretty, and my mother said, "Since when do you whistle?"

I was in such a fog that when Mort said he wanted to talk to me in his office, I thought he was going to give me a raise. But when he pointed at the chair across from his desk, I knew I was in trouble. Sitting down in there was never a good sign.

Mort's face was usually easy to read, but not that time. He said Cornish had seen my story in *The Nation* and sent it to the owner

321

of the *Transcript.*

"What were you thinking, Addie?" Mort said. "You must have read the paper's editorials against the amendment — a plot against states' rights and the sanctity of the family and all that. This was like spitting in the owner's eye. I was upstairs all afternoon getting my ass handed to me."

I told him I never meant to get anyone in trouble, especially him.

"I'll be all right, but it took some doing to talk him out of firing Katherine Walters. I told him she didn't know a thing about it and I never want to know otherwise, you understand?"

I apologized. I asked if there was anything I could do. Would it help if I wrote the owner and told them it was completely my fault?

Mort shook his head. "Why the hell did you have to use your own name? If you'd signed it Sally Smith, you could have made your point and we wouldn't be sitting here. I thought you were smarter than that."

He looked like his dog had just died.

"I have no choice, Addie. I have to let you go."

THIS IS AUNTIE ADDIE'S FELLA.

I didn't tell them at home I'd been fired. Betty would push for the details and Levine would tell me to come work for him again. Most of all, I didn't want to see the "I'm not surprised" look on my mother's face.

The next morning, I left the house at the usual time as if it were a regular workday. First I went to the telegraph office to let Aaron know not to send any more letters to the newspaper. Then I went to see Gussie about her offer to help me get another job. It was so early, her office was still locked. I leaned against the wall in the hallway to wait and I guess I closed my eyes because the next thing I knew, she was next to me. "Addie, what's wrong? Did somebody die?"

Gussie asked me if I wanted an aspirin or a cup of tea. I kept telling her I was okay but she said she was getting me a glass of water, which was good because it gave me a minute to take in the decor.

Did I already tell you about how Gussie dressed? Boxy suits, flat shoes, no lipstick. But her office looked like the powder room at the Ritz. There were embroidered pillows on all the chairs and pictures of flowers on the walls. Even the lampshade on her desk was pink. It was hard to keep a straight face when she came back and asked what was going on. This being Gussie, it turned into a real cross-examination. She was up-to-date about the story I'd written, but I hadn't said much about Aaron other than how we'd met and that we were writing letters to each other. Since Gussie saw Betty at Hadassah meetings, I didn't want her spilling the beans before I did. It's not that Gussie was a gossip, but sometimes she got excited.

When I finished telling her the whole story, she let me have it. Her feelings were hurt. She was mad that I didn't trust her. What did I think friends were for, anyway?

And then, before I could say I was sorry, she asked if I wanted to start working right away for a lawyer down the hall. One of his secretaries had sprained her wrist and he was in a jam.

That was Gussie in a nutshell: full of herself *and* ready to give you the shirt off her back.

I started working for the lawyer that morning, and even though typing contracts and letters was not nearly as interesting as newspaper work, I made a lot more money for fewer hours than I had at the *Transcript.*

There was a phone on my desk at the lawyer's, and Gussie called every few hours to see how I was doing and to tell me what she was up to. She had done the same thing when I was at the newspaper until I said I'd get fired if she didn't stop.

Gussie loved the telephone like nobody else. She had one at home as well as in her office, and whenever a new model came out she bought it. She said everyone was going to have a telephone sooner or later, but not soon enough for her.

Betty and Levine had a phone at home, too, though I think they only used it to talk to each other during the day. Nobody ever called at night, so when Betty came downstairs and said there was a call for me, I knew it had to be Gussie.

But she didn't call to tell me about an idea she just had or to ask if I wanted to have lunch with her tomorrow. She had a message from Katherine Walters, who wanted me to go to her apartment after work the next day. Before she hung up Gussie said, "And afterward, you are going to tell me everything she says."

I was praying that Katherine had a letter from Aaron and when she opened the door with an envelope in her hand, I did a little dance. "You'll notice I didn't open it," she said, "but I was tempted."

Aaron was on his way home. He had to stop in Washington to pack but he would be in Boston as soon as possible. "Two weeks tops." The letter was postmarked almost a week earlier, which meant he could be home any moment. It also meant he left before he got my wire about being fired.

I let Katherine read the letter. She said she couldn't wait to meet him and she had some other news for me. "I didn't want you hearing it from anyone but me."

Cornish had caught her in the mailroom with Aaron's letter to Miss Cavendish. "When he told me to hand it over, I stuffed it down the front of my dress, wished him a lovely day, and quit."

I was horrified. "I made you lose your job?"

Katherine said I had nothing to do with it. "It was just a matter of time before he fired me and I was more than ready to go." She said that helping me with the child labor story had made it hard for her to keep writing about hats and hairdos.

"Especially with everything going on these days, I need to do something important. The Sacco-Vanzetti Defense Committee needs a person who doesn't sound like a maniac to talk to the newspapers. Someone like me."

Even though Katherine kept saying she was glad to leave the *Transcript,* I felt responsible and working for the Sacco-Vanzetti group could be dangerous. They had just lost an appeal for a new trial and there had been a bombing. Some of the hotheads were talking like bombs were a good thing.

I did a lot of worrying after that. How was Katherine going to manage? What if the child labor people roped Aaron into staying in Washington again? What if Aaron was hit by a car?

I was sitting in my room driving myself crazy when Betty came downstairs and said there was another telephone call for me. "If this keeps up, you're going to have to start paying me to be your secretary."

But when I got there, the phone was on the hook.

Betty yelled, "Herman, I'm back."

He yelled back, "I'm coming." But it was Aaron who walked in.

First I was speechless. Then I said, "Why

327

are you here?"

He laughed, "Why do you think?" I started crying and we held each other until I pulled away and looked at him. "It really is you."

Then he got all teary-eyed and I laughed.

Levine and Betty and the boys watched our big reunion and Eddy said, "Is Auntie Addie sad or happy?"

Betty said, "She's very happy. This is Auntie Addie's fella."

Aaron put his arm around my shoulder and made it official. "If it's okay with you, I'd like to be her husband."

Betty shrieked and grabbed me. Levine shook Aaron's hand and poured the last drops out of a secret bottle of whiskey. Prohibition wasn't over yet. He lifted his glass: "Mazel tov and may you be as happy together as me and my bride."

WHAT'S HIS NAME?

Betty thought the whole thing with Aaron was so romantic, she wasn't even mad that I hadn't told her sooner, and she decided a Friday night supper at her place was the best place to introduce him to our parents. She told Mameh that Levine was bringing a young man, the brother of someone he knew from business. "A lawyer," Betty said. "Herman thinks he's a catch."

Just as those words were coming out of her mouth, Eddy walked into the kitchen and said, "Are you talking about Uncle Aaron? He promised to play stickball next time he's here." If Betty had been the kind of mother who smacked her kids, he would have gotten it, but she changed the subject and just told him to go outside.

My mother was not going to ignore the fact that we had been sneaking around behind her back. So Aaron started with one strike against him.

It wasn't so easy with Papa either, not after he heard that Aaron's family belonged to Temple Israel. "That's a church, not a shul. I wouldn't step a foot in the place."

"You already did," I said. "It's where Betty got married."

"Once was enough."

Jake was the one who softened Papa up a little. My father was tutoring him for his bar mitzvah, which was probably the first time the two of them spent more than a minute together. Papa said Jake was smart and a serious student and Jake started calling him Rav Baum. So when Jake said Aaron was a good guy, it counted for something.

I wasn't looking forward to that dinner. I was going to marry Aaron no matter what my parents said. I didn't want them to hate him, but I was probably more worried what he would think of them. You never marry just one person; you get the whole family as part of the deal.

As soon as Aaron arrived, Betty made us go right to the table — no chitchat. She lit candles and Papa made kiddush with one eye on Aaron to see if he knew when to join in; he did. After we passed around the challah, and they schmoozed a little, he told Aaron that he spoke a good Yiddish.

But Mameh looked at him like he was a sick cow someone was trying to trick her into buying. She shook her head when she saw him pick up his spoon with his left hand and she winced when he unfolded his napkin and put it on his lap. To her, left-handed people were dishonest or unlucky or both, and doing anything but wiping your mouth with a napkin was putting on airs.

She even smirked at his bow tie, which he had bought to make a good impression.

Betty did her best to build him up. "Papa, did you know that Aaron's first cousin is a big doctor at Beth Israel Hospital?"

Levine said, "And his brother is a very successful attorney."

Mameh pretended she hadn't heard any of that and asked Betty, "*Vas iz zaneh nahmin?* What's his name? Where does he work?" As if Aaron hadn't been talking in Yiddish to Papa since he got there.

Levine said, "Michael Metsky is one of the biggest real estate lawyers in town. Very successful. We've had dealings with him."

Mameh shrugged. "That's the brother."

Aaron laughed but I wanted to scream. Wasn't her whole purpose in life to get me married to someone exactly like him?

I went to the kitchen to make coffee and calm down. When I got back, Aaron was on the floor and playing tiddlywinks with the boys.

Betty said, "Look how good he is with children. He'll be a wonderful father."

To no one in particular my mother said, "They all think I'm stupid."

From as long as I could remember, Mameh talked to herself under her breath. She muttered spells to ward off the evil eye and kvetched about how Betty never made the tea hot enough. But her hearing wasn't as good as it used to be, so she didn't whisper anymore and that time you could have heard her from the other room.

"He didn't eat a thing. What's the matter with him? Her meat was a little dry, but nobody makes better carrots than me. When you visit someone, you eat."

Betty tried to shush her, but Mameh didn't notice. "She turns up her nose at a man who owns a store? This one doesn't even have a job."

Eddy said, "Bubbie, why are you talking to the saltshaker?"

That seemed to wake her up. She said. "Come eat your compote."

Aaron said, "Mrs. Baum, my father owns a hardware store and I worked there when I was growing up. But Pop wanted us to go to college. I think he was hoping for doctors or maybe pharmacists, but he says he's proud of his lawyers anyway."

Betty said, "Aaron's sister is going to law school, too."

"A lawyer is not a job for a woman," Mameh snapped. Then she pointed at Aaron and said, "Young man, eat the fruit at least."

I walked Aaron outside and made excuses for the meat — it really was dry — and for my mother. But he thought it all went well.

"Your father was nice to me. Betty and your brother-in-law are in our corner and their boys are terrific. Eight out of nine ain't bad. And maybe if I clean my plate next time, your mother will come around, too."

Aaron never gave up on people. Sometimes it drove me crazy, but it's a good way to live.

The next Saturday, we all were invited to Aaron's family for supper. Betty promised that Mameh would behave. "She was probably nervous about meeting him, and anyway, everyone is more polite in someone else's house."

We squeezed into Levine's car to get to Brookline. You remember that house, don't you? Around the corner from where JFK was born?

The front yard at the Metskys' was like

nothing else on the street. There was no grass, just flower beds and roses climbing up the porch like the ones at Rockport Lodge.

The flowers were Mildred Metsky's doing. She was Aaron's stepmother and the opposite of evil stepmothers in the fairy tales. Murray Metsky married her five years after Aaron's mother died, and the three kids were as devoted to "Mom" as she was to them.

She opened the door and hugged us like we were long-lost cousins. The Metskys were all big huggers: Aaron, his father, and his sister, Rita. Even his brother, Michael, who was kind of stiff, put his arms around each of us. My mother looked like she was being licked by cats, and she hated cats.

When we sat down to eat dinner, which they didn't call supper, Mameh asked the name of the kosher butcher where Mildred Metsky had bought the meat. She'd never heard of the place and leaned over to Papa and whispered in a voice that everyone could hear, "It smells funny, no?" Aaron said, "That's rosemary, Mrs. Baum. Mom grows all kinds of herbs in the backyard."

Mameh said, "So, herbs and flowers. Me, I grow cabbages and potatoes. Things you can eat."

Thank God, Mildred didn't understand a lot of Yiddish.

Rita and Mildred gushed over the boys, which was all Betty ever wanted to hear. Levine and Michael figured out they knew a lot of the same people. Murray and my father went outside and smoked cigars. Aaron and I held hands under the table.

When Mildred put out coffee and cake, Murray stood up and made a speech about how happy they were that Aaron had found me. "When he went off to Washington, I was afraid he'd find a girl from there and never come back. When he went to Minnesota, I worried he'd meet a girl there and she wouldn't want to leave her family."

He said they liked me not only because I was a Boston girl but also because Aaron was so happy and I was so lovely and my father was a chacham, a scholar, and the boys were extraordinary. Murray shook his finger at me and gave me one of those "naughty-naughty" looks. "These boys only need some cousins to play with."

I swore I would never embarrass my own children like that. And I never did — at least not in public.

When it was time to go, the Metskys started again with the hugging, which took a while, because everyone had to hug everyone else. It was as if they thought we might crash into an iceberg and disappear on the way back to Roxbury.

My mother hated all the "grabbing." When we were back in the car she said, "It feels like they're trying to pick my pocket." It was strange for me, too, but I got used to it.

Remember when I used to chase you and your sister around the house to get my daily minimum requirement of hugs? I said if I didn't get one hundred hugs I would float up into the sky like Mary Poppins and you would never see me again. We stopped playing that game when you started school, but we never stopped hugging.

LOOK AT ME, I'M
BECOMING A METSKY!

I wanted a wedding like Betty's: small, quick, and simple, but that wasn't in the cards. For one thing, there was no rabbi's office big enough for all of Aaron's relatives, so "small" was out. Maybe we could keep it simple, but it wasn't going to happen quickly because Jake's bar mitzvah was coming up in October and Betty was already up to her eyeballs getting ready for that.

Bar mitzvahs weren't the productions they are today with caterers and hotels and flowers, but they were still a big deal and Betty wanted it perfect. She tried out I don't know how many recipes for strudel and cookies, painted the dining room, and made new curtains for the living room. Everyone got new clothes and Levine took Jake downtown to buy him his first grown-up suit, with long pants and a vest. Like I said: a big deal.

On the morning of the bar mitzvah, my

mother got up on the wrong side of the bed. Usually she was the first one up, drinking her tea, washing her cup, and putting it away before my father and I even got to the kitchen. But on that day of all days she didn't even have her shoes on when it was time to go. When I asked if she was feeling all right, she answered like I had insulted her. "When am I ever sick?"

By the time we got to the synagogue, which was only three blocks away, she was practically shuffling and holding on to my arm. She closed her eyes when we sat down in the synagogue and I was sure she was asleep but when my father was called up to sing the blessings, she sat straight. And when Jake chanted his portion from the Torah, she was smiling.

"Wasn't he wonderful?" I whispered.

"Not bad," she said.

Jake still looked like a chubby little boy but he did a wonderful job. He didn't stumble or slow down and he chanted everything loud and clear. I was so proud of him I had tears in my eyes, but Betty just about collapsed from the naches. You'll understand naches when you have children: there's nothing like the feeling you have when your child stands in front of a crowd and shines. It was like that when your mother made the speech at her high school graduation, and how I felt at your bat mitzvah, and your sister's.

After the service, everyone went downstairs for sponge cake and wine. My mother was not the old lady I had helped down the street anymore. She moved fast enough to avoid most of the Metsky hugs and when someone asked if she was proud of her grandson, she said, "Of course. What do you think?" For once she didn't mention that Jake wasn't really "her" grandson.

Aaron and I took our time getting to the party at Betty's house. It was one of those perfect fall days when the air is cool enough to wake you up but the sun is also kissing your face. Aaron kicked around in the leaves and I made a bouquet out of red and gold ones; we were like a couple of kids. It felt wonderful to be alone and we had a lot to talk about.

Someone at the Massachusetts Society for the Prevention of Cruelty to Children had heard Aaron had moved to Boston and offered him a job but his brother was trying to talk him into staying at his firm. Michael said if he stayed put, we could buy our own house in a year or two.

Aaron had been working in Michael's office since he got back to Boston, but he hated it. Writing contracts and arguing with bankers made him grumpy and grouchy like I'd never seen him.

But after one meeting with the children's society committee, he was glowing. "These are the same people who started the National Child Welfare Committee," he said. They were his heroes and they wanted to hire him to help the governor's office make better laws to help children and families. It was a dream job and I knew that the only reason he didn't say yes on the spot was because they couldn't pay him the kind of money he was making in private practice. But I said what good is a house if I have to live in it with a crab?

It wasn't hard to talk him into doing what he wanted. Besides, I was working, too.

Gussie, God bless her, had found me a full-time job at Simmons. The minute she heard that the vice president's secretary was leaving, she called him and said not to bother looking for a replacement. Betty joked that I got my wish. I was finally going to college. But it wasn't a joke, because I could take classes after work for free.

Once we decided that Aaron was going to take the job he wanted, he couldn't wait to get back and tell the families that we were setting a date for our wedding. It couldn't be soon enough for me; every time I walked into my parents' house, I felt like I was putting on a corset.

Betty's place was mobbed. She had invited the neighbors, Jake's friends, and my father's synagogue friends, everyone from Levine's office, and all of Aaron's family. His brother had surprised everyone by bringing Lois Rosensweig, the woman he'd been seeing for five years. Rita said he'd never brought her to a family event before. "That's Michael for you. Now that Aaron's got a fiancée, I bet he pops the question any day."

Levine was running around with a new camera asking people to say "cheese" and driving everyone crazy. But as usual, the pest with the camera turned out to be a hero. He had a terrible time getting my parents to cooperate, but he didn't leave them alone until he got some good shots of them. That picture you put on the cover of your family history paper in seventh grade? That was from Jake's bar mitzvah.

When I finally found Betty, she winked and asked if we'd gotten lost.

I winked back and said, "What are you doing December nineteenth?"

"Why?" she said. "Am I going to a wedding?" All I had to do was smile and she threw her arms around me and gave Aaron a kiss and a hug. "Look at me," she said, "I'm becoming a Metsky!"

Betty said she had to round up the boys before the announcement and we had to find Mameh, too.

Betty said she'd never seen Mameh in a better mood. She had been friendly and eaten everything without any complaints until Betty put out store-bought cherry preserves for tea. "Then she made that sourpuss face and said she had to show everyone how much better homemade was. I told Herman to go downstairs and get it but she said he didn't know where to look. Maybe she got lost, like you two."

Aaron said he'd get her. "She has to get used to me sometime."

When everyone was crowded into the living room, Aaron's father shook his finger at me. "I bet I know what this is about," he said. "And here comes the groom."

But the groom ran in looking very serious and said, "Somebody call an ambulance."

My World Got Very Small.

It was a stroke.

They took Mameh to Beth Israel, the old brick one, which wasn't far from where we lived in Roxbury. They opened the modern building a year later, but it wouldn't have made any difference. There wasn't much they could do for strokes in those days other than keep them warm and massage the muscles.

It was hard to know what was happening in the hospital. The doctors didn't tell you anything and patients were allowed only one visit a day and only one person at a time. When Papa went in, he couldn't say if she seemed better or worse, but he always looked older when he came out.

Betty brought clean nightgowns and said the sheets felt like wax paper, but she couldn't tell if Mameh was in pain or comfortable or what. "Sometimes she opens her eyes, but I don't know if she sees me."

She said her face wasn't as bad as at the beginning, when the right side looked like it had melted off the bones.

They only let me go once and it was pretty awful. The room was overheated and smelled like bleach. My mother's face on the pillow was yellow and her hair was combed straight back and tucked under her head so I could see the shape of her skull under the skin. Her cheeks were sunken and her eyelids were twitching. I wasn't sure if she was awake, so I whispered, "Mameh, it's me, Addie. How are you feeling? Can I do anything for you?" I tried to sound cheerful but my stomach was in the same knot as always, waiting for her to wake up and demand to know what was I doing there, where was my father, who put her in this place?

After a few weeks, she was a little better, opening her eyes, and drinking through a straw. She could sit up in bed if someone helped her and even though she didn't say anything, we were sure she recognized us.

The doctor said she might get back some use of her right arm and leg, but that could take months if it happened at all. She could start talking or maybe not. Like I said, they couldn't do much for her in the hospital, so we took her home.

Her right side stayed paralyzed and the right side of her mouth drooped so the words were garbled when she started to talk. She got agitated when we didn't understand her, so we knew she was still all there inside her head.

During the day, Papa and Betty took turns sitting with her. I came home straight from work and took over while Betty made supper and my father walked to shul.

We were the only three she let in the room. Mildred and Rita offered to watch her, but when they came to visit, Mameh clamped her mouth shut and refused to open her eyes. If Levine, Aaron, or any of the boys came into the room, she muttered and grimaced until they left. She scared the little ones so much they wouldn't come downstairs at all.

My world got very small, the way it always does when someone in your family is sick. I was at work or at home, where I was either sitting with my mother or helping Betty with the boys. I didn't go out on the weekends, either, so Aaron came to the house and taught me to play gin rummy and hearts, and, of course, we postponed the wedding.

My new boss was very sympathetic when I got phone calls at the office. Gussie and Irene stayed in touch. And whenever he could, Aaron met me after work and rode the trolley home with me. He put his arm around me and there were a few times he had to wake me up when we got to my stop.

It was about two months after the stroke, Jake's best friend was having his bar mitzvah. Papa had been his teacher and Betty was friendly with his mother, so I said I'd stay home with Mameh and told them to have a nice time and not to hurry back.

I hadn't spent much time with her in the mornings. Betty said she usually woke up around ten o'clock, and that was when she seemed clearer in her mind and it was easier to understand if she tried to talk. But that day she didn't open her eyes until noon. I offered her soup and tea but she shook her head and nodded toward the door, which meant she needed the bathroom.

She hated the bedpan worse than anything, but she'd lost so much weight since the stroke, it wasn't hard to carry her.

She let me wash her face and hands, but she turned away when I offered a cup of tea or bread soaked in broth. I asked if she wanted me to read to her but she squeezed her eyes shut.

I don't know why it's so exhausting to sit with a sick person. It's not like you're doing anything, but it's a hundred times more tiring than hard work. Maybe it's the helplessness or maybe it's the strain of waiting for the body to decide if it's going to get better or not.

The sky had been overcast all day and when it started snowing, the room got dark. I must have dozed off because the next thing I knew, Mameh was sitting up straight, something we didn't think she could do on her own. Her eyes were wide open and she was looking around the room as if she was trying to figure out where she was, like she was Rip Van Winkle. She frowned at the dirty glasses on the bureau and at the reading lamp I had moved in.

In Yiddish, I said, "Mameh? Can I get you something? Do you know who I am, Mameh?"

She searched my face and frowned. I could hear her breath get faster and I said, "Don't worry. Just rest."

Her eyes got big and she reached out to me with her good arm. I sat down next to her on the bed and she whispered, "Of course I know my own daughter." Her voice was raspy and the words were slow but I could understand her. "How can a mother not know her own beautiful daughter?"

She ran her hand over my hair and let it rest on my cheek. "I didn't know right away it was you, sweetheart, zieseleh. Your hair is so short. Have you been sick?"

I told her I'd cut my hair and that I was fine and she didn't have to worry. But she was anxious and started talking fast, as if she was in a hurry to say something before she forgot. "I want to tell you that I'm sorry. You were right and I was wrong. If I had listened to you, you would have been happier."

She started crying. "Ich bin moyl. I'm sorry. But you'll forgive me; I know you will. You were always such a good girl, so pretty, so good . . ."

I had never heard her apologize to anyone, not even once. I couldn't remember my mother ever looking at me that way or telling me I was pretty or sweet. She never called me darling.

It was like a miracle.

All that talking wore her out and she sank back on the pillows. I kissed her hand and said not to worry about me, that I was getting married to a wonderful man. I asked if she remembered Aaron and she squeezed my fingers.

I said how happy I was to talk to her like this and that I wished I had tried to explain myself to her before.

She shook her head and whispered, "I

thought I had lost you, but here you are, just like my mother, your grandmother. You have her golden hands, goldene hentz, like an angel with a needle and thread.

"I was wrong to make you go. I chased you and beat you to force you, even when you were telling me you would die if I sent you away.

"I thought he would keep you safe and that Bronia would look out for you but you knew better. You knew this country would kill you. I am sorry, little Sima. My poor, poor Simmaleh."

She sighed. Her breath slowed. When she fell asleep I let it sink in.

I had waited my whole life to hear her say those things. That she was sorry. That I was a good girl. And pretty and sweet. But it was all for Celia: the tenderness, the apology, the love. She didn't even know I was there.

I was too sad to cry.

It was late when Betty came back from the party. She turned on the light and asked why I was sitting in the dark. "Did she sleep all day?"

I said yes and that I was going for a walk. I needed some fresh air.

It was a beautiful, clear evening. The snow

had stopped and the moon made everything look silver. I was walking a long time before I realized that I was going to Aaron's house. From Roxbury to Brookline is a long way, five miles at least, and I took a few wrong turns on the way. It was so late by the time I got there, his house was dark except for one light in the living room. They never locked the door, so I just walked in. Aaron almost fell out of the chair.

I said, "Don't ask. I'll tell you in the morning."

■ ■ ■ ■

1927

■ ■ ■ ■

ALL I FELT WAS PAIN.

My mother died a few weeks later. Levine took care of the funeral the same way he took care of most things — without anyone asking him and without much in the way of thanks.

I had been to the cemetery when Myron and Lenny died, but burying Mameh was a completely different experience, like night and day. Even getting there wasn't the same. The roads were better, so we got there in no time, and instead of three mourners, there were twenty people and a whole line of cars behind the hearse.

The biggest difference was how "normal" it seemed. Mameh was sixty-five, which wasn't so young in 1927. Nobody was shocked. She had been sick and died at home in her own bed, so it was sad but nothing like the tragedy it had been with Celia, or Myron and Lenny.

Only Papa and Levine had been there for

Celia's funeral. That was probably because we didn't know many people back then, but maybe it had something to do with how she died. There was so much guilt mixed in with the grief. And how do you explain a healthy young woman dying from a slip of a kitchen knife?

With the flu epidemic, everyone was afraid, and walking into a cemetery seemed like tempting fate. I went to the boys' funeral to stand in for Betty and it's a good thing she didn't come. The idea of her seeing those little coffins was so awful. Just remembering it still makes me feel like crying.

Before the service for Mameh, I went to look at their graves and tried to think of my sister and nephews when they were young and healthy, but all I could remember was the blood on Celia's hands and the look on Betty's face when they took away her little boys. Standing by those gravestones, I didn't get any comfort or what you'd call "closure" today. All I felt was pain.

One thing hadn't changed: the cemetery was just as bleak as I remembered. The trees had grown and they had planted bushes, but it was January and hard to believe that anything would ever be green again.

I started to shiver when the service began.

There wasn't any wind and nobody else seemed bothered by the cold, but I could hear my teeth chattering. I had to lock my knees to keep from wobbling, and if Aaron hadn't put his arm around me, I might have keeled over, honest to God. At least Jewish funerals are short.

When they lowered the coffin into the ground, I remember thinking, She won't be able to make me feel like there's something wrong with me anymore.

But when the first clump of dirt hit the coffin, I realized that I would never stop wanting my mother to tell me that I was all right and that's when I started to cry.

LIFE IS MORE IMPORTANT THAN DEATH.

After we sat shiva, Papa told Betty and me that we were official mourners for a whole year, which meant we were supposed to stay away from celebrations and music or entertainment of any kind. So no parties, no going to the symphony, not even a movie.

After the first month, Betty stopped paying attention to the rules. If her boys wanted to see the new Our Gang movie, she took them and stayed to watch. "You think I'm going to leave them in a dark theater all by themselves?"

I felt like I was living "in the meantime" and I actually didn't mind being quiet. Papa and I ate suppers upstairs with Betty and her family, then he would go to the synagogue and I usually went to my room to read. It was sort of like living in the boardinghouse.

Not that I was a hermit. I was with people all day at work and I kept going to class. I think it was American history that term. My friends called on the phone and came to the house. Aaron and I saw each other all the time; we just didn't talk about the wedding.

But when the flowers started blooming and everyone put away their winter coats, I started to feel like a dog on a chain. Everywhere I went, I saw couples holding hands and whispering to each other. Aaron showed me an advertisement for an apartment we could afford. I got up my nerve and asked my father how soon we could get married.

He said, "Anytime you want."

I couldn't believe it. "You told me I had to wait a year."

"Did I say anything about weddings? According to the Talmud, if a funeral procession and a wedding procession cross paths, the wedding party goes first. Life is more important than death."

You'd think he could have told me that before.

"Just don't make it fancy," Papa said. "No music or dancing."

That wasn't a problem. I'd always wanted it to be simple, and Aaron didn't care about fancy as long as it was soon. But when I told Betty and Mildred we were thinking about getting married at the beginning of May, which was just a few weeks off, they acted like it was a disaster only a littler smaller than the *Titanic.* Betty said that since she didn't have a daughter, this was going to be her only chance to make a wedding. And why did I want to ruin it for her?

For *her,* right?

She and Mildred complained and noodged until we agreed to wait until June so they could make everything nice. Rita asked if she could give me a bridal shower to introduce me to the other women in the family before the wedding. I'd never been to a shower — it was a new fad at the time — but my sister-in-law-to-be had read an article about them in *Ladies' Home Journal* and she had her heart set on doing it just like it said in the magazine — right down to pink icing and sugar roses on the cake. She wanted to invite my friends, too, so I gave her Gussie's phone number and said she'd get in touch with everyone else.

Rita planned it as a tea party on Saturday afternoon at three o'clock and told everyone to wear nice dresses and white gloves, if you can imagine.

Irene called me to ask if she could come to my party even if she didn't embroider a pillowcase, which Rita had asked all the guests to do. When I said I didn't know anything about pillowcases she said, "Gussie didn't tell me the pillowcases were supposed to be a surprise. Now I've ruined the whole goddamn thing."

The older Irene got, the more she swore. I remember when her grandson pooped in his diaper at his christening, she said, "Holy shit," loud enough for everyone to hear. The look on that priest's face!

On the day of the shower, the Metsky house was full of doilies, lilacs, and a dozen aunts and second cousins. After they all got finished hugging me, I smelled like the perfume counter at Jordan's.

Rita presented me with a trousseau of pillowcases and towels embroidered with my new initials and I acted as if Irene hadn't spilled the beans.

There were some other surprises, though. I knew Irene and Helen would be there but I was bowled over when Miss Chevalier and Miss Green walked in with Katherine Walters, who I lost touch with after I left the *Transcript.*

Miss Chevalier kissed my cheek and said, "I'm so happy for you, my dear." Miss Green seemed to have shrunk two inches but she still had a twinkle in her eye. "I like to think we had something to do with your marriage, since you met your fiancé in our home."

The Ediths hadn't been asked to embroider anything, thank goodness, but Miss Green brought me one of the lovely ceramic boxes she designed; you used to put Barbie shoes in it when you were little.

Having all those women together in one place was like looking through a photo album of my life: from when I was a baby to the Saturday Club to Rockport Lodge to working at the newspaper to meeting Aaron.

And it was amazing how well they got along. Miss Green, who had been to Ireland, talked to Irene about the town where she was born. Katherine and Betty had a debate about who was funnier: Harold Lloyd or Buster Keaton. I could have told them it was Charlie Chaplin, but I didn't want to butt in.

I asked Helen where Gussie was. "She's just a little late," Helen said. Gussie gave me so much grief if I was even two minutes late, I looked forward to giving her a little of her own medicine. When she finally got there, she put up one hand like a stop sign. Then Irene sang, "Ta-da," and Filomena appeared.

I don't know if I shrieked or just stood there with my mouth open, but everyone clapped and Betty shouted, "She didn't have a clue!"

As soon as we'd set a date for the wedding, I wrote to Filomena to ask if she could come. She wrote back that she couldn't because that was the week she had promised to take her teacher to a powwow in the mountains and she couldn't go back on her word or that would be the end of their friendship. I had figured it was a long shot and I could tell how bad she felt because it was the longest letter I ever got from her. Betty was there when I got her wedding present, which came with the note saying not to open it until the wedding day.

They were all in on it: my friends, my sister, even my new in-laws. It might have been the only secret Betty ever kept. She'd rummaged around in my room for Filomena's address, Gussie sent a telegram, and everyone chipped in for the train tickets.

It had been more than ten years since I'd seen my best friend. Filomena still wore a long braid. Her hair wasn't pure black anymore, but the streak of white next to her cheek made her look glamorous — not old. It was the same face, though, darker and a little weathered by the sun, but just as beautiful.

She was dressed in a long skirt and a striped shawl, like the Indian girls in her picture postcards. There were stacks of turquoise and silver bracelets on both wrists and she smelled like something fresh and woody. She told me that it was sage, something the Indians used for health and good fortune. I'm making her sound like a cartoon hippie from the 1960s, but she didn't look messy. No matter what she was wearing, Filomena carried herself like a queen.

When she saw Miss Green, Filomena took both of her teacher's hands in hers and said, "Thank you for giving me my life."

It was such a sweet moment. Katherine said it reminded her of how students in India honored their teachers by touching the ground at their feet. I didn't feel quite up to that, but before the afternoon was over I thanked Miss Chevalier for everything she had done for me since I was a girl.

I wish I'd had a camera. Not that I need pictures to remember that day.

I've forgotten a lot more than I like to admit, but I have all the details memorized: the pink icing, Katherine's beautiful yellow shoes, the lilacs, and the sound of Filomena's bracelets when she threw her arms around me. Like a wind chime.

You Never Looked at Me With Anything but Love.

Sometimes friends grow apart. You tell each other everything and you're sure this is a person you'll know the rest of your life but then she stops writing or calling, or you realize she's really not so nice, or she turns into a right-winger. Remember your friend Suzie?

But sometimes, it doesn't matter how far apart you live or how little you talk — it's still there. That was Filomena and me.

The day after the wedding shower we got together in the North End. She had to go to a big family lunch after church so she wasn't sure exactly what time she'd get away, but I didn't mind waiting. I was sitting on a bench in front of St. Leonard's in the North End on a beautiful day and people were strolling on Hanover Street. Old ladies in black dresses were feeding the pigeons and watching their grandchildren play. It was exactly how I remembered it from when I was growing up, except the hats were different.

There isn't enough room to say much on a postcard, so I had a hundred questions for Filomena. I knew that some of her New Mexico friends were painters and that she spent a lot of time with an Indian potter named Virginia. I knew she was living by herself and watched the sunset every day. She was selling enough of her pottery to scrape by. But that was about it. It was like I had an empty coloring book for her to fill in.

At first, I didn't recognize the frumpy woman in a baggy black dress who was waving at me. Filomena's sisters had made her take off her "costume" before church and dressed her like a grandmother. They were furious at her. How could she come to Boston for a friend's wedding when she hadn't bothered to make it to her own nieces' and nephews' first communions and graduations? They calmed down a little when she told them her friends had paid for her tickets. I guess they forgot she'd been sending them money ever since she moved to Taos, and believe me, she never had much to spare.

Filomena unpinned her braid, pulled a woven sash and some bracelets out of her bag, and in one minute was back to looking beautiful. She said she was dying for an espresso. "I've been dreaming about coffee ever since I got on the train."

We went to a café where not even the hats had changed. I never saw a person enjoy anything more than Filomena enjoyed that espresso. The waiter must have noticed, too, because he brought over a second cup before she could ask.

She said, "Grazie," and it was like they were long-lost cousins, talking with their hands and interrupting each other, just like Jews, except everything sounds better in Italian.

Filomena had brought a stack of pictures to show me and laid them out on the table in rows, like she was playing solitaire. There were a few of her sitting at a table with Morelli and three couples who were making silly faces at the camera. They had been his friends in art school and shared a big house on the outskirts of Taos. Filomena said, "We stayed with them at first, but it was like living with the Keystone Cops.

"They loved each other but they fought all the time and I could never figure out who was mad at who. Crazy people, but they were always good to me." Eventually she and Morelli moved into a cottage on their land.

I had always imagined her living in a little shingled house like the ones in Rockport, but the house in the picture looked like a big anthill. Filomena explained what adobe was and how cool her house was on hot days. I said it sounded like living inside of a clay pot.

She got a kick out of that.

There was a picture of Bob Morelli sitting at a pottery wheel, looking down at a lump of clay between his hands. It made me remember how handsome he was.

"That's an old picture," she said. For the first few years, Morelli had gone to New York to visit his son in the summer, but one fall he didn't come back. He said his son needed him, but Filomena knew that wasn't the only reason. He couldn't work in bronze in New Mexico and he missed the city. "Did I write that he died last year? Car accident. I'm still getting used to the idea."

I said I was sorry and I meant it.

Filomena was excited to show me pictures of her work and there were a few vases that reminded me of Miss Green's designs. But most of it had a different shape: round at the bottom, sharper like a tulip bulb, and mostly very dark. To me, it looked like streamlined modern art, but it was an old

Pueblo style called blackware.

She said the minute she laid eyes on it she had to find out how to make it. She handed me a picture of an Indian woman with wrinkled cheeks and white hair bending over a fire. She said, "This is my teacher, Virginia; my Pueblo Miss Green."

Virginia was one of the few people who still made blackware but when Filomena asked to study with her, she said no. "The Pueblo people don't have much use for the whites. To them, we're like badly behaved children."

But Filomena kept pestering until Virginia let her dig the clay for her pottery and collect the manure she burned in her kiln. It sounded to me like work that the slaves did in Egypt but when I asked if she got paid, she laughed. "Virginia thought I should be paying her and she's probably right. She only started teaching me how to build the pots when she broke her arm. But now that she's getting older, I think she keeps me around because she knows I'll keep the tradition alive. Not that she'd ever say so."

Virginia called Filomena's first attempts "half-breeds" and "bastards." But once she stopped smashing them when they came out of the kiln, Filomena knew she was making progress.

"I'm really getting the hang of it now, but the tourists aren't interested." People want colorful souvenirs that people back home would recognize as "Indian." So she was giving art lessons to make ends meet. "Of all the Mixed Nuts, I always thought you'd be the teacher. It turns out I like teaching."

Filomena was in Boston for a few weeks before the wedding and we saw each other a lot. Irene had a dinner party for us with Gussie and Helen, who brought her husband and kids. One evening, Aaron took Filomena and me out for ice cream. She had a lot of family obligations, but we made sure we had time alone and we never ran out of conversation because nothing was too trivial or painful to talk about. I don't know how many times we each said, "I never told anyone but . . . ."

I told her how I wished I'd been more sensitive and sympathetic to poor shell-shocked Ernie and how I had a dream about trying to save that poor farm girl in Minnesota. I confessed that I was relieved my mother wouldn't be at my wedding, and how sad I was about feeling that way.

Somehow, telling Filomena about those things made them seem lighter and less terrible. I remember asking her if that's what it was like after going to confession in church. She said "God, no. When I was a girl I thought I'd get in trouble if I didn't say all the Hail Marys and Our Fathers. But nothing bad happened if I didn't say them and I didn't feel any better when I did. It was like putting a penny into a slot and nothing comes out. By the time I was twelve, I only went to church when my sisters made me."

She said she felt better talking to someone she could see, someone who cares about her. "The time I almost died in that bathtub, what kept me going was the look on your face and Irene's and that wonderful nurse. I could see how worried you were, not mad or angry or disappointed. You just didn't want me to die. And afterward, too, you never looked at me with anything but love: no pity, no judgment. I've thought about this a lot, Addie. You made it possible for me to forgive myself."

I had no idea it was so important to her, just like she was surprised to find out what I remembered from our conversations that first week at Rockport Lodge. She changed the way I thought about myself. "You told me I had a good eye and that I was good listener. You laughed at my jokes and took my ideas seriously."

You know, Ava, it's good to be smart, but

kindness is more important. Oh dear, another old-lady chestnut to stitch on a sampler. Or maybe one of those cute little throw pillows.

I guess I hadn't written much about the classes I'd taken, because Filomena wanted to know about college and my teachers and the subjects I'd studied. When she asked what I was taking in the fall, I said I wasn't planning to sign up. I already felt like an old lady with all the eighteen- and nineteen-year-olds and anyway, once I had children, I wouldn't have the time and I'd really be too old.

It wasn't like today. In those days you never heard of a married woman going to college. But you'd have thought I'd said I was going to join the circus or enter a convent. Filomena gave me a lecture about women in Taos who started businesses at fifty, even sixty. She said Virginia's niece was in her forties when she left her kids with her mother and moved to Albuquerque for three years to become a nurse.

She said, "You're not even thirty years old, which means you'll be in your fifties when your children are grown up, and you don't have to wait anyway. When they go to school, you can go to school, and you don't even have to move to Albuquerque."

I said maybe, but that wasn't enough for Filomena. "Give me one good reason why you shouldn't keep taking classes at least until you have a baby."

The reason was that I still didn't know why I was taking classes at all. It would have been different if I wanted to start a business or be a lawyer. But I was still just "dabbling" and I wasn't even enjoying it.

I had taken literature classes thinking maybe I should be an English teacher like people had been telling me since I was a kid. It was true that I loved reading stories and novels. But the only courses I could take were about Milton or Dryden or Chaucer. They weren't easy to understand. And the professors? They didn't care whether we understood the poems, much less loved them. None of my homework was as interesting as the writers I was reading in the magazines or books I took out of the library: Willa Cather, F. Scott Fitzgerald, Sinclair Lewis.

Filomena said she was going to talk to Aaron about my staying in school. "He'll be all for it. You still don't know how smart you are, just like you don't know how pretty you are. But Aaron knows. He also thinks the sun and moon revolve around you. What

371

wouldn't I give to have someone care about me that way."

I said, "But I thought you didn't want to get married."

"That has nothing to do with wanting to be loved," she said. "I know you never liked Bob and things didn't turn out the way I wanted, but he was the love of my life. The time we spent in Taos was the happiest I've ever been. He found us a studio and made me believe in my talent. We were together day and night. He used to say we were made out of the same clay."

Filomena said she was "keeping company" with someone. "He's very nice, but you only get one great love in a lifetime."

Then it was my turn to make a speech. "Who made that rule?" I said, and ticked off the war widows I knew who were happily remarried.

Filomena said she wasn't complaining. She liked her independence and privacy and the fact that nobody judged what she did or didn't do.

She admitted that she got lonely for her family — and for me. She missed Italian food and good coffee and the smell of the ocean. "But I belong to that landscape now, to the sky and the mountains. I wouldn't be happy anywhere else."

From the moment Filomena walked into my wedding shower, I had wanted to ask if she was ever coming back to live in Boston. That wasn't the answer I wanted to hear, but I meant it when I said, "Then I'm happy for you."

Don't Let Anyone Tell You Things Aren't Better than They Used to Be.

It wasn't a fancy wedding. No long gown or veil, like Betty wanted, but I think I looked pretty great in my tan dress with the pearl beads, and I wore the most beautiful hat I ever owned. There was no music and no dancing the hora, but it was much bigger than I'd imagined and not only because there were so many Metskys. Between my family, all of my friends, and their families, there were plenty of people on the Baum side, too.

Levine held one of the poles for the huppah. He almost cried when I asked him. Aaron's brother held another and I don't remember who the other two men were. It never occurred to me to ask Betty or Rita. Fifty-eight years ago, asking a woman to do that would have been like asking when a man was going to walk on the moon — something only a crazy person would say.

Don't let anyone tell you things aren't bet-

374

ter than they used to be.

We had lunch in the synagogue because there were too many people to fit into Betty's house. There were long tables with white tablecloths, big platters of herring, rye bread, salad, and pickles — the usual. There was plenty of wine and even a bottle of whiskey with a real label, a wedding present from someone. Since we were in a temple, we didn't even have to put it in a teapot so we wouldn't be raided. Prohibition didn't end until '33, which I only remember because it was the year your aunt Sylvia was born.

After we ate, there were toasts and jokes about how Aaron and I met. Filomena stood up and asked us to open her present in front of everyone because there was a story to go with it.

Her gift was a big blackwarc vase with two spouts. "It's called a wedding pitcher," she said. "The two openings stand for the bride and groom and the handle in between makes them into one."

At an Indian wedding, the bride drinks from one side, the groom drinks from the other, and then they're married. If the husband or wife dies, the other one is supposed to give it to a young couple getting married. It sounded sort of Jewish to me.

Anyway, I'm giving mine to the grandchild who gets married first. I don't think you should rush into anything with Brian just to get a nice piece of pottery. But it's something to keep in mind.

I wish Levine had taken a picture of me with Aaron and Filomena and the pitcher. He took a dozen of us in front of the wedding cake Mildred had baked — four layers and white frosting. My mother would have called it goyishe, but it was delicious and there wasn't a crumb left over.

I noticed my father bringing a slice to an older lady I didn't know. I figured she was with the Metskys, but it turned out that she was a member of the synagogue. Betty said, "She was at Mameh's shiva, but there's no reason you would remember her." There had been a whole flock of widows at the house after the funeral and they brought pots of soup and kugel over to the house for weeks afterward. Betty called them "the vultures," which was kind of mean but kind of true. Whenever an older man lost his wife, there was a competition to get him. Of all the widows, Edna Blaustein had brought strudel as well as casseroles. She was one of the younger ones and kept herself looking nice. She was also the only one with the chutzpah to invite herself to the wedding party. I'm pretty sure that she asked Papa to marry her.

Betty thought it was terrible that Papa didn't wait a whole year to marry her, but he said there was no law against it so they did and he moved into her house, a triple-decker that gave her a nice little income.

It turned out that Edna had expected Papa would take care of the building like her first husband had, but my father didn't know anything about fixing sinks or putting glass in a broken window. And after a few years of reading and teaching in shul all day, he wasn't about to shovel coal for the furnace.

"I almost feel sorry for her," Betty said. "Almost."

You're that Addie, Aren't You?

Aaron and I went on a little honeymoon: three nights at the Hotel Edward in Rockport, Massachusetts. Our room faced out to the sea and the full moon on the water was so bright that we had to close the curtains to sleep. It was very beautiful, very romantic.

During the day, I showed him everything. We took the train that used to run around Cape Ann. We walked on the beaches and up to the big rocks in Dogtown. We poked around in the art galleries and bought taffy to bring to our nephews. We ate fish every day and ice cream two times a day.

The cliff house where Filomena and I had met Morelli was gone. Washed away in a storm, I guess. All that was left were the granite steps and the slab that used to be in front of the red door.

Of course, I took Aaron to see Rockport Lodge. The woman who answered the door didn't want to let us in but I kept saying

378

that I had been a lodge girl myself and please could we just look around. She finally said I could come into the parlor for a moment but not Aaron. The house was quiet, so I knew the girls had to be on an outing; there was no good reason to keep him out. "We won't be long," I said. "It's our honeymoon. It would mean so much to me."

I didn't stop talking until she let us both inside, where she didn't let us out of her sight, as if we were going to steal something. I don't know what she thought when the first thing I did was head straight to the kitchen.

The closet I'd slept in was back to being a pantry and there was a big new refrigerator and fresh linoleum on the floor. The cook was standing at the door, blowing cigarette smoke through the screen. Mrs. Morse would have thrown her out for sure. But when she turned around, I realized it was her sister, Mrs. Styles. She was thinner and grayer but she still had that "Who do you think you are?" look on her face.

I had sent her a letter when I heard Mrs. Morse had died, saying how sorry I was and how I would always remember how good she'd been to me, but I wasn't sure she even got it.

Mrs. Styles said, "I know you. You're that

Addie, aren't you?"

I was surprised that she remembered my name.

"Maggie used to talk about you and what a big fuss you made over her pies. I never understood why she did so much baking when she was here. There's nothing wrong with a plate of stewed fruit, and you only have to make it twice a week."

I introduced her to Aaron, who said he liked a plate of stewed fruit himself. Mrs. Styles might have been flattered, but it was hard to tell.

A few weeks later, I got a note from Mrs. Styles with a recipe for piecrust. "My sister would be glad for you to have this. I never bother with it myself."

I know you think my pies are the best in the world, but believe me, they're not nearly as good as Mrs. Morse's. Sometimes I wonder if that sister of hers left something out on purpose. Or maybe it's just because I use butter instead of lard.

■ ■ ■ ■

1931 . . .

■ ■ ■ ■

SOME OF THE BEST YEARS OF MY LIFE.

Your grandpa loved his work. His whole life he tried to make things better for poor children, but his real calling was being a father. It was a talent with him.

As soon as our girls could sit up, he was wheeling them to the library and taking out books to read them bedtime stories. I used to listen, too. It was the first time I'd ever heard some of those fairy tales, and I was surprised at how scary some of them were. Your mother didn't sleep for a week after "Rumpelstiltskin."

We liked the Little House on the Prairie books so much that he would run to the bookstore whenever there was a new one and we'd stay up late to find out what was going on with the Ingalls family.

Aaron was heartbroken when Auntie Sylvia and your mom were old enough to read on their own and "fired" him. When your sister and you were born, it was as if he'd been holding his breath for all those years. Sometimes, we'd drive to your house and stay just twenty minutes so he could read you a story. He had most of Dr. Seuss memorized. Do you remember how you jumped all over him for *Hop on Pop*?

We were the only ones on either side of the family to have daughters, and the aunts went overboard. Betty bought every doll she ever saw, and Rita, who had two boys, kept our girls in pink until they were in high school. Grandma Mildred taught them how to bake bread and took them to the flower show every spring and bought them corsages.

It was like we were in that fairy tale where all the fairy godmothers bring gifts to the princess. Gussie bought savings bonds for every birthday. Helen, who was the best-dressed woman I ever knew, gave us her daughter's beautiful hand-me-downs. Miss Chevalier gave them books, and Katherine Walters bought them each a new diary every year.

When Betty found out we had asked a neighborhood girl to babysit, she read me the riot act. That was *her* job.

When I was pregnant, I was petrified about being a good mother. I would lie awake at night and worry about all the mistakes I was going to make: dropping, yelling, nagging, even poisoning. It took me a few years to get the hang of cooking.

It's a good thing babies don't give you a lot of time to think. You fall in love with them and when you realize how much they love you back, life is very simple. Of course, I was fascinated by every sneeze and yawn, and when my babies started to talk, I was sure they were geniuses and your grandfather and their aunties agreed.

I remember Irene saying everyone thinks their children are geniuses until they go to kindergarten. I was a little offended by that until I saw that two other children in class had started to read three months before mine did.

Being a mother wasn't as scary as I thought it would be, not only because Aaron was a good father, but because I didn't have to invent the wheel. I learned from Betty that it was good for children to have fun with them, to get on the floor and play. And I watched the way Irene talked to her son and daughter almost as if they were grownups. There was no baby talk and no beating around the bush in her house. Irene always told the truth and called a spade a spade and a penis a penis. That was unheard of in the '30s. When her little boy, Milo, said "penis" at a family dinner it was as if he'd murdered the pope.

When Irene's kids were both in school, she got a job as the office manager for the Birth Control League of Massachusetts; she didn't keep it a secret from Joe's family, either. They were horrified and tried to get him to make her quit, but Joe knew better than anybody that there was no way to *make* Irene do anything. And he loved her for it.

Irene and Joe, Aaron and I were a foursome. We spent so much time together, our kids were like cousins and when Joe lost his job in the Depression, it didn't feel so much like charity when we had them over for supper twice a week.

Not that we didn't feel it, too. We ate a lot of beans and I remember putting newspaper in a pair of shoes to get another summer's use out of them. But compared to most people, we had an easy time. Aaron didn't lose his job, but what made the biggest difference was that Levine moved us into one of his buildings in Brookline and wouldn't let us pay rent. "You'll mow the lawn," he said.

The lawn in front of that triple-decker was so small you could cut it with a pair of scissors. But that was my brother-in-law. He was a know-it-all his whole life. If you asked Levine what time it was, he'd give you a lecture about how his watch was the best one on the market and only a nudnik would buy anything else. But I don't think he ever evicted a single tenant from the buildings he owned.

It's strange to say, but I had some of the best years of my life during the Depression, because that was when I had your mother and aunt. They were nothing like their namesakes. Your mother, Clara, was the opposite of Celia. Clara was a spitfire who started talking at seven months, and once she started walking, I never sat down. Your aunt Sylvia was nothing like Aaron's birth mother, Simone, who was famous for her sense of humor and for starting the Metsky hug. My Sylvia didn't say a word until she could talk in sentences and always took things to heart too much, but she was the kindest, most loyal person you ever met.

So much of who a person is has to do with temperament. I think my sister Celia was probably born without any defenses, like Betty was born with skin like a rhinoceros.

I'm somewhere in between. It helped that I was born in America and that I got to go to school. But there was something built into my makeup, too; something that let me

387

connect to the friends and teachers who helped along the way. I think my girls inherited that from me.

They both did well in school, too. Your mother was the valedictorian at Northeastern.

You didn't know? That's terrible! You should do an interview with her next. Or maybe it would be better to wait until you're a little older, when you're completely cooled off from adolescence.

Oh, yes, your mother and I butted heads when she was in high school. I didn't like her friends — a bunch of rich girls who treated her like a pet dog and started her smoking cigarettes. She thought I was telling her how to live her life and treating her like a five-year-old. We were both right, but it took until she was out of college for us to admit it.

OLD FRIENDS ARE THE BEST.

The year both of the girls were in school, I decided I would take some daytime classes. Aaron picked up the Simmons catalog and asked if I'd be interested in Social Work Practice with Delinquent Youth. I'm sure he would have taken that class if he could, but after years of listening to Aaron's stories from work at the Child Welfare League, it sounded interesting to me, too. I'd never given social work a thought because those classes were held all the way downtown. But Aaron said so what; the trolley went downtown, too, and we could have lunch together, just the two of us.

So I signed up and that was that. The minute the teacher opened her mouth, I knew what I was supposed to do. Ann Finegold was one of those people who lights up a room. You wouldn't think so to look at her: she was in her forties, five feet tall, plump, frizzy-haired, and brilliant.

She told us that social work was a young profession still finding itself. She called it a "creative science" and said that, in her opinion, the best social workers were intelligent and compassionate, and while she could give us ideas and tools to help our fellow man, she couldn't teach us how to put ourselves into another person's shoes. She said, "If you don't already know how to do that, you should drop this class and consider another line of work."

She reminded me of Irene: no bullshit. She made me think of my Shakespeare teacher, too, because he was so passionate about his subject and curious about us. Ann insisted that everyone use first names in class, which was unheard of back then.

I took every class she taught and we got to be good friends. The husbands, too. You probably don't remember, but they were at your bat mitzvah.

When I had to do my fieldwork, Ann sent me to Beth Israel, where I did intake interviews with women who were waiting in the emergency room.

I was given a list of questions to ask: age, where they were born, years of schooling, marital status, reason for coming to the hospital. There was one woman — she was my age but looked twenty years older —

who answered everything in a flat, quiet voice. When I asked how many children she had, she stopped and gave me a hard look. Then, as if she was admitting to something terrible, she whispered, "Three living children, but six times pregnant."

It was all I could do to keep from throwing my arms around her and telling her that I had two living children, but I'd been pregnant four times.

I had two miscarriages before your mother was born and I was sure it had been my fault: I'd eaten the wrong thing or ridden on a bumpy streetcar or maybe I shouldn't have gone to see that scary movie. Or else it was a sign that I shouldn't have children because I wasn't fit to be a mother.

I didn't talk to anyone about how brokenhearted I was or how hopeless I felt. I had no idea how common it was to lose a pregnancy. Betty came to see me in the hospital after I lost the second one. She noticed I hadn't touched the cookies she brought the day before.

I said I didn't feel like eating.

But instead of her usual noodging, she sat down next to me on the bed and told me that she had lost a baby, too. "It was after you got married. We really did want a little girl."

I said, "Why didn't you tell me?"

She said, "I don't know."

Women used to think we were supposed to act as if nothing had happened, as if losing a baby you wanted wasn't a big deal. And if you did say something, people told you that you'd forget all about it when you had a healthy baby. I wanted to punch them all in the face.

Betty cried. I cried. We had never been closer.

After those interviews in the emergency room, I never did another intake without asking a woman how many *pregnancies* she'd had, and just asking the question like that opened a door nobody had noticed was there.

I heard about abortions and unwed girls whose fathers or mothers beat them or threw them down stairs so they would miscarry. I heard from women who had miscarried without knowing what was happening to them, and then nearly died from infections. A lot of them said they'd never told their story to anyone before, and most of them thought what happened to them was their own fault.

When I told Ann what I was hearing, she said I had the makings of a book. I think I laughed at her; I was raising children and had a hard time getting my reading done and my papers written, much less a book. But I never forgot the idea.

When the girls were in high school, I started working on my master's degree. I interviewed more than two hundred women by the time I was done. I didn't just ask about their pregnancies but about how they had learned about sex and their first sexual experience. I couldn't believe how many of them knew nothing on their wedding nights, or worse, how many had been raped. There were days I went home shaking and Aaron would hold me until I calmed down. After all his years in child welfare, he wasn't surprised by anything.

I talked about what I was learning with my Saturday Club friends, too. We always stayed close, but during World War Two, we really held each other together. Irene lost a nephew in the Pacific. Helen's son was wounded in England. And our own Jake was killed over Italy; he was a pilot, a hero. We all did whatever we could to get Betty and Levine through the shock, but they didn't really come back to life until their first grandchild was born. Eddy named him Jonah Jacob, after his brother.

All those years, Filomena kept sending

postcards, and once in a while I'd get an envelope with a sketch or a picture of what she was working on. As soon as it wasn't ridiculously expensive, we called each other long distance once a month at least.

Old friends are the best and I dedicated my book to them. It took me almost twenty years to finish. *Unasked Questions* came out the same year as *The Feminine Mystique*. Gussie was outraged that my book got lost in all the hoopla about Betty Friedan. "That woman stole your thunder."

I told her not to be silly. I wrote my book for social workers; it was never going to be a best seller. But it was a success in its own way. It got me the teaching job at Boston University, and I got a lot of letters from women thanking me for writing it. I can't tell you how much those meant to me.

I STILL MISS HIM LIKE CRAZY.

Your grandfather and I went to New Mexico twice. The first time was when the girls were twelve and fourteen. It was our first big family trip.

We went horseback riding and hiking, and Filomena took us to the Pueblo village where her teacher lived. Virginia was pretty frail by then, but she lit up when she saw Filomena. We were all invited inside to eat.

One night, Filomena kept the girls at her place for a sleepover. They camped outside and she woke them up in the middle of the night to watch a meteor shower. Your mother and your aunt Sylvia didn't stop talking about it all the way back on the train.

Aaron and I made a second trip when the girls were in college. It was just the two of us that time. We got a sleeper car and drank wine in the dining car. It was like a second honeymoon.

We stayed with Filomena, who was living

in a big house with her husband. I bet you weren't expecting that. She got married when she was almost sixty and always said she was more surprised than anyone.

Saul Cohen was an art collector from Philadelphia who fell in love with Filomena's pottery on a visit to Taos and bought everything she had to sell. Four weeks after they met, I got a telegram that started "Sit down." It's in the box with all her postcards.

They lived in Taos most of the year but Saul came back East a lot to see his children and grandchildren. Filomena came with him, so I got to see her pretty often. She was here for Miss Green's funeral and for the fiftieth reunion of all the Saturday Club girls.

When Aaron died, she flew from New Mexico for the funeral and stayed with me for a whole month.

I still miss him like crazy. You should only have my luck in that department. Not that he was perfect. Your grandpa snored like a buzz saw and I never saw him eat a piece of fresh fruit. How can you not like apples or watermelon or even raspberries? It drove me nuts and I'm sure I drove him nuts hocking him about it.

As he got older, Aaron got set in his ways about a lot of things. He hated television —

wouldn't even watch PBS with me. To him, all popular music written after 1945 was garbage, and he thought I was only pretending to like the Beatles so my students would think I was cool.

But he did like trying new things: bread baking, guitar lessons, fishing. When we started renting the cottage in Gloucester, he read everything he could find about Cape Ann and asked the old Sicilians at the coffee shop on Main Street for stories. They adopted him and taught him how to swear in Italian and drink sambuca.

But after he found out that they were going to vote for Ronald Reagan, he took his newspaper to Dunkin' Donuts and never talked to them again. He hated Reagan. I always thought that election had something to do with his getting sick.

Your grandfather was a peach. If he'd been at my birthday party, he would have made a speech so schmaltzy there wouldn't have been a dry eye in the house. It's a shame he wasn't there, but it's worse that he missed being at your sister's wedding and at your graduation from Harvard. He would have been so proud. Harvard.

Like I said, I miss him like crazy. But life goes on.

■ ■ ■ ■

1985

■ ■ ■ ■

Now There's Something to Look Forward to.

My birthday party was wonderful, wasn't it? So many people: the family, colleagues from Simmons and B.U., my graduate students, and my friends. Irene turns eighty-five next month, and Gussie with her walker but still going strong. Of course, I thought about everyone who wasn't there, too: Miss Chevalier, Helen, Katherine, Betty and her Herman.

Filomena felt bad that she couldn't make it, but her hip didn't heal fast enough for her to travel. I'm thinking about flying out to see her. Don't tell your mother, okay? She worries about me taking trips alone. Of course, I'd much rather be going with your grandfather.

But maybe you'd like to come with me? It's such a beautiful part of the country and you've never been. You're not going to have time for a real vacation once school starts and it would be my treat. Just you and me.

As much as your Brian loves me, he's not going to want to go on vacation with his grandmother-in-law. *If* you get married, that is.

Oh no. Maybe I am becoming a yenta after all!

But think about it anyway.

It was a little uncomfortable, all those birthday speeches about what an amazing human being I am. But hearing your mother and aunt say how lucky they are to have me as their mother? That's a level of naches everyone should know.

Still, I have to tell you, it was a little like being at my own funeral. Which reminds me, I want you to make sure there is just as much joking and laughing when I die. You were the funniest of all: I can't believe you told them that we smoked pot on my eightieth birthday.

Maybe you'll put that in when you do the eulogy. And please, *you* do it. It would be too hard for your mother or your aunt, and it's always so moving when a grandchild speaks.

Don't look at me that way. I'm fine. The doctor said she only hopes she's as healthy as me when she's eighty-five. And anyway, there is no way I'm dying before I get to hear someone call you Rabbi Ava Miller.

I keep trying to imagine what my father would say about his great-granddaughter becoming a rabbi. I think his head would explode.

Rabbinical school is five years, right? So I'll be ninety when you graduate. Oh, excuse me, when you're *ordained.*

Now there's something to look forward to.

ACKNOWLEDGMENTS

Grateful thanks to the staff of the Schlesinger Library at Harvard University, who rearranged their schedule to catalog more than fifty boxes of papers related to Rockport Lodge for my use: Susan Earle, Kathryn Allamong Jacob, and Sarah M. Hutcheon.

Thanks for their generous assistance to Bridget Carr, Boston Symphony Orchestra; Katherine Devine, Boston Public Library; Susan Herron, Sandy Bay Historical Society; Jane Matlaw, Beth Israel Deaconess Medical Center; Maureen Melton, Museum of Fine Arts Boston; Ethel Shepard, Crittenton Women's Union; Ellen Smith, Brandeis University; Donna Webber, Simmons College.

Chris Czernik, Rosalyn Kramer, Deb Theodore, and Pattie Chase shared memories of Rockport Lodge. Dexter Blumenthal and Joe Mueller provided early research assistance. Thanks to Ellyn Harmon, Amy Fleming, Joyce Friedman, and Marilyn Okonow for their support and suggestions, and to Denise Finard, Ben Loeterman, Harry Marten, Nancy Schön, Sondra Stein, Jonathan Strong, and Ande Zellman for being there when I needed you.

Thanks to Amanda Urban at ICM and the Scribner team, Roz Lippel, Susan Moldow, and Nan Graham: I so appreciate your belief in me.

My longtime, wise, and gentle writing group partners, Amy Hoffman and Stephen McCauley, were on this long march with me every step. Janet Buchwald provided fresh eyes when they were sorely needed.

My family endured more than the usual mishegas from me. Thanks to my mother, Helene Diamant, brother Harry Diamant, daughter Emilia Diamant, and especially my husband, Jim Ball, who bore the brunt and never lost faith.

Bob Wyatt talked me off the ledge half a dozen times. Without his help, you wouldn't be holding this book in your hands.

ABOUT THE AUTHOR

Anita Diamant is the bestselling author of the novels *The Red Tent, Good Harbor, The Last Days of Dogtown*, and *Day After Night*, and the collection of essays, *Pitching My Tent*. An award-winning journalist whose work appeared in *The Boston Globe Magazine* and *Parenting*, she is the author of six nonfiction guides to contemporary Jewish life. She lives in Massachusetts. Visit her website at AnitaDiamant.com.